I0700341

Holland, my Heart

Jennifer J. Coldwater

Holland, my Heart

Jennifer J. Coldwater

ISBN: 9798848738339

For Ruth.

PROLOGUE

three years ago

As Naomi adjusts my gown's sweeping train, I run my fingertips over the antique Irish lace. Handmade more than a century ago, the elaborate flower and vine motif in openwork ivory cotton is luxurious against my skin.

"I'm a fairy princess in this dress," I say to my future mother-in-law as I admire the gown in the full-length mirror.

"You look like an angel." She beams back at me in the mirror's reflection.

A searing stab of anger and guilt and regret follows my initial joy at Naomi's words. My own mother would not have been as happy to see me in this Victorian vision with tiny handmade crochet buttons running down my spine. My own mother would have found a way to ruin this day as she has ruined all the most important days of my life.

"Please think about sweeter things today, my darling girl," Naomi says softly as though she can read my mind.

"Naomi," I start, turning to my friend and confidant, "I cannot thank you enough for—"

"Holland, my heart," she cuts me off, her eyes glistening with unshed tears. "Your love for my son is the only thanks I'll ever need. You have brightened both our lives. It is you we should thank."

♡

When I fell in love with Aidan, I never dreamed I would fall in love with his entire family. His youthful, beautiful mother was graceful and gracious when we first met at a Gallagher family Christmas party two years ago.

"My husband would have loved meeting you, Holland," she said as a caterer came by with crystal flutes of champagne. "Oh, here." Naomi took two and handed me one. "This was Elias's favorite wine."

"The only wine he'd drink, in fact," Aidan said, taking a glass for himself. "Right, Mom?"

"He was a beer man, it's true." Naomi's warm smile lights up her whole face. She offers a toast. "To Dad."

"To Dad," Aidan and I echoed. I blushed when I realized what I'd just said. Oh, galoshes, that sounded presumptuous of me. Aidan sipped his wine and then kissed my temple softly. "He'd have loved to hear that," he whispered for only me. Sigh.

That same dazzling winter night in Naomi's huge ancestral home in Charlotte, I was instantly smitten with Aidan's brother and sister-in-law, the kindest and most charming of couples.

Hashtag relationshipgoals. Ethan and Ximena looked more like they'd stepped off the pages of Vogue Paris than out of the office they ran for Naomi.

"So nice to meet you, Holland," Ximena said. "Come with me to the ladies' room?"

Dumbstruck at first, I was also kind of excited to be so instantly invited to do girl stuff. As soon as we were out of earshot, Ximena said, "I've never been more relieved in my life to make a new girlfriend! My dress has a mind of its own and I could use a hand." She laughed as she led me to a tiny powder room. Her giggling was infectious but when she showed me how the strap of her beautiful holiday-red dress was about to break away from the bodice, I immediately went into fix-it mode.

"Oh, we've got this," I said confidently. I whipped my emergency kit out of my clutch and took out the itty-bitty scissors. "May I do a thing?" I asked my new instant friend.

"You're in charge back there, Holland. I put myself completely in your hands," Ximena said.

I made a few snips, tied a lovely (and secure!) bow, and checked Ximena out in the mirror before us.

"No way." Ximena's jaw dropped. "It's better than when I bought it."

"I don't know about that, but the new halter neckline is very flattering on you." I tucked away my sewing kit and handed Ximena my lipstick. "Try this."

"This is the exact color of my dress!" Ximena took the tube and put it on.

"It's yours, it looks great on you." I smiled.

"I can't keep it!" Ximena protested. "Oh, wait, let's trade." She opened a drawer and took out a gorgeous sparkling hair comb. "I found this on Etsy. I tried it on, but it just didn't work with my red dress. I think it's perfect with your gorgeous blue one."

She swept my hair over my shoulder and fastened the gold comb in my hair. It had tiny pinecones, the most delicate greenery, and elegant gold accents—it looked festive and kind of perfect nestled in my dark brown hair.

"Oh my breathless," I said. "I can't keep this. It's stunning."

"Sister, you saved my dress, and you gave me a lipcolor. We are more than even." Ximena gave me a quick, tight hug. "Let's get out there and wow those Gallagher men."

When I found a moment alone with Aidan, I said, "Your family is…" I couldn't find the right words.

"Eccentric?" Aidan offered as he brushed his lips in a soft kiss over my knuckles where our fingers were entwined, holding hands. "Annoying? Way too much?"

"They're perfect," I said as his sweet gesture set butterflies dancing in my belly—a common occurrence even after we'd been dating for nearly a year. "They are so generous."

"Yes, well." he laughed as he nuzzled my neck with his lips— more butterflies and now goosebumps chasing up and down my spine. "You're quite charming—it's easy to be generous to you."

"They're all so open and so kind." I smiled and shivered, staying on topic despite my temperature rising at his attention. "I always assume people that beautiful—"

"And that rich?" he pulled back to wink at me.

"Stop it." I squeezed his hand, still laced with mine. "It's not their so-very-rich wealth. It's their so-very-huge hearts." I beamed at him.

"You're right, my love." His boyish grin belied the pride his teasing was trying to disguise. "My family is pretty great. But what you're seeing is that they have fallen madly in love with you. Just as I have."

♡

Remembering that candlelit evening, my eyes fill with happy tears.

"That's better." The mother of the groom smiles at me, and I can't help but smile back. "I love seeing you happy, Holland."

A man clears his throat from the doorway to the bride's room of the church. Naomi and I both spin to see—

"Ethan! I thought you were Aidan," I confess. The slim, athletic redheads look so much alike, they could be twins.

"My brother is waiting for you at the altar, Holly." Ethan grins. "He's practically vibrating with excitement."

I am exactly the same way. I've never been more sure of anything in my life.

"Are you ready to do this?" Ethan asks me, his grin turning devilish. "Aidan's kind of a handful. I'm sure my mom is more than ready to pawn him off on you."

"Ethan, don't pick on your brother when he's not here to defend himself," Naomi reprimands her younger son. She turns to me to ask, "Holland, how do you feel? Are you ready?"

"Naomi, I'm more than ready to marry your son," I say. "Well, not this one," I tease, looking at Ethan. His mock-scandalized look makes me giggle. "Let's go, brother-in-law-to-be, I want to get hitched to Aidan."

Ethan rolls his eyes. "There's no accounting for some tastes." He chuckles. But his mood shifts instantly, more serious suddenly. "I'm so happy for you and that nerd, Holly. More than that, I'm happy for all of us, our whole family." As though conjured by his words, Ximena appears in the doorway. The two look at each other like today is *their* (second) wedding day—so happy, so in love.

"Look at you!" Ximena squees at me. Or maybe at her hubs? Probably both of us because she's hugging us both fiercely and I'm laughing uncontrollably. We finally calm down and Ethan looks at me, takes my hand to the bend of his arm, and says, "Let's officially become a family, sis."

1

Oh my. I catch my breath when she enters the bar. Time has been exceedingly good to my friend. "Naomi, it's so good to see you."

"Kai, my old friend." She wraps me in her scent of jasmine and fond memories as she hugs me. "Time has been kind to you," she says.

I grin at her echo of my thought.

"Our table is ready, but shall we start with a drink?" I ask, offering her the barstool I just vacated when I stood to greet her.

"No, no. Let's sit and catch up," she says, her elegant hand touches my sleeve.

"Of course." I lightly place my hand high on the middle of her back as I catch the eye of the hostess.

We settle in at a quiet table, and I can't help but stare at my oldest and dearest friend.

"Are you coming from work?" I ask, taking in her impeccable suit and tasteful jewelry. Her youthful elegance makes me feel all forty of my years.

I mean sure, I can bench press my car—I'm exaggerating even in my mind *(ha!),* but not by much. I could potentially have a full head of hair, but I've been shaving my noggin clean since college. My beard is equal parts salt and pepper these days, but I hope that is more about running my company than it is age.

Naomi looks ten years my junior, not fifteen years older. She's as gorgeous now as she was when we met.

I remember an instant attraction to her and then a repulsive electric shock when I realized who she was—the coach's wife. From the minute I walked on to play football the summer before I started college, Elias was both my coach and my mentor. As time went on, he became my best friend—he and his wife Naomi were like family to me. Eventually, the three of us became inseparable. Not to be cheesy, but those really were the days.

"Yes, we celebrated our new cohort of social justice fellows this afternoon." She looks happy and proud. "I wish we could grant every applicant a fellowship—you wouldn't believe how many energetic kids are coming out of college looking to make the world a more equitable place, Kai. They remind me of you, really." Her eyes glisten. Despite her words, I know she is thinking of Eli. If I think about him daily, I cannot imagine her pain. "Enough of that. I want to hear about you. Catch me up," she says.

I notice how she makes eye contact with the server, my new instant friend Marcus, and thanks him for filling her water glass. She hasn't changed a bit.

"I've taken the liberty of ordering dinner," I smile at Naomi and then nod to Marcus. "I didn't want to lose out on a moment of conversation, and I know your time is limited."

"What a treat!" she says, sounding genuinely delighted. Then she quirks her head to give me side-eye, like she's got a secret she can't wait to share. "Kai, my daughter is going to join us—I should've let you know earlier. I hope it's not too much trouble to add one more to our little party."

Confusion writes itself all over my face. Daughter? How did she get a daughter?

"No trouble at all," I say as I carefully try to smooth my features. "Marcus, please set us up for a party of three?"

"Of course, Mr. Ipu," the professional says quietly. "May I inquire if either of your guests has allergies or sensitivities?"

"Oh, how thoughtful of you to ask," Naomi says. "We are both adventurous eaters, but my daughter does, in fact, have a shellfish allergy."

"I'll let Chef know, ma'am," Marcus says as he pours wine for her.

After meeting with me in the bar earlier this evening, helping me choose a menu, pair wines, plan dessert, this kid now thinks to ask about allergies? I'm going to have to tip him big. I chose this place because of its excellent reputation for service, but this is above and beyond what I hoped for.

With wine and a starter before us, I bring up the topic that's been tickling my brain.

"Please tell me about your daughter, Naomi." I study her face for some kind of clue. "I'm so sorry, but I remembered that you and Eli had two boys."

"Oh, Kai," emotions I cannot decipher race across her beautiful face. "Yes, of course. We had two sons. They were—" She cuts herself off suddenly. "Holland, my heart! I'm so glad you could join us. Let me introduce you."

I stand before looking up to see the woman my friend greets. And thank God because fuuuuck. The most radiant creature I've ever seen apparates at my elbow. I think if I'd seen her first, I might've tripped over myself trying to stand.

"Kai Ipu, this is my daughter-in-law, Holland Gallagher," Naomi gestures to the heavenly vision glowing next to me. "Holland, honey, this is my old friend Kai."

The angel beams at me a smile that makes her sea-glass-green eyes sparkle—and sends my internal temperature soaring while my heart does this triple-beat.

"Kai, it's such a pleasure." She reaches out. I am a lumbering hulk taking her delicate hand in my monstrous paw—the lightning flash at our touch steals my breath. But she goes on as though she doesn't feel a thing, "Nomi has told me so much about you. It's like I'm meeting an old friend of my own."

"I'm at a loss—Holland—lovely—um," I stammer. I am never at a loss for words. What is this enchantment?

Naomi is giggling at me. "Kai." She calls me back to earth, back to this moment, back to the table.

"Forgive me," I say as I pull out the chair next to Naomi for Holland. She smells intoxicating, like a summer day, clean and green. Her proximity makes every nerve in my body sit up and take notice. "Please, join us," I say. I close my eyes and make an effort to compose myself before returning to my seat. I shudder—releasing both my tense muscles and these intense emotions—that's how overwhelming my reaction to her is.

Marcus settles Holland with wine and water. I mentally triple my tip for this kid—he's so attentive. Marcus's professionalism makes *me* look good, like a most excellent host. As many times as Naomi has fed me, I want to impress her with this meal. And now Holland. I want to… impress her. Yeah, that's it.

"Holland, my heart." Naomi takes the reins of the conversation I cannot find the presence of mind to begin. "I was just telling Kai about our boys." With this I finally hear what Naomi said when she introduced Holland—daughter-in-law.

"Yes, please." I hear my voice gruff as I force the words past the lump in my throat. And my heart breaks clean in two. She's married. I glance quickly at her left hand to find an ornate diamond wedding set that looks authentically art nouveau. Of course. Married. To Naomi's son. Of course.

"Oh yes," Holland says with sad eyes but the same bright smile. "We lost Aidan and Ethan last summer, Kai. Did you know my husband and brother-in-law?"

Lost? Shock and devastation crash over me. I look over at Naomi who is watching me closely. I look back at Holland who looks hopeful—they're both waiting for me to …what? Searching my mind for details of the two young boys I'd last seen not long after their father died, I come up short.

I'm failing Holland. Distraught I'll never be able to give her details of the men they became, I feel like a failure. This is a new one for me—I have never felt like a failure.

"I'm… I'm so sorry. No, I knew them—uh, when they were boys. I—" I can't complete a sentence without tripping over my tongue. This is all too much.

Saving me, Naomi explains with the grace I remember from so long ago. Her sons died in a tragic accident nearly a year ago, leaving Naomi childless and both her daughters-in-law widows.

My heart shatters into shards and scatters around my feet—even as it was still recovering from its breaking over Holland's status as a married woman. Now this.

"Ethan's wife Ximena remains the CFO of the Foundation." Naomi wraps up her story.

"But now she works out of Mexico City so she can spend more time with her family," Holland adds.

"Her family of origin, Holland." Naomi places her hand on Holland's. "We're all still a family."

"Of course, Nomi," says this ever-more-beautiful-with-each-word-she-utters brunette with a warm smile for Naomi. "And I followed my sweet mother-in-law here to Los Angeles just a few months ago."

Holy shit. I've been through the wringer and it's not even my story—the strength of these two—it humbles and amazes me. My broken heart goes out to them—even as my libido slams its fist on the inside of my brain, reminding me that Holland is my no-holds-barred ideal. Dammit.

"Kai." Holland smiles at me, and all the blood in my body rushes south. "I fear Nomi and I have not allowed you to get a word in edge-wise." She pronounces my friend's name with only two syllables: No-mi. It's the cutest contraction I've ever heard, and it wrenches my heart even further. If you'd asked me two hours ago, I would've insisted my hardened heart was simply a functional organ—but here it is, smeared all down my sleeve for this woman.

"Please, I know she was looking forward to catching up," Holland presses. "Don't let me interfere with your visit. Tell us both about yourself."

Well, I'm a giant ham-fisted lummox who cannot complete a sentence because you're intoxicating, I think as I take a near-gulp of my wine.

I see Marcus—well on his way to earning a car in lieu of a tip—refill my wineglass for the, um, fourth time? Oh, well. Maybe the wine will help prop up my (uncharacteristically) inept conversational skills.

"Kai?" Naomi prompts. "Hey, buddy, how ya doin' over there?" The Carolinas slip into her voice as she prods me gently out of my brain fog.

Shit, shit, shit. What was the question? Who asked?

"Oh, Holland." I love saying her name as I snap back to attention. "This evening was meant to be—" something. Fuck. What? "I'm enjoying hearing you two—" enjoying?! They've been talking about their dead men. I'm such a dumbass. "I'm sorry for your loss." I recover. "I wish I'd had the pleasure of knowing Aidan and Ethan as men. And I'm glad you two have each other." I pause to sip—sip, dammit!—my wine. "Please tell me how you two got to be so close." Stupid brain. The death of a man you can never compare to, Ipu, you stupid git. That's how they got to be so close! My anger at myself bubbles up in my chest.

"Did you just growl?" Naomi exclaims.

"I did not growl," I lie. "I was clearing my throat." As if that's somehow better. Jeez.

"Well," she huffs. "I was about to excuse myself, but I'm suddenly afraid to leave my darling girl with an enormous snarling bear of a man." Naomi gives me her best I've-got-my-eye-on-you-Mister look. I remember that look well. "I hate to rush off, but I have a trip to Chicago early tomorrow. Before I go, I wanted to see you both. Kai, thank you for letting me hijack our visit by having my sweet Holland join us." I notice Naomi's own dazzling wedding set sparkle as she squeezes Holland's beautiful hand. Eli's been gone for so many years, but she still wears his rings. And then to lose both their sons…

I don't think I can take much more of her loss—how disgustingly selfish and thoughtlessly cold is that?

"And Holland," hearing Naomi say her name makes my heart triple-beat again. This time I really do clear my throat to start it beating normally again. "I leave you in the capable hands of our host. Kai, be a good boy and make sure this one gets home safely."

Wait. What? She's leaving? Us. Here? Alone?

"Good night." Holland hugs her mother-in-law. Is there a word for the mother of your dead husband? Former mother-in-law? Widow-in-law? I'll google it later.

"Good night, love. Lunch when I'm back?" The two arrange to meet up after Naomi's trip. I watch them together. They look more like sisters than two unrelated women with a generation between them. Oh, look, Aidan married a woman so much like his mother. How precious is that? I stop myself disparaging a dead guy. And my two best friends' dead son at that. What a jackass I am.

Shaking off my negativity, I rise to hug Naomi goodbye. "It has been such a pleasure to see you," I say. "Please let's keep in better touch now you're back in LA."

"Oh, I have no doubt we'll be seeing much more of each other, Kai dear," Naomi says with a wink. Before I can even ponder what that's supposed to mean, she asks, "Walk me to my car?"

I look at Holland.

"Please, do." Holland holds up her phone. "I'll be fine here."

Reluctantly, I leave her at the table. Marcus nods as I pass him with Naomi on my arm. What a champ—kid's got this.

Once we're at the valet stand, Naomi turns to me. "Let's talk about Holland." Naomi beams. Shit, I'm probably smiling like a fool myself. "I have a favor to ask you."

Hell, yes. "How can I help?" I ask.

"Listen. My sweet Holland has been drifting a little this last year," Naomi says quietly.

"I cannot imagine how hard this has been for you both," I say. "All three of you." I correct myself, remembering her sons had both been married. The ache in my chest makes me grit my teeth and clench my fists.

"I don't worry about Ximena." Naomi straightens her spine. "She has landed on her feet surrounded by loved ones. She says," her voice cracks just a little, "she says she's working for two, for both Ethan and herself." Naomi sounds genuinely sad for the first time tonight.

"Naomi, my dear friend." I reach for her hand. The gesture is so natural, as though we haven't been separated by decades and an entire continent. And a sea of grief. "I know you love your boys. And I can see how proud of their wives you are. Tell me. How can I help Holland?" I mean, I'm not trying to rush you, woman, but let's get on to the Holland part of this conversation.

"Yes, of course." she gives me an unreadable look, squeezes my hand with affection, then lets me go. "Holland." There's the faintest hint of a smile in her eyes. "Listen, she would never ask, and I probably shouldn't ask for her, but Holland needs to find a job."

"Done." Thank fuck. I take a deep breath. Here is a problem I can fix.

"You don't even know—" Naomi starts with a heartfelt laugh.

"I don't care," I interrupt her. "I'll hire her. Literally, there is a place for her at Innovated regardless of her skill set."

"You sweet man," Naomi says. "I knew you'd be the right person to ask." She steps away to accept her keys from the valet. "I'll leave it in your capable hands, Kai," she says. "Just remember to make it your idea, and not mine." She tosses this directive over her shoulder as she slips into her car and drives away.

"My—" Wait. What? My idea? Fuck.

2

As Kai returns from walking Naomi to her car, I see him talking with our server. The nice young man came by to check on me in the short time I sat alone. So polite. I swear I hear Kai say something about a Lamborghini to Marcus as he heads my way. Men and their machines.

"I'm sorry we abandoned you," he says as he sits.

"No worry at all, I was catching up on email." A blush creeps up my neck before I even finish saying this. He's going to think I mean work email. Because I said it as though it were work email. Ugh. Old habits.

Sure enough, he says, "What is your work, Holland? Your sister-in-law is in the family business. Are you as well?" He must truly not know how very not-working I am because his question sounds sincere.

"I'm between jobs right now," I say as though it's not a joke.

One eyebrow sneaks up his forehead. "Between jobs is usually a euphemism for unemployed." He looks exceedingly skeptical. "Somehow I don't think that's what you mean."

"Technically, I'm on a bereavement leave," from a job I'll never return to, I *don't* add.

"Oh, of course," he says flatly. I hate that my reluctance to answer the question has made this uncomfortable—for both of us.

"Thank you for asking, Kai, it's just–" I start but get stuck in the sentence. "I didn't particularly like the company I was working for when Aidan was killed. It's been very difficult to wrap my head around returning to work—in what already felt like an overwhelmingly toxic environment."

"I see." He knits his brow, looking sad. I guess it's not sadness, really. More like empathy.

"Plus, the commute would be like twenty-seven hundred miles," I deadpan. "Each way." We both laugh.

"Tell me about Aidan."

I don't exactly gasp, but it's a sharp inhale. Then, almost as instantly, I relax. This is easy. This I can do. I love to talk about my husband. It hurts, yes. But it's better than being numb.

"I met Aidan when we ran for the same student council seat," I begin. My advisor recommended I throw my hat in the ring with the two temptations he knew I couldn't resist: an opportunity for leadership and lots of public speaking experience. "I had my application all filled out, and I stopped by this tiny broom-closet of an office to drop it off. This guy was there for the same reason, turns out." I was so laser focused on turning in my paperwork, I don't even think I noticed him at first. He was more of an obstacle than anything else.

"That was Aidan?" Kai asks.

"Yeah." I can hear my voice go all nostalgic and dreamy. The wine isn't helping. "The woman accepting applications invited us to do our initial interviews—together—right that minute. Guess she wanted to kill two birds with one interview." I smile. "So, the three of us sit at a picnic table outside. The woman introduces herself as Gracie and says, 'You are both applying for the open at-large seat, so just tell me a little bit about yourselves.' Before I can even take a breath," I tell Kai as I pause for a breath here in the present moment.

"Oh no." Kai can see where this is going. "He didn't."

I put on my best Aidan voice. "'Sure, I'll go first,' he says," I say. Kai is already shaking his head. "'I'm Aidan Gallagher, I'm a business major in my third year. I'm from North Carolina, and…' I stopped listening," I tell Kai, laughing.

"I'll bet," he deadpans.

"Right? I mean, who does this guy think he is? North Carolina, my asparagus! What southern boy doesn't let a lady go first?" I'm on a roll now, remembering that day. I didn't even know I had a type until I realized this Aidan guy was definitely not it. All my previous love interests had been tall (and taller… and super tall), dark, and handsome. Aidan had red hair, green eyes, full lips, freckles. I remember noticing he was almost exactly my height. *"May I ask a question?* I interrupted this Carolina boy,"* I continue to tell the story to Kai.

"I have no doubt," Kai grins.

"'Um, sure,' he said, clearly perplexed by me. *It's Aidan, right?* I double checked. 'Yes, Aidan Gallagher,'" I'm still doing Aidan's voice. He had a beautiful tenor with a hint of a southern accent. "At least he had the decency to blush a little. He was clearly nonplussed I wasn't falling at his feet." I recount to Kai how I proceeded to interrogate Aidan—with Gracie's full support. "I asked him, *What's your personal mission statement?* After a stuttered answer that sounded like it was lifted wholesale from his fraternity, I went on. *Coffee or tea? Who's your favorite Beatle? What's your favorite constellation? Do you collect anything? How many bottles of sand from beaches all over the world,"* uh, privilege much? But I don't say that out loud to Kai, "*do you have? What are your goals after college? Why do you want this student council position?* I peppered Aidan." As I tell the story now, I realize with bittersweet nostalgia I was interviewing my future husband with that barrage of questions. In the moment, I was sure I was grilling an opponent. Now, I recognize my flirting-via-interrogation habit I started in middle school. Huh. "Gracie told me after I won the seat by student vote a few weeks later," won by a landslide, I omit as I wrap up the story to Kai, "that she loved the way I shaped the conversation. She told me Aidan tried to look like a leader while I actually led the entire meeting," I say with just a hint of pride in my voice.

Kai is nodding now. He's a good listener. "And that's when you knew you and Aidan were meant to be," he says. It's not a question. It's a statement.

"I guess. Maybe," I say as heat creeps up my neck. As we'd talked on that picnic bench, I made eye contact for the first time with the man I would marry. It felt like fireworks. Our eyes were the exact same not-quite-green-not-quite-gray color, I realized. I always felt like my eyes were the color of a murky pond. But seeing the same hue in Aidan's eyes, I understood what people meant when they said my eyes were sage green or sea green or light-blue-green. Because here were my eyes reflected at me in this man's face. It felt like a sign. Providence.

"Speaking of commutes, Naomi mentioned you didn't drive here," Kai says. Were we speaking of commutes? Oh, yeah. Wow, that was a lifetime ago. Nope. It's been mere minutes.

Catching up to Kai, I say, "To dinner? No. I mean, I didn't drive to Los Angeles either. I sold nearly everything when I moved. Including the cars."

"Cathartic," he says.

I nod. "But now, I think I've run out of gas," I say. "Figuratively." I smile weakly at my lame joke. "It's been a long day." Year, really. This is the only thing on my calendar for today—well, it's the only entry on my calendar at all, and it's been sitting there solo since Naomi invited me weeks ago—just coming out to dinner has exhausted all my energy.

Kai smiles kindly, stands, and says, "I'll walk you out." He offers me his arm. "I have a car waiting for you." What, like a magician? Waiting for me?

"Oh, I'll just call an Uber," I say—cognitive dissonance ringing in my head as I simultaneously refuse his offer and accept his arm. His big, strong arm in this luxurious suit jacket. Holy roly poly, what is wrong with me? This close, I smell his delicious creamy vanilla, cocoa, wood, warm, spicy scent. My head is spinning.

"I'm afraid I promised a dear friend I would get you home safely," he says. "I know our Naomi well enough to trust that she would have my head if I dropped the ball on this most delicate and vital of tasks." He smiles down at me.

A sleek black town car waits at the curb just outside the restaurant.

"Jamil will get you home safely, Miss—er, Mrs.—er, Holland," he stumbles on the Mrs.

I mean, I still stumble over it too. How long should a widow keep the honorific? I'll have to google it later.

"It was my most sincere pleasure to meet you," he says as he places his huge hand over mine on his arm. The warmth and the weight of it overwhelm me.

The next thing I know, I'm in the back of the town car being whisked away home.

3

Alone in my big, empty living room, I'm restless. I've lit a fire. Poured a whiskey. Paced the living room… all acting as if I'm not about to pick up my laptop. Fuck it.

I launch Google. Let's start with familiar territory. I type in Elias Gallagher. Of course, it's his obituary that pops up first. With a stabbing pang in my heart, I click it. I'm reading it (even though I was there for most of it) when the elevator dings. I unlock the door and let in Micah before he even announces himself. Who else would it be in the middle of the night?

"There's a distinct vibe in this room, man," my ever-so-loyal assistant says. "A melancholy …deep …blue …funk." I don't dignify it with a response. "Seriously, dude. What's up? How was your dinner with your friend?"

I put down the laptop. Pick up my glass. I notice Micah's helping himself to a measure of whiskey, too. "All good," I say as I stretch my neck and back. "Naomi's good. She brought her daughter-in-law."

"Okay…" Micah prompts.

"It was fine. It was nice to see Naomi. I just—" I don't even know what I just. "Seeing her is painful, man."

"Because of Elias?" Micah asks. He knows the answer. Why does

17

he do that? Ask. When he knows.

"Eli was in the best of health, man. He ran every day, ate healthier than any sane person should, had the love of a good woman, two young sons, the world's *best* best friend," I say. Smart ass, I berate myself. On a deep breath, I continue. "When he dropped dead on a ride."

"I know, man," Micah says quietly. I get up from my seat, head for the bar.

"I was right here, Micah." I mean, I wasn't in this apartment. But I was in LA. "Why the fuck didn't he ask me to go biking with him that day? We'd biked those trails a hundred times together." Why did he go alone?

That day, I found Naomi at the trailhead parking lot where police and an ambulance were staged. I wrapped my arms around her, held her close. Rubbed her back as she sobbed when the covered backboard appeared from the brush, carried by paramedics. I stayed strong so she could fall apart. My only comfort was my hope that I could comfort her. Neither of us said a word until police questioned us. And then we could say frustratingly little. Neither of us had spoken to Eli that morning—he'd left so early, didn't have his phone, pretty normal for him... Eventually, they sent us home. Alone.

It was tough to go on without my best friend; it was nearly impossible for her to go on without her husband. Naomi was a director at the American Heart Association at the time. Fucking painful irony, that. She lost the love of her life to an undetected hole in his heart, the autopsy said. Devastating.

I had wanted to step up and step in as Aidan and Ethan suddenly needed a father figure. I even thought about courting Naomi— thought about offering to become her new partner and their stepfather. But our long friendship was too much of a hindrance to even say it out loud.

Despite having had a huge crush on her in college, we'd simply become too much like family. That, and she will forever be Eli's girl. As evidenced by his rings on her hand tonight, all these years later.

I was as supportive as I could think to be for as long as I could manage it. But after Naomi moved the boys out to her folks' place in North Carolina, we drifted apart. For years we spoke at Christmas and on the anniversary of Eli's death. But eventually even those phone calls tapered off. I'm such a shitbag. Why didn't I keep in touch with her? Tonight was our first real chance to reconnect in many years. I could've been there for her when her boys were killed.

"Self-hatred isn't going to do you or Naomi any good," Micah says. I nearly jump out of my skin—where did he come from? Wait. Did I just say all that shit out loud?

"Why are you here?" I demand. Thank god this jackass puts up with me. I'm not being very nice to either of us.

"I was reviewing your travel schedule for the next month. We're going to have to clone you." I can't help but laugh. It's not a happy laugh. "No, seriously, I think we need to look at hiring," Micah says. "I'm never going to tell you to stop being hands-on with our international offices, but there's a limit. We're growing too fast for you to be this involved, dude."

"This neither seems like bad news nor worth a trip up here in the middle of the night, Micah," I say as I look at my watch. "Jeez, man, don't stay at work this late. It can't be good for you," I say even as I thank all that is holy and unholy for the loyalty of this unstoppable machine who is my right-hand man.

"You're one to talk," Micah says. "What were you working on when I came in?"

"Funny you should ask. A new hire," I say.

Micah's eyebrows climb his forehead. "That is a coincidence. Who'd you have in mind?" he asks.

"I'm not ready to disclose that just yet," I evade.

"I see how it is." He nods a smile at me and sets his glass on the kitchen island. "I'll talk to you tomorrow."

"I have no doubt," I say to his back as he heads down to the garage and home to his place. As empty as mine. We are a sad pair of losers, really.

I open my laptop to review the travel plans Micah was working on. Oh, who am I kidding? I google Holland Gallagher.

4

HOLLAND: Well, I messed that up.

I message Naomi to confess to her my absolute airheadedness at forgetting to thank Kai for dinner, or even to say goodnight.

NOMI: In what way? I cannot imagine you being anything other than charming.

Naomi, ever the maternal and supportive advisor, sends me his contact info with an admonition to rectify my oversight immediately.

As soon as I see his contact card pop up, I call her.

"I can't text him," I protest in lieu of a greeting. "It's the middle of the night. He'll think I'm nuts."

"You don't have to send him a note tonight, Holland," Naomi retorts. "But if it bothered you enough to mention it to me, it's something you should sort out."

I roll over to stare at the bare white wall of my stark white bedroom in my minimalist white loft. "Maybe," I say with a big sigh.

"Get some rest, honey," my mother-in-law says.

"I'll try." Hearing how whiny my voice is, I buck up. "Really, I'll try."

As is her habit any time we chat late at night, Naomi runs through our sleep hygiene checklist.

"One. Go to bed and wake up at the same time every day." We both laugh. That one gets us every time.

"Two. Create a relaxing bedtime routine to get your body and mind ready to sleep?" Naomi's voice goes up at the end. She's asking.

"I will," I promise.

"Three. Stop working an hour before bedtime and avoid talking about stressful or emotional issues in bed—" She can't even finish this one before I snort-laugh. "Are you already in bed? Holland! We should not be having this conversation."

"I know, Nomi, I know." I placate her.

She ignores my tone and continues, "Four. Make your bedroom dark, quiet, cool, and comfortable."

"Like a religion," I say. This is my favorite item on the list, and I take it incredibly seriously.

"Me too," she says quietly. We bask in the dark quiet of our respective rooms for a moment. "Did you skip caffeinated beverages the last six to eight hours before bedtime?" she asks.

"Sure," I lie.

"Hm. I'll bet. We both know it's your drug of choice. Did you avoid eating a big meal close to bedtime?"

I'm shaking my head even though she can't see me. "Nomi, you were there," I scoff.

"Okay, but dinner was definitely more than an hour ago. I think we'll be okay," she says.

I take over the list. "Seven. Exercise at least twenty minutes each day, preferably in the morning" I say.

"Also, like a religion," she says. Me too, and she knows it. My early morning runs and her even earlier morning pilates were our only means of dealing with all the pent-up energy accumulated when we each finally hit our lowest low. Ximena's outlet was her boxing gym. That woman is all badass.

"Eight. No TV, no tablet, no smartphone," I say into my smartphone.

"It's the thought that counts," Naomi says with an audible smile. "But we both promise the phone goes into a drawer."

"Promise." And it's true. I can't even attempt to sleep if that thing is looking at me. "Checklist checked."

"We've got this," my sweet mother-in-law says. "We are sleeping champions."

I giggle. "Thanks for Kai's number," I say, already calmer. "I'll reach out. Good night, Nomi."

"I'm proud of you, my sweet girl. Good night." She ends the call.

I don't know what I'd do without her. Following Naomi west has been the best decision. In this blank-slate apartment, I find I finally have enough psychic space to feel my feelings. Far from the ocean air—the smell of salt and the sting of sand—in this urban space where traffic sounds nothing like waves crashing on the shore, I can stop expecting Aidan to come bounding through the front door.

I can imagine a world where I learn to be alone, learn to cook for one, learn to make lists (don't forget to water the plants, the trash doesn't magically take itself out to the curb, laundry must be moved from washer to dryer) and set timers and reminders and alarms and calendar invites to myself. When the phone rings, it won't be Aidan. Here in this white on white with white accents space, I can see my things for what they are rather than what they remind me of. The monkey-wearing-a-top-hat lamp we bought laughing until we cried at a flea market in Wisconsin is now in a Goodwill in North Carolina. This light fixture was ordered by my sister from a website specializing in things without a soul.

I hated being alone in our warm, wonderful, welcoming Kill Devil Hills bungalow. It broke my heart to walk on the honey-colored wood floors Aidan and I refinished ourselves. The home we made our own with gallons of paint, a nursery-load of plants, and tons of sweat equity.

And as I find my space for one here in Los Angeles, I find I don't miss Aidan. I crave the Aidan-spaced shape my side is permanently curled into. I don't long for my husband; I long for the way his citrusy cologne (which does not smell the same on me and I am not ready to forgive the perfumer nor my body's chemistry for this affront) smelled when he wasn't in the room. I miss missing him. I pine for the delicious hope that I felt at the end of the day—picturing his getting home before me so I could pounce on him with a demand to tell me about his day while I covered him in kisses.

Kai Ipu. I add his contact information to my phone. It's very weird to create a new contact for a handsome single man. Not quite like cheating on my husband. But it's definitely not something I'm used to.

Poor Aidan. We were essentially still newlyweds when he died.

We were happy. We were still in that giddy can't-believe-we're-really-married stage.

And now he's gone.

I think that thought for the thousandth time. Today.

I'm numb to it. Until I'm not numb. Until, uninvited, the opposite envelops me. Or smacks me upside my head. Or makes my ears ring. But right here, right now I am simply blank. Like these walls.

Think on sweeter things, I hear Naomi in my head. So I replay this evening's dinner: the delicious food, the amazing service, the way Kai was so attentive, the way he stumbled over my name… The cringeworthy way I left things.

I mean, it's not that late. It hasn't been that long since I got home. Right? And I was pretty rude when I left. I'll just send him a quick thanks.

HOLLAND: Kai, it's Holland. My MIL gave me your number. Hope that's okay. I owe you an apology and a thank-you. Dinner was spectacular. And I greatly appreciate the ride home. Your driver was very protective.

I hit send and immediately regret each and every word. I should have said Holland who. He won't know what MIL means! He will be– Oh! Three dancing dots! I freeze.

KAI: Why are you awake, new friend? Shouldn't you be asleep? You owe me nothing. It was my pleasure to meet you—and to treat you. And Naomi.

Before I can think of a response, the three dots pop up again.

KAI: Tell me more about Jamil. Tell me he was professional. He didn't hit on you, did he?

HOLLAND: Oh goodness, no! He got me home in one piece, just like you asked. Walked me to my door. Waited until I was deadbolted inside. That's all. Very professional.

KAI: Good.

HOLLAND: Thank you for dinner. And thank you for getting me home safely.

KAI: My pleasure. In fact, I'd like to take you to lunch tomorrow. Or coffee? I have a business proposition for you.

Oh. Wow. Okay. Sure. Maybe.

HOLLAND: Yeah, I think I can do coffee tomorrow.

Like my day is so full of appointments. Ha.

KAI: Excellent. Let's meet at 11 AM.

He suggests a place on La Brea. I agree.

KAI: Looking forward to it. Sleep well, Holland.

That'll be a first in a long, long time, but I appreciate the sentiment. And even as I put my phone away, I think maybe I am a little sleepy....

5

It's quarter-to-ten when I leave the office to head to the historic old building to meet Holland Gallagher. I need Holland to think my reason for this coffee date—it's *not* a date, dammit—is simply because I was dazzled by her upon our first meeting. With no interference from her mother-in-law. I need her to believe I want to work with her based solely on my first impression of her.

Which is honestly how it should have gone. Which means it shouldn't be difficult at all. Right?

Last night, I did a little research. I roll my eyes at myself—*a little research, ha!* It was three in the morning before I finally put down my tablet.

I caught up on Naomi's life in North Carolina—Naomi comes from old tobacco money, and I have always suspected that her drive to make the world a more equitable place is based on generational guilt. She's a goddamn saint trying to make up for the sins of her fathers. She raised Aidan and Ethan, according to my research into their adult lives, to be good men with kind hearts and shrewd minds for business.

I read an article in a business magazine about Aidan and Ethan early in their careers. The profile included photos of the fit, attractive, redheaded brothers looking almost like twins. They'd been wildly successful entrepreneurs. I wish I'd followed their lives more closely, kept in better touch.

Regret washes over me again.

Rubbing my temples at a stoplight, I recall the articles I found about the boys' tragic deaths—how did this get past me? It was apparently national news at the time. The brothers' single-engine plane crashed into the water "under unknown circumstances" eighteen miles off the coast of North Carolina, according to the reports I read. I should have been there for Naomi. How much these Gallagher women have suffered. No wonder they are so close.

Including Ximena Hernández vda. de Gallagher. Ethan's childhood sweetheart, best friend, and wife, Ximena manages the Gallagher Foundation's finances. According to an article I read, it was Eli who inspired Ximena at a very young age to pursue her love of math. Always an inspiration, our Eli. I can picture Eli and Ethan befriending the little girl with her dark pigtails, new to Pasadena from Mexico. I can imagine Eli encouraging her to love numbers if she wanted to—naysayers be damned.

As I park my car, I find I am missing Eli, rooting for Naomi, suffering the loss of their sons, intrigued by Ximena... and obsessing over Holland.

Long after I stopped googling the rest of the family, I was still looking for anything I could find about Holland.

She is dazzling in photographs—and even prettier in person— the camera loves her beautiful face with her bold brows, sometimes-gray-sometimes-green eyes, straight sweet nose, kissable bow-shaped lips as much as I do. No two photos of her capture the same pose or expression. Even in stills, I sense her animated energy. Every cell in my body craves more time with this woman.

I read articles about her and articles by her. I could hear her voice as I read her writing. It made my heartbeat triple and my—ahem, let's go with—*pride* swell.

I found her on the About pages of two companies I admire— one where she was hired in a strategy and business development role inside a multibillion-dollar marketing and communications business. The second at a two-hundred-million-dollar business where she started as a senior accountant and was offered the CFO position just eight months after being hired. How old is she? I don't think she can be over thirty. Impressive.

I think I'm so clever showing up early, but I see the luminous, brilliant brunette perusing a menu as soon as I walk in.

"Fancy meeting you here," I say. So lame. But she looks up with a smile. Her smile is so beautiful—I thought she was glowing before, but this smile nearly makes my eyes water.

"I bet you say that to all the girls." Her smile wobbles a little bit. "That sounds an awful lot like a pick-up line." I can't tell if she's teasing.

"I'm not here to pick you up, Holland, this is a job interview." I grin back at her. And immediately regret my words. She looks stricken. "Wait. No. Wait. That's not quite what I mean," I stammer. Will I ever be able to speak clearly in front of this woman?

She smiles, but it doesn't reach her eyes. Those look skeptical. She says, "Hm. Let's get coffee."

"Of course. Coffee." I cross my arms across my chest. Mostly so I don't reach for her. My fingers ache with the need to touch her.

As we walk to the counter, the awkward silence gets awkwarder. That's not even a word, Ipu.

"Tell me what you mean exactly, Kai," she says. "In what way is this a job interview?"

"I– I didn't mean that. I–" fuck, fuck, fuck. Speak up, man. I sound like an imbecile. I plant my feet and take a deep breath. "Holland, I'd like you to come work for me. This isn't a job interview because I'm fully prepared to bring you on board. I greatly enjoyed our conversation last night, and Naomi is one of my oldest friends. If she loves you, I…" get yourself out of this sentence, Ipu. "I have no choice but to hire you."

She looks slightly less terrified than she did when I tipped my hand—job interview? What was I thinking?

When I stopped stumbling over my words, she turned to face me. She isn't small by any stretch of the imagination. In fact, she might be nearly six feet tall. But I love looking down on her. Love the thoughtful tilt of her chin. I love everything about this woman. This woman I just invited to join me at my company. Holy crap. What am I doing?

6

I turn away from Kai to face the server at the counter.

"May I please have a hot dirty chai tea latte? For here," I say.

Kai coughs until I think he might need medical attention. Then he orders coffee and a smoothie, and I ask for toast and jam. I'm going to need carbs if this is a job interview.

We look for a table in the half-full café. "This sounds suspiciously like something my mother-in-law put you up to," I say. "Let's sit outside."

"Absolutely not," he says with authority. My eyes grow wide.

"I mean, yes—let's sit outside. But this is one hundred percent me being impressed by you. Last night we talked about how you're not going back to your last job," he says. He pauses as we find a seat. "Anyway, I thought you might be ready to return to work. And where better than at a Fortune Best Company to Work For seven years running?"

Everything about his demeanor changes. He is very proud of Innovated, I can see it.

"I can offer you a competitive salary, a ridiculously generous benefits package, as much travel as you're ready for." My ears prick—now I'm listening. "Top-notch colleagues who love their work. And a job description tailor-made for you."

"Ridiculous is the right word," I say, curious but also salty. "I'll hear you out."

Our food arrives and Kai obviously uses the break to organize his thoughts because he proceeds to ask me, well, a bunch of interview questions. So much for this not being a job interview. Figuring turnabout is fair play, I ask each question back to him.

"Great question, Kai, and my answer isn't complicated. If I'm going back to work, I want to be running the joint in five years—wherever I am, whatever that means," I hedge. "I have a chance now to make my career my sole focus." I concentrate on keeping my tone professional even as this statement heavily weighs me down. Aidan is really truly gone, and I am alone. How did we get here? "That is if I go back to work." I know I'm repeating myself. But it bears repeating. Before I can get lost in thought, or more accurately, lost in the waves threatening to engulf me, I ask, "How about you? What's your five-year plan?"

"Who's interviewing whom, Holland?" He asks with a crooked grin.

"You told me this isn't an interview, Mr. Ipu." I give him my saltiest glare.

"Ha!" He barks a laugh. "You're right. It's a conversation. Ask me anything."

"Well, I'd like to hear your five-year plan," I remind him. "For you personally, for Innovated, both…"

"You asked a question and I have yet to answer it, Holland. I apologize." He sounds sincerely serious suddenly. "I have a five-year plan, but I fear it makes me sound old." He smiles shyly.

Shy Kai? Who knew?

"This I have to hear." I actually lean in. "Are you five years from shuffleboard or something?"

His smile turns all the way on again. "Not shuffleboard, no. But you are eerily close," he says. "It is my goal to find and train my successor in the next few years. I'd like to retire so I can start a family—be a full-time dad—by the time I'm forty-five."

I blink. "Wow," I say. "That's not at all what I expected you to say. I guess that's a personal and professional plan, both. What does your girlfriend think about that timeline?" I hide behind the action of sipping my coffee as soon as I say it. I will my neck and cheeks not to blush.

"Well, yeah." He laughs. He's got a great laugh. Each laugh hints at a new and different layer of meaning. "I don't have one of those yet," he says.

"Sorry, what? You don't have one of what?" I ask, genuinely confused. I was following this train of thought but now it has left the station without me. I'm distracted.

"A girlfriend. My five-year plan includes meeting someone great and sweeping her off her feet," Kai says. "That's not unreasonable, is it?" he asks, sipping his coffee much more gracefully than my own nervous prop action had been.

"I– I guess not," I stammer. "Are you on Bumble?"

"What's a bumble?" he asks. I can tell by the twinkle in and crinkle around his eyes that he's giving me a hard time.

"I'll take that as a no." I smile at him. "Ambitious, sir," I announce. "To find both a wife and a CEO in the next five years."

He mumbles something into his coffee. It sounds like "done and done" but that doesn't make any sense.

"Let's talk about your ambitions, Holland," he says. I sit up straighter. "How would you like to work with our executive team? I'd like to introduce you to our Chief Information Officer first. I think you two will get along."

"I'd love to shadow Zahra Johnstone." I nearly giggle, I'm so excited about the opportunity. I hope he doesn't realize I'm admitting to cyberstalking him and his company. I was curious for goodness's sake. Well, that and I research like other people watch YouTube. It's a hobby, a habit, and something I do to relax. It's fun.

"You've done your homework," he says, obviously on to my nosy ways. "Yes, Zahra is a gem. I don't want you to shadow her, though—I want you to evaluate her. Holland, I'd like to bring you in as an observer. I want to hear your insights into what we're doing at IPU." He says EYE-pea-YOU—like the acronym it is—instead of EE-puu, like his surname. The distinction sends my busy brain down the rabbit hole of imagining twenty-year-old Kai dreaming in his dorm room of a business advisory firm and what to call it. Innovated Processes Unlimited. After himself. Bold. Just short of obnoxious. Wait. What are we talking about? "I want to know what you think we can do better," he says.

"I'm hardly qualified to do that," I protest. "You're asking me to consult for a consultancy?"

"Holland, I've also done my homework. You're more than qualified." His dark brown eyes are warm and kind. "The last year has been tough for you, obviously. However, your experience at two multinational companies, your published work on leadership, your efforts to bring social justice to the corporate world, all give me confidence you have what it takes to make us better. Zahra will love you," he says. "Perhaps you two can consider your time together a co-mentorship."

"Did you say co-mentor?" I nearly choke. "You really did do your homework." I wrote my thesis on the concept—women in business partnering to lift each other up, to push each other cooperatively to win in the workplace.

He's very proud of himself over there, grinning.

"I'm impressed." I smile back at him. I can't help it. Plus, it really is impressive, and so is his company. Maybe I'll take a week or two and do some more digging, make a measured decision about applying for work at IPU. "Thank you for thinking of me, Kai."

His face is unreadable, but he looks like he's having an entire conversation with himself. The pause is so long, I find myself fiddling with my silverware, stacking it neatly on the plate.

Then as though there'd been no pause at all: "I'd like to have you start as soon as possible," Kai says casually and confidently. "I have a meeting with Zahra at nine o'clock. Join us."

"Tomorrow?" I ask, my heart racing. "You mean tomorrow."

"Yes, in twenty hours, in fact," he quips as he looks at his huge watch—the face of it as big as my first phone.

"I… I don't… I worry…" I stutter. Tomorrow?

"Zahra leaves for a trip tomorrow evening," he says, "It's nine a.m. or not for two weeks. Do you have a valid passport? Bring it with you." He nods, looking self-satisfied. "Just in case."

7

I check my watch for the thirtieth time in twenty hours. I really need to get my nerves under control if I'm going to work with Holland Gallagher. This behavior is out of bounds. Nothing makes me nervous. Except this woman. Holland makes me nervous. I keep picturing how she will fit perfectly in our office, how she will fit perfectly in my arms…

"Ahem." Zahra sticks her head in my office door, fake-clearing her throat to get my attention. "You wanted to meet before our meeting, Ipu." I can hear the sarcasm from across the room.

"Yes, Zahra, hello. I have a consultant coming in at nine o'clock and I thought it wise you and I touch base before she gets here." I sound like I'm overcompensating for something. She's going to see right through me–

"Kai, I know this. I can't wait to meet Holland Gallagher." Even Zahra's eyes twinkle when she talks about Holland. Maybe she really is some kind of magic. "What's going on?"

Well, she's the most captivating creature I've ever met. She addles my brain; therefore, I wanted an excuse to talk about her so I can get my mental feet under me before she arrives. But I can't say that out loud.

"Nothing's going on." I run a hand over my beard. Now I even look nervous, probably. I have got to calm down. "I just want to ensure you're prepared to work with Holland right away."

"Kai, I'm prepared to put her on the plane and take her to Melbourne with me this evening." Zahra laughs. "I can't wait to pick her brain. Did you read the article she wrote in Harvard Business Review last spring? I was fangirling before you even mentioned her." Then she says, "Why don't you tell me what this is really all about." This gifted woman who was my first hire and remains the best professional decision I've ever made sits back in her chair and crosses her long legs. Looking both relaxed and ultra-professional in her pale lavender suit, she says, "You're all hot and bothered. You're not… attracted to Holland Gallagher, are you?" Zahra knows me way too well.

"Attracted? Hell no." I scoff. "Hardly. Of course not."

"The gentleman doth protest too much, methinks," she quips.

"No. Holland's mother-in-law is a dear friend of mine. She introduced us. I just want to impress her for my friend's sake," I lie. Of course I know I'd be lucky to have someone with Holland's brilliance and brains on this team. And beauty. Let's not forget how she'd bring her radiance to the office as well. She's practically a supernova.

Then, in an attempt to sound like I have my priorities in order, I say, "And for Innovated's sake. Like you, I think Holland brings a great deal to the table. She'll be an invigorating addition to the team. I'm just covering all our bases and such." How believable does that sound? Zahra's wry smile speaks volumes. Okay, so not believable at all. Fuck.

"Well, I cannot wait to meet her. I know you don't want me to take her to Australia just yet, but I am disappointed to only have today to spend with her," she says.

Just then Micah announces Holland's arrival over the intercom on my desk.

"There's a hottie with a body in the lobby for you, Ipu," he snarks. I decide I might have to castrate him. Why are these two torturing me this morning? "Holland Gallagher has arrived." At the sound of her name my heart does that annoying triple-beat thing. I may have to drag my old ass into a cardiologist at this rate.

"Sit," Zahra says as I get up. "I'll grab her."

I snarl my disapproval at her.

"Or not." Zahra laughs at my back. I'm already out the door and headed to the lobby.

♡

Micah stops by midafternoon. "I've been compiling the dossier you requested. I'm pretty sure Holland Gallagher and I are destined to be best friends for life," Micah quips.

I growl.

Micah presses on. "No, seriously, I think I'm already a little bit in love with her. She's smart and makes good decisions. Plus, so much heartbreak. It's going to be difficult to work for a jackass like you when there's someone as great as Holland on the team." I am pretty sure Micah is teasing me, but I'm also pretty sure I could hide his body with very little effort. I growl more forcefully. He continues to ignore me. "I'm sending you a couple of items that stood out and the rest will be in her file."

"Do that." I'm silently seething at Micah for indirectly flirting with Holland, and I find myself distracted by thoughts of Holland even as we are discussing her—the soft brown waves of her hair begging for my touch, the glow of her snow white skin exposed by the sleeveless shirt she's wearing today with a skirt that hugs her perfect curves, the twinkle in her green-gray eyes when she laughs… Micah is still talking? Shit.

"I've pulled together a ton of photos, too," Micah says. I am no longer distracted suddenly.

"Send me all of those," I say. Maybe a little too quickly. Cool it, Ipu.

"Done." Micah doesn't take the bait. Good man.

"Let me know if you get anything on her parents. I'm drawing blanks."

"Sure, boss." Micah sounds the tiniest bit …something. If I know this cocky fucker, he's about to give me shit. "Is that new? I mean, is this a procedure you want me to employ going forward? Researching a new hire's parents? Should I go back any further? Grandparents, too?"

"No. Definitely not," I bark. "I'm—" what now? "tracking down a hunch about her mother," I lie.

"Sure, boss," Micah says.

Best to end this conversation before I say anything else stupid.

"Thanks, Micah, keep me posted." I give him a look that invites him to leave my office without giving him a chance to respond.

♡

Late in the day, I get a text from Zahra. She must be in the air.

ZAHRA: Good day. Good woman. Time to talk?

About Holland? Always.

KAI: Gimme five to get on the treadmill.

Five minutes later, I call Zahra as I start my warm-up pace.

"Tell me," I say when she picks up the phone.

"I love her. I loved today. I've been sitting here firing off emails to my team since before takeoff." I can hear Zahra's smile in her voice. "I haven't felt this energized in months. She's a breath of fresh air."

I couldn't agree more. I sigh.

Zahra snickers. Is that a snicker? Shit.

"I hope you'll bring her on board." Zahra lets it go. Bless her. I'm not sure how to explain away sighing over someone I'm not supposed to have a crush on.

"Her first meeting tomorrow is with HR," I bark. The irony is not lost on me. Perhaps I should drag my sorry self into HR even before the cardiologist. Just in case.

"Good to hear. I can't wait to see what she does with the rest of the crew." Zahra sounds genuinely excited. "If you had asked me yesterday if I thought we were doing our best work, I would have been unequivocal. Yes. But talking through our processes with Holland—hearing her ideas and sensing her exuberance for excellence—makes me want to do better."

"I get it," I say honestly. Just having a meal with Holland makes me want to be a better man, live a better life. I have no trouble believing Zahra's assertion.

"Micah says he's already a little bit in love with her," Zahra says. I can hear her grin.

"Hmph. Does he now?" Not just to me, but he's saying this all over the office. Good thing he is the most capable, well-educated, and organized man I know, or else I'd have to carve Micah's heart out with a dull knife.

"My warm-up is over, Zahra. Safe flight."
"Don't let her go," Zahra says. "We need her, Ipu."
I grunt my agreement, hang up the phone, and pick up my pace.

8

I rest my head against the exceedingly comfortable leather… headrest. Guess that's why they call it that. Just as I'm about to close my eyes, Ximena's ringtone interrupts the cool silence of the town car's backseat.

"*Manita.*" My sister-in-law uses the LA-Spanish slang for little sister. "How are you?"

"Menita." I use the play-on-words-diminutive for Ximena I gave her years ago. "I am toast."

"Oh, Holland, you sound wrung out." Ximena's voice drips with the warm honey of empathy. "How did it go at work today?"

"I mean, I suppose my day could have been longer," I say. "I could be on my way to Australia…"

"Oh my! On your first day?" I hear in Ximena's voice all the excitement and anxiety warring in my own heart.

I don't argue. It was just a visit. Not my first day. Instead of correcting my sister, I say, "I'm as elated as I am exhausted. I met one of my heroes today. I have followed Zahra Johnstone's career since the first time I read about her in Forty Under Forty," I tell her. "In the eight hours we worked in her comfortable, sunny office, we broke down the entire structure of the company's current IT processes."

After nearly a year out of the workforce, I am pretty squeaking proud of my contributions. I recommended a handful of software upgrades, and some updated best practices—especially regarding Innovated's employee experience and inward-facing technology. At every turn, I was thrilled to find that Zahra was receptive and appreciative. I felt welcomed and valued, seen and heard by this woman I respect so completely.

"The only time we took a break was when Kai magically appeared with lunch," I say. I felt a familiar Kai-flavored heat creep up my neck and cheeks when he brought us sandwiches, salads, sodas, and brownies. "He's so capable and competent. I really admire his… well, um."

"Ass?" Ximena offers.

"Mena! No!" I am aghast.

"Abs? Arms? Ankles?" she's laughing now.

"Ximena! No!" I'm choking back giggles. "I admire his mind. Over lunch he asked Zahra how it was going, and her debrief was fast and furious—but he kept up, interrupting to ask insightful questions and to praise her flexibility and ingenuity."

"Did he flex his biceps while he asked? Did he mention his desire to get in-to-you-ity?" Ximena and her terrible puns.

"That's not funny," I protest through giggles.

"I googled his hotness," she says. "The man looks good in a suit, Holland." She stretches out the o's in good like a four-year-old would describe a particularly excellent ice cream cone.

"Stop it." I'm so glad she didn't FaceTime me—I am most likely beet red from my chest to my ears. Because, of course, she's absolutely wrong. I have no interest whatsoever in Kai. As if.

After talking through the morning with Zahra, Kai turned his penetrating eyes and glowing praise on me. He was thorough and thoughtful in his assessment of what he saw as my contributions to the day's progress. I tried to keep a seven on my face while I felt an eleven in my heart. But that was pride in my work. Nothing else.

My phone beeps in my ear, jerking me out of my reverie. "Oh, sis, I'm getting another call. Talk soon?"

"Ha! I knew it! You've got it bad for this g–" Ximena starts.

"Gotta go," I say as I cut her off and click over to the incoming call. "Hello, Zahra, how nice to hear from you so soon. Are you on a plane?"

"Yes, I am, it's a long flight to Tullamarine." Zahra doesn't sound the slightest bit fatigued—an embarrassing contrast to my weariness. "I just want to touch base before I get bogged down in time zones and jet lag and business meetings. I greatly enjoyed our work together today, Holland."

"Oh, me too, Zahra," I say. Sincerely. I loved the exchange, and I love this sense of accomplishment after only one day with her. And Kai. At the end of the day, he walked me to the lobby and I had déjà vu when I got out my phone to request an Uber—wait! Zahra's telling me something!

"And I very much want you to become a permanent part of the Innovated team." Zahra sounds… something? Hopeful? I don't know her well enough yet.

"Oh gosh, Zahra, that means a lot," I say. "I confess I'm equal parts exhausted and exhilarated by our time together. You inspire me—and I had an absolute blast with you today." We cracked each other up throughout the day—making connections and finding patterns in the mountains of spreadsheets and org charts and such. I can imagine working with Zahra regularly would be a ton of fun.

"Let me make myself clear, Holland. I'm a firm believer that a rising tide lifts all boats, as they say," Zahra says. "And I think you and Innovated can help each other get better, do better, be better. We need you. And I hope you can see how this will be mutually beneficial. We will pay you back in dividends not measurable in dollars alone. We lead as a team at Innovated. We will invest heavily in you, Holland."

"Zahra, this is a heavy pitch coming from the CIO," I start to argue.

"Actually." She doesn't exactly cut me off. "This is an impassioned plea from the only woman in the C-suite. I need you. And I think you and I can help each other. I'd love to work with you. Plus, I think we made pretty great progress toward a friendship today."

"I love to hear you say that, Zahra." I must be tired because I'm a little choked up, "I feel exactly the same way." I haven't made a new friend in so long. That must be what's making me so emotional about this phone call.

Zahra and I wrap up the impromptu meeting of our newly founded mutual admiration society. We make plans to dig in further to some cybersecurity updates we talked about earlier.

As I hang up the phone, the car drops me off at my building. I am bone-weary and very aware of how much more draining a full day of work is than I remembered. And yet it is also infinitely more rewarding than I remember. I thank the driver (who is not Jamil, I noted when Kai walked me to the car he insisted I take home) and drag my thousand-pound limbs up to the door. But as I wait for the elevator, I decide it's a good kind of tired. Maybe I'll accept the job at IPU. Unless, of course, I already did? And today was my first day? I wonder.

9

Over the next ten days, I perfect a complicated dance of seeking out and then avoiding Holland Gallagher.

On Tuesday, she was on the elevator when it reached me, so I faked having forgotten something in my office. I can't be in an enclosed space with her. That would be too much.

Wednesday was a blur, but I still found time to casually check on Holland twice. Okay, so, not so casually since I had to ask at reception both times where I might find her.

On Thursday, I realized I hadn't seen her all day, so I went in search of her. I stood outside the door of Micah's office listening to her answer a million of his (all very professional and appropriate, thank god I don't have to kill him today) questions. I looked at my watch—it was nine-twenty in the morning. I am so screwed.

I took meetings off campus all day Friday so I could avoid my deepening desire to see her, talk to her, hold her. But after a dinner meeting with clients, I found myself rushing out of the restaurant, speeding back to work, relieved to find Holland just leaving for the day.

"Headed out?" I say nonchalantly, as though I haven't been thinking about her, worried for her, daydreaming of her all damn day.

"Oh, Kai, hi." She beams. That smile is more than I can handle. "Welcome back."

So, she noticed my absence today. That seems like a good sign. Or is it? I imagine HR would have a thing or two to say about my excessive need to be near this woman (note to self: stop by HR for real this time).

"How was your day?" She looks shocked that I asked. What's that about?

"My day was good," she says slowly. Her response is like she knows the answer but isn't sure I want to know. "I had a great meeting with some of your lawyers today." A million bad lawyer jokes rush to the front of my brain.

I settle on, "I hope it was *brief*." My day is completely made when Holland starts to respond, visibly replays my statement, and then starts to laugh. Her laugh is a miracle. I want to spend the rest of my life making this woman laugh.

"Nah, but it never lost its *appeal*," she says. I shake my head and walk away, laughing. That exchange will get me through the next week.

Wrong. By Sunday night, after suffering through a Holland-free weekend, I find I can't wait any longer. As I touch her phone number, chills shoot from my hand, down to my toes, and back up my spine.

She answers. "Hello, Kai."

"May I take you to dinner this week? How's Wednesday night?" I ask. Before she can say no, I say, "I'll pick you up. Don't look for Jamil. It'll be me." What's this? Am I jealous of my driver? That's precious. She's going to say no, I just know it.

"Sure, Kai, I'd love to have dinner with you on Wednesday," she says.

"Excellent," I bark. "Look for the 1960 Ferrari 250GT LWB California Spider Competizione."

"Um. What color?" she asks. My stomach drops. What a jackass—am I trying to show off? Why did I say that? "I don't know if I'll recognize something based only on that long string of words…"

I laugh nervously. I've never laughed nervously in my entire life. "Very funny. Red," I say. "I'll pick you up at home at seven sharp."

"I look forward to it," she says.

I attempt to end the call without sounding overwhelmed and clumsy. "Same." Well, fuck. I failed that assignment.

10

When Wednesday finally rolls around, I wake up drenched in sweat. I was dreaming about stealing some stranger's boyfriend. I don't know him or her in my real life, but I knew I wanted him in my dream. I am aware even now as I turn over in the sopping tank top and damp sheets how much I wanted this anonymous man to be mine. Not hers.

Shaking off the dream, I drag myself to the restroom, peeling off my tossing and turning as I go. Without flipping on the light, I relieve myself, wash my hands, splash cool water on my face. Stumbling back into my room, I pull a cleanish sports bra out of the suitcase and onto my overheated skin. Clean shorts. Clean socks. Ancient sneakers. I am just on the verge of calling out to Aidan to announce my departure for a run.

Oh. Right.

An icy heat works its way from my core to my limbs and lifts my fingers to my hair. Deep breath. Tight ponytail. I'll try a new route around the neighborhood this morning. My skin pricks painfully as I put the unfamiliar house key in my pocket, walk out the door Aidan has never walked through, letting it lock soundlessly behind me.

♡

Later that afternoon, I find myself sitting in my living room, staring at the blank wall, completely freaking out. Is this a date? What if it is a date? Do I want it to be a date? Am I ready to date?

When Kai called the other night, I was caught off guard. I mean, it seemed like the most natural thing in the world to have the boss I haven't seen all week ask me out to dinner. (Well, except for the lawyer pun exchange in the lobby the other night. Honestly, besides that, he's been a ghost all week.)

Tonight, I still don't know if dinner with my boss is a good idea or a very bad plan. I don't know if I'm nervous or excited. I definitely don't know anything other than Ferrari in his description of his car. So I look it up. Oh, *Ferris Bueller's Day Off!* Well, won't that be fun? No sooner do I have that thought than I start freaking out.

Most experts agree there is no set-in-stone appropriate amount of time for widows and widowers to mourn. Some say that one might start moving out of the "widow brain" stage after about six months. *Ha!* I still cannot find my phone or keys or sunglasses half the time.

It's one of the reasons I dragged my feet about returning to work. For months (well, more than six, lemme tell ya) I'd find myself standing in the kitchen with absolutely no idea why I was in there. Not hungry, not thirsty, not looking for my phone… As a person who values my ability to think my way out of any problem, I find it infuriating. It has improved, for sure. But it's not gone.

Anyway, experts in the myriad articles, books, and posts I've read also seem to agree that, in regard to dating, I am the only person who can decide if I'm ready. That I should trust my gut. But how can I trust my gut if it's all tied in knots?

Before I even realize what I'm doing, I dial Ximena's number.

"Holland," she says. "So nice to hear from you."

"Menita, I missed your voice."

"Always good to talk, Holland," Ximena says. "But what's wrong? I can hear it from eighteen hundred miles away. How can I help, *manita*?"

I sigh. "I think I have a date tonight," I squeak.

"Oh, Holland." Ximena must hear something in my voice because hers is grave and nearly a whisper. "It's okay, let it out."

Even as she's encouraging me to cry, I hear *her* sniffle.

"Don't cry, Mena! I'm so sorry. I don't mean to inflict this on you." I don't recognize my own voice as I'm laughing through tears (or crying through laughter?). In the year we've been widows together, my favorite sensation has become the catharsis of sharing hysterics and misery simultaneously with my closest friend.

"I love you so much, Ximena." I blow my nose loudly in her ear. "I wish you were closer."

"I know, baby girl," Ximena replies with a loud nose-honk of her own. "Being here is what works best for now, my sweet girl. This is my place. You will find your own. I promise." She takes a deep breath and, following her example, so do I. "Now, tell me about your date," she says.

I swallow around the unnamed nothing choking me. This physical sensation is so familiar I actually crave it when it's absent. If I'm not choking on emotion, I fear I'm somehow forgetting to feel. "Maybe it's not a date." My voice is a full octave higher than it was just a moment ago. "Maybe it's just dinner. Maybe it can't be a date."

"Well, isn't that up to you?" Ximena asks. "If this person is worthy of you, they will let you decide if you're ready to date. Without pushing you."

"You're right." I swallow hard. "And I don't even know if he thinks it's a date. He asked me out to dinner. But it could be, I don't know…" I search my brain. Foggy, as usual. "Something other than a date?"

"Oh, boy," my sister says with great gravity. "You're going to dinner with Kai."

My eyes sting, and my nose starts running again. "I'm going to dinner with Kai," I whine.

Ximena laughs. This is far and away my least favorite. Every time I'm in crisis while my sister laughs at me—something that occurs all too often in my estimation!—I feel like such a big baby.

"Stop laughing at me," I grouch. "And don't call me baby girl." I pout—my belated response to something she said many minutes ago. "You're like eight months younger than I am. How is it you clearly have your act together and I'm a blubbering mess?"

"Holland, baby." Ximena stifles a giggle—I can hear it. "You have your act together. You're wildly successful, exceedingly beautiful, gracious and graceful, considerate and generous, driven, and a total badass."

"I've been a wildly successful stay-at-home widow for the last year, Mena," I howl. "That's not a real thing!" I can't help the tears or the giggles that accompany this statement of cold, hard fact.

"Stop it. You were taking some time off. That's completely understandable. I took time off. So did Nomi," Ximena says softly, her compassion pouring through the phone to wash over me. "We all needed time to absorb the impact of our boys' deaths."

"It's too soon to date. I was far more prepared to re-enter the workforce than I am to dive back into the dating pool," I whine. "It's only been a year."

"Yes, it has been nearly a year. In fact, I'll see you in just a few weeks." Ximena sounds brighter and lighter. "We'll commemorate the day. Celebrate our men. Treat Nomi to a girls' weekend. That's something to look forward to, right?"

"Yes, of course it is. It's more like six weeks," I grump. "I can't wait to see you." I take another slow, deep breath. "I just have to get through tonight."

"Just set some boundaries. Establish some ground rules. Let Kai know what you're ready for and what you're not," Ximena says. "You're so good at communicating boundaries in a professional setting, Holland. I know you know how to do this."

"Yeah, okay," I hedge. I'm not sure what I'll say to Kai because I'm still not sure what he thinks this is. But a good cry and a good conversation with my good friend put me in a better state of mind. "I'm going to go for a run, then shower and change, start fresh." I don't tell her it'll be my second run of the day.

"Great idea. I love you so much, sis," Ximena says.

"*Te quiero*, Menita," I say, and then I end the call.

11

Changing out of a suit and into jeans earlier, I felt like a blundering teenager getting ready to pick up a girl for our first date. Parking my sixty-year-old car on the street, I curse myself for being a dirty old man scamming on a girl half my age.

She is not half my age, I remind myself. I've done the math. She's half my age, *plus* seven years. And according to the internet, that's just about right. Right? I've been with younger women before. Hell, I've been with women younger than Holland. This is different.

She is different. My first impression of her was both the girl-next-door and the sexy minx. Now I know her better and I spend half my day wondering how I can get her to show me more of that se— hold up. Get your mind out of the gutter, Ipu.

My head is swimming with Holland. I want her, there's no question. And I admire her, respect her. I am responsible for her— for Naomi's sake. Maybe also for Aidan's sake, if that's not too weird. And I have responsibilities for my new employee, of course. I blink at the inanity of my ability to compartmentalize that shit.

I get out of the car, circle to the passenger side, and reach in to pick up the bunch of daisies I'd rested on the floorboard to protect it from the wind. Shit. I should not have gotten her flowers. This isn't a date. Dammit, what was I thinking? Wait. Is this a date?

Before I can change my mind about the daisies, the front door of Holland's building opens, and I swear the sun comes out from behind a cloud. In a simple sky-blue sundress and tiny light blue sneakers, her nearly six-foot self looks sassy and sporty and delicious. I'm aching to know what her lips taste like, how soft her skin is under my fingertips, my lips.

"Holland." I don't even recognize my own voice. Oh, I'm doomed. I'm saying this woman's name like it's a prayer. I clear my throat. Start over. "Holland, hi." I try to sound pleasant—or at least sane—this time. "You didn't have to come down. I would have come up to collect you." I hand her the bouquet. Like at the coffee place, I'm looking for a reason to keep myself from reaching for her. I just know, know like I've never known anything before, that she would feel as good as she looks. This woman.

"Flowers? Oh, goodness, look at these happy daisies. Thank you," Holland says. "Does this mean you're taking me on a date, Mr. Ipu?" I can't tell if she's teasing. Inquiring? Freaking out? Wait. This feels exceedingly familiar.

"Actually, this is… not a date. This is just dinner." I can't even answer the question of to-date or not-to-date when asked a direct question. "A friendly dinner. Dinner between friends. Daisies are friendly flowers." I mentally roll my eyes at myself.

"Hm. Let's walk," she says.

Walk? I panic. I try to look calm and cool, leaving my pristine vintage convertible unattended. On the street. Downtown.

I sneak my phone out of my pocket and surreptitiously text Jamil to come pick it up. Immediately.

"Of course. Let's walk." I fold my arms across my chest so I won't be tempted to try and hold her hand. She's holding both her flowers and her bag on my side of her. Good. Excellent. Fuck. "It'll give us time to talk about your first week at Innovated," I suggest.

"Yes, walking lends itself to talking about work. Of course. I'm just relieved we're not on a date," she says with a kind of snort-laugh. And I laugh along with her—and try to hide how she's once again smashed my heart into tiny little bits.

12

"This is such a treat." Naomi gives me a jasmine-lemon-rose-scented hug. She smells like hugs feel. We're meeting at a little café near Innovated. "Where were you this time, Nomi? What's new in your world?" Naomi surprised me this morning with an invitation to lunch. I didn't even know we were in the same zip code before I got the note.

"I'm returning from Miami. I missed you, my girl." Naomi smiles. "I had to get home in time for our West Coast cohort to launch their first initiative. I definitely needed to be here for that."

"That's impressive." I truly am impressed. Part of me is, in fact, envious of the group of Fellows making such quick work of their new placement. I feel so far behind in my new role.

"Unknit that beautiful brow, Holland, please," Naomi says. "What's wrong?"

"I feel like I'm not moving quickly enough at Innovated," I confess. "I love the work. I love the people. I love the company and the culture. But I feel like I can't get to every team, every issue, every idea fast enough."

"Holland." Naomi sounds like she is scolding me. "You are being unfair to yourself. You are decisive, adaptable, engaging. I'm sure you're exceeding Kai's expectations."

"That's just it," I say. "I'm not sure of his expectations. Kai lets Micah set meetings for me. He doesn't seem to be involved in my schedule at all. When he asks for debriefs, it's never in person. I can't get him on the phone nor catch him in his office. When he leaves me messages, he's incredibly positive and I feel like he's happy with my work."

"You sound like you're complaining, Holland." Naomi laughs softly. "Positive feedback and 'happy with your work' are good things. I'm confused." So am I. I accepted the position partially because I hoped I'd have a chance to work closely with Kai. Wrong.

♡

When he invited me to dinner, it seemed like the evening was going to be a good chance to catch up.

He was leaning into the open top of that ridiculously sexy car, reaching for flowers for me when I first saw him. Goodness but his jeans were clearly meant to show off his best asset. Then he stood and turned my way. Assets, I had to correct myself. A plain white long-sleeved tee with a shallow v-neck showed a hint of a tattoo. He had on the kind of man-sandals only confidence can pull off on his well-groomed and how-is-it-possible-they-are-attractive feet.

The flowers were a nice touch. If a bit confusing. They were the prettiest natural brown-butcher-paper-wrapped bunch of daisies (*Bellis perennis*, if you were wondering) made special with the inclusion of cheery yellow goldenrod stems (*Solidago canadensis*, for those of you taking notes) and tied with a real hemp string. The arrangement sat on the empty chair next to me on the patio of my favorite fun and funky pizza place.

Kai sat across the piping hot, bubbly cheese and mushroom pie we were sharing.

"Are you a vegetarian?" Kai asked over his glass of house-made watermelon lavender lemonade.

I laughed as my attention snapped back to my dinner date. It's not a date, I reminded myself for the fifty-seventh time. How long had I been staring down at the flowers, thinking about Kai and not actually in the moment, here with Kai? Sheesh. "No, not a vegetarian," I tried to relax my features, afraid that he would think me unstable watching all the emotions crossing my face.

His eye crinkles tipped me off—maybe he finds me amusing and not annoying? He was smizing at me.

"I just imagined the three different mushrooms would be delicious. Do you not like it?" I asked.

"I do like it, very much," he said. "I only mean, I would never have ordered it myself. Thanks for helping me try something new, Holland."

I liked the way he said my name. He didn't have an accent per se, he just had a very specific way of speaking. His voice was big and deep and always sounded like he was on the verge of a laugh. Each time he said my name, it sounded different to me. Like it held some layer of meaning beyond just getting my attention. Earlier that evening when he greeted me, I could have sworn he said my name with reverence. And now it sounded like my name was the setup for a promising joke.

"Are you teasing me?" I asked.

"Not even a little bit." He beamed a huge smile at me. "I'm being sincere. I rarely remember to try new things, I'm afraid. At least when I'm in LA," he said, turning contemplative. "I've lived here all my life and I fear its charm is lost on me. I can't remember the last time I walked to dinner, for example. Thank you for that as well."

"Oh, gosh, no need to thank me." I pushed my hair behind my ear, a little shy at his gratitude. "I just hate inefficiency. It would have taken longer to drive here and find a place to park than it did to walk. And that's if we could even have found a parking spot closer than my building," I said.

"I see that at work," he said. I didn't know how to respond to that.

He took a deep breath and a long drink of lemonade. "Would you like some wine? I think we should drink." Heavily, I agreed silently. Without waiting for my response (or did I say that out loud?), he waved over a server and ordered a bottle of something I didn't recognize.

The wine arrived, and I sipped the Sicilian deliciousness. "I'm embarrassed to admit I didn't realize Sicily makes wine. This is scrumptious, thank you."

"Have you ever been to Italy? To Sicily?"

"Italy, yes." I saw flashes of sun-soaked Tuscan hills, laughing with Aidan and Ethan and Ximena on a stone terrace, drinking wine.

My throat tried to freeze up, but I forced myself to say, "The island, no. I really don't know much about it—only what I've gleaned from mafia movies." Kai's smile was wide.

"I'll take you," he said as though it were no big deal. I laughed nervously. I felt my butterflies staging La Bohème in my belly.

"Do you take all your new employees to Italian islands?"

In lieu of a response, he offered a toast. "To new friends." He held his glass my way.

"To friends."

♡

I get out of my head and return to Naomi. "He asks for debriefs via email and leaves voicemail messages on my work phone to let me know he's happy with my progress. It is awful," I say. "I know I sound like such a whiner." I have to laugh at myself. "I'm not sure why I'm so disappointed. Irritated. I really just wish I knew what Kai was thinking. If he likes me." Wait. "My work, I mean."

Saying this to Naomi aloud, I'm starting to realize what my problem might be. It could be the issue that Kai is observably, undeniably, empirically gorgeous. Probably the largest man I've ever met. Six foot—what, five?—and obviously strong and healthy. I can tell in his perfectly tailored suits—does a man that large have to have them custom-made?—that he is not just fit but extremely well-built and Just. All. Muscle.

Lots of tattooed muscle, I am pretty sure, even though I can only ever see a hint of ink where his top two shirt buttons are perpetually open. Tantalizing copper skin and a cleanly shaved head. Salt and pepper beard that belies the fact he is just enough older than I to be incredibly appealing and not taboo. His ridiculously infectious smile crinkles his eyes in the sexiest way. Not since I met my husband— and obviously not since I lost Aidan—have I found anyone this insanely attractive. I'm in so much trouble.

"Holland, I'm sure it really is that he's just very busy. You, of all people, know what it means to juggle multiple tasks." Naomi makes perfect sense, but I still feel annoyed. Maybe at Kai, maybe at myself. "It's one of the reasons I thought you and Kai would be so great together. You are both so hyper-focused and perhaps a little too driven."

I squint at my mother-in-law, trying to hear her more clearly by focusing on her face. "You did what?" I whisper-demand. She tries to look innocent. "What do you mean, you thought we would be great together?"

Naomi sips her water. She's stalling. "Let's order. The food looks delicious," she says in a clear dodge, looking around at other tables.

"Nomi, explain." I try to keep my tone even and not bite her head off in anger.

Naomi sighs. "I knew you and my old friend would work well together. I set you up." She at least has the decency to look abashed. "Not romantically, please don't misunderstand. I just wanted you two to meet so you could see that you would make a fantastic team."

"Naomi." I deliberately pronounce all three syllables. "How could you?"

"Don't be angry, dear," Naomi says. "Please understand. You'd been talking about getting back to work. And I knew Innovated would be the best place for you."

"What did you do?" I am clenching and relaxing my fists to keep myself from getting really angry. Or maybe to keep myself from getting really embarrassed.

"I asked Kai to interview you for a position at Innovated," Naomi says, blushing. "That's really all I did. He was thrilled. Jumped at the chance. He adores you."

"Naomi. This is mortifying." I drop my forehead to my hands. "I've been acting as though I got this job on my own merits," I tell the table. "And now I find out it's nepotism." I look back up at her. "This is horrifying."

"No nepotism whatsoever, Holland." Naomi tries to reach for my hand, but I am not ready for that. I pull both my hands into my lap where I can dig my fingernails into my palms unobserved by the traitor (even if she's a well-intentioned backstabber, I sigh). "His exact words were 'regardless of your skillset' he'd find a place for you at Innovated." Naomi is smiling sweetly, looking hopeful for some forgiveness.

"That. Is. So. Much. Worse!" I seethe through clenched teeth. My throat tightens. I try to take a deep breath but find it painful. I bore my eyes into my mother-in-law's skull. "Nomi, this is... I'm—I can't even—" Naomi's eyes are brimming with tears and I start to feel bad for making her upset. I'll lighten up in a minute. Right now,

I am burning up with humiliation.

"Oh, Holland, I love you so much and I really was just trying to help." Naomi reaches for my hand again. This time I let her take it, but as soon as she touches me, it is all I can do not to snap my hand away. This motherly touch is usually the comfort I seek from Naomi, but in this moment, my mortification makes me recoil from it.

This is the only mother you have, Holland, I remind myself. She means well. Assume best intentions. You can fix this thing at work. Don't let it ruin the only love you have left.

"I know you love me, Nomi." I sigh. Not a teenager's exasperation, but an exhalation of my anger and tension. "Let's just eat. We both have to get back to work. Let's enjoy each other's company. Tell me about your cohort's new project." I forcibly relax my jaw and squeeze Naomi's hand with sincere affection. Dagnabbit.

13

HOLLAND: Kai, I'd like to find time to speak in person. How's Wednesday at 7 PM?
KAI: I can make that work.
HOLLAND: Meet me at my flat. Bring wine. Not flowers.
KAI: Har har. I'll be there.

I feel my heart do its obnoxious triple-beat each time I re-read the brief text exchange. I've been avoiding Holland since our roller coaster of a dinner the other night because I am trying very hard to deny my ever-growing ...let's go with... feelings for her. But also because I have absolutely no idea where we stand. Dinner was fun and flirtatious one minute—icy the next. When I walked her back to her place after pizza, the electricity was palpable. I knew my side of the equation was sexual tension, but even now I have no clue what she was contributing. At her door, I wanted so desperately to kiss her goodnight, but for the first time in my dating life, I was scared of rejection. It's obvious Holland has no idea what she wants. Yet.

I can do all the wanting for both of us. For now.

In the meantime, Holland has been lighting my business on fire—in the best way—since Day One. After igniting the IT department with Zahra, she tackled cost with the marketing team, tax with the accountants, even ergonomics and wayfinding with the interior designers. I am blown away each and every day by her progress. I cannot believe the audacity I had naming this business "innovated" anything before I knew her. And yet, I've been dodging her, hiding from her, using every excuse I can. I must avoid having to confront my feelings—or her beautiful face.

I mean, I give her plenty of feedback, and I try to convey how impressed and pleased I am in my (let's face it, cowardly) late-night voicemails to her office phone.

I imagine this invitation to meet face-to-radiant-face is her effort to force me to grow a pair. Dammit.

And now my workday is flying by and falling apart. I have no idea how, with so many capable and competent people in my employ, the shit can so quickly hit the proverbial fan. I can't even pinpoint what is driving me so insane this afternoon. Every single person I've spoken to today has pissed me right the fuck off. I am at my wits' end with these people.

"I've had about enough of this," I grumble to no one.

"I hardly think you'll ever get enough," a lovely feminine voice I've been hearing for half my life responds.

"Naomi, hello." I jump up to hug her, immediately less irritated. "What a pleasure to see you again so soon. Is this what I can expect now that you're back in LA?"

"You're sweet," she says with a restrained grin on her sweet face. "I just wanted to stop by to thank you for dinner the other night."

"In person." I raise a skeptical eyebrow at her. "That seems unlikely. What's on your mind?" I motion her to a pair of chairs in my vast wasteland of a ridiculously oversized office.

"Oh, Kai." Naomi sighs. "I'm not a stupid woman. You know this. But I really messed up."

I cannot imagine what this can be about. "Whatever it is, Naomi, we'll fix it. Tell me what's going on."

"I had lunch with Holland yesterday. We—I—we talked—she was so upset." I've never heard her this flustered in all the years we've been friends.

"Who? Holland?" I prompt her to get to the point. If this is about Holland… I envision my sympathetic nervous system preparing my body for a fight response. Fuck flee or freeze. I'll kill anything that threatens Holland.

"I told her I asked for your help to find her a job." Naomi sounds distraught.

"That's what you're upset about?" I'm relieved. I feel the

adrenaline already starting to drop off. "That shouldn't—"

Naomi cuts me off. "I'm not the one who's upset, Kai. Holland is livid. She thinks your job offer was nepotism. She thinks you hired her simply because you're doing me a favor. She's truly humiliated." Naomi's voice is wavering.

"I see," I say. I'll have to think about this. "She invited me to dinner on Wednesday. Now I can see why she wanted to speak off-campus."

"She did? I think that's a good sign." Naomi sounds slightly hopeful. "Is that a good sign? She won't want to make a scene."

"Hm. We're meeting at her place." I stop myself from imagining the worst. "No worries, Naomi. I've got this. You and I both know Holland is more than qualified for the work she's doing for Innovated. In fact, she's probably underemployed with us. I can easily convince her that her fears are misguided."

"I hope so, Kai." Naomi's sweet voice sounds strained. "I feel like I really let her down."

"Don't even think about this another minute, Naomi. I've got it handled. I'll handle it. I'm on the handle." Wait. What?

Naomi laughs her biggest, brightest, most charming laugh, tossing her auburn head back and holding her stomach. I nearly start to laugh, hers is so infectious and unexpected. But I'm too annoyed at myself to give in.

"Oh, Kai." She finally stops laughing long enough to catch her breath. "She's beguiling, isn't she? I loved watching Aidan get tongue-tied over her, too."

I search her familiar, flawless face for something to read between the lines. Is she scolding me? Warning me? No.

Is she encouraging me? I shake my head at my wishful thinking.

On this note, I assure Naomi one more time that I've got everything under control. We say our goodbyes and I walk her to the door.

Now what, hotshot? I've got it handled? We'll see about that.

I suddenly see the value in a huge office as I remove my suit coat and dress shirt and start doing push-ups in the middle of the floor.

14

On Wednesday at precisely seven o'clock, I take a deep breath as I buzz up my boss. I left the office at lunchtime today to prepare for the very serious discussion I plan to enter into this evening. The loft is spotless. Dinner is ready (thank goddess for delivery). I spent as much time perfecting the lighting as I did rehearsing my opening salvo. And I made sure that every vase in the house has fresh flowers—not one of them a daisy—because somehow I feel this proves my independence.

The knock on the door brings my attention back to the mirror in front of me. I'm a professional. This is a business dinner. I've got this, I silently reassure myself in the mirror. With another deep breath, I open the door. And all of my resolve melts away. Kai is mouthwatering in a black cashmere sweater, perfectly cut jeans, and—be still my beating heart—cowboy boots. What is he trying to prove by looking so incredibly attractive? The soft wool accentuates each of his sculpted muscles. His jeans look bespoke—are custom jeans a real thing? All six-feet-five-inches of him stands looking casual, comfortable, and magnetic in the hallway before me. I stop myself from self-consciously looking down at my own effort to look effortless—I was sure the oversized linen French-tucked button-down, high-waisted jeans, and pale pink ballet flats said post-pandemic-business-casual-work-from-home when I chose them. Now I feel like I'm playing dress-up in someone else's clothes. Graceless.

"Holland," he says, still in the hallway. I jump.

"Kai, please come in." How long have we been standing in the doorway staring at each other? Holy guacamole. I am way in over my head here. What was I thinking, inviting him to my home? I was so sure it was a power play when I devised my plan. Now it feels like the fast track to serious drowning. In him.

"The wine you requested." He hands me a cool-to-the-touch bottle of Veuve Clicquot. "And the chocolates you did not." His copper skin tints the slightest bit red—is he blushing? Maybe this evening isn't completely out of control yet. If he's making himself blush by bringing me chocolates, I may not be the only one in the deep end. Food for thought.

"Champagne?" I raise a single eyebrow. "Were you under the impression we're celebrating?"

"Yes," he says, walking confidently into my living space, now the doorway spell is broken. "We are indeed celebrating. I'm sorry you had to prompt tonight's meeting, Holland. I'm thrilled we have a chance to celebrate together." I wonder what he could possibly be thinking.

And I wonder what he's thinking *about* as he takes in my space. I long ago removed the horrible corporate paintings that came with the apartment and have finally replaced them with an installation of postcards Aidan and I sent home to ourselves on our travels. Nearly ninety postcards fill the wall behind the couch—I put up a four-foot-square white enamel metal surface next to an identical black enamel metal surface and used tiny nearly-invisible silver magnets to hang the cards. Some nights when I can't sleep, I sit on the ottoman facing the wall, staring at them.

More than once, I've climbed up on the couch to rearrange the postcards—and the memories. Currently, they are in color order— more about aesthetics than sentimentality—working from the blues of Greece's beaches and Montana skies to the glorious greens of Ireland and Iowa. Before the hues-based organization, the last arrangement had been chronological. That hurt too much to look at, so I meticulously reorganized them this way. My plan is to add to the collection on solo travels someday. That also hurts too much, so I try not to think about it.

"Nice place," Kai says. He nearly fills the room I normally view as massive.

"It's not mine." It sounds like an apology. "It was furnished."

"These are yours," he says without question, gesturing to the postcards.

"Yes. When my husband and I traveled, we mailed ourselves souvenirs. These span my junior year of college right up to last summer." I am proud I keep my voice from wavering.

"You like to travel." Again this isn't a question.

"Very much. Even before I met Aidan, it was a hobby. An obsession." My mother's wanderlust was really the only trait of hers I adopted. Years before she started moving us each summer, my mother and I had gotten "the hell out of Dodge" on a spontaneous and regular basis. "My mom would wake me up in the middle of the night sometimes, throw me and a bag in the car, and just drive," I say. Out loud. Oof, I didn't mean to say it to him. Recovering myself, I say, "Can I get you a drink?"

"Please," he says, turning to me for the first time since the hallway. His eyes on mine have me ready to say and do things I've never considered in my lifetime. No really, this is too much. "Whiskey?" he asks. His first question of the evening.

"Of course," I say in a voice that sounds raspy and whiskey-warm already. At the bar, I pour us each a neat glass and then motion to the living room. "I'd like to discuss my performance at Innovated Processes Unlimited, Mr. Ipu," I say formally.

"Holland, I'm not Mr. Ipu. My father wasn't ever even called Mr. Ipu. Please call me Kai." He looks more hurt than perturbed.

"Kai, I'd like to talk about how you think this is going." I soften my approach. I don't want to hurt his feelings, but I also didn't want to change the subject.

"I could not be more pleased with how things at Innovated are improving under your influence, Holland." He says my name like it has weight—like it is bigger than just my label—as though it has heft and carries meaning to him beyond the obvious. "I've tried to be clear in my daily communications, and again when we went to dinner last week: you are killing it." He smiles broadly. Good goddess in her heaven, he has a great smile. His entire beautiful bronze face smiles when he lights up like that. I feel my heart and my brain start to melt. I can't afford to melt. This is a dinner meeting, not a date.

"I appreciate the voicemails." I try to sound snarky—and not as hurt or neglected as I truly feel.

"Yes, well." He growls. Just a little. I try not to smile at his snarl. I remember how Naomi reacted to his growling at dinner the night we met—with humor even as she censured him. "We've both been very busy. Again, I'm grateful to you for arranging this evening so I can tell you to your—" He clears his throat. "So I can say to you personally how very much I appreciate all you're doing for our teams, our people. Our processes. I see it every day, Holland." This time, the way he says my name has a connotation of respect—how does he do that? Fit so much meaning into my name?

He gives a short speech (that sounds only a little rehearsed) about the feedback he's been hearing from the teams I've been working with. He wraps it up with, "You're changing the culture—which is remarkable because our culture was something I was exceedingly proud of before you came on board. The idea that it could be so vastly improved is a little disconcerting for this old man."

"You're hardly old, Kai." It's a reflex. I fear it might sound like flirting and I wish I could take it back.

"You're kind." He half-smiles. I suppress a sigh. Even his half-smiles make me want to whole-sigh. "What I am is a man prouder of the company I've built because you're in it." I suppress a swoon. But that's not what this is all about. I straighten my spine. Where was all this praise and poetry when we went to dinner last week?

"Look," I start in my most businesslike voice. My boardroom voice, Aidan called it. It is my armor and I don it protectively now. "I'm an extremely pragmatic person. I consider your success my success. I can see the numbers. In the time I've been consulting, Innovated has seen some gains that make me proud." I watch his face carefully to see if he is truly hearing me. "That said, I am also aware that you hired me as a favor to my mother-in-law."

"Wait—" He tries to interrupt me, but I press on.

"Please let me finish. You hired me because Naomi asked you to. I've thought a lot about this since she confessed her foolish interference to me. I'm no longer angry at her—or at you—for this nepotism. This was my mistake for taking too long to decide what my next steps were after my husband died." I pause to take a breath. This was why I was so angry when I found out Naomi had meddled: it isn't fair I have to discuss my personal life and my professional life in the same sentence. If Naomi hadn't gotten involved, I might've eventually gone back to work in a place where no one knows me, no one knew Aidan, no one knows my story. Now, I am saddled with this burden of mixing my two worlds and I really hate it. "I'm grateful for the opportunity. You have built a business that is truly remarkable, and I admire you and the people you've gathered. I'm proud to have counted myself among them."

"Thank you. I—" he starts.

"I'm speaking, sir," I scold. "Allow me to finish. I'm proud to have worked for you and with your team. However, please accept my two weeks' notice." His face falls. "I cannot possibly continue to work in a position I did not earn on my own merit." There. That's done. I wait for his response. And I wait.

"I'm done," I say, referring to both my speech and the job.

"My turn," he announces.

Oh, here we go.

15

I shouldn't have interrupted her. But now I have the floor.

I take a breath before I launch into my retort and—six rapid reverberating knocks—are you kidding me? What now?

Someone is demanding attention at Holland's front door. She looks as perplexed as I do. Without a word, she gets up, looks to see who it is, looks back at me, and opens the door.

"Mrs. Gallagher, I'm sorry to disturb you," Jamil says. "Kai, we gotta go."

There are exactly two situations in which Jamil would do something like this. One is if the building were on fire. The other is even more urgent and important. I watch his eyes to see which it could possibly be. Understanding he's not just asked *both* Holland and me to go with him—years of working closely together make it clear which "we" he meant when he said "gotta go"—I turn to Holland. "I hate to do this. But he's right," I say. While I don't know exactly what's going on, I trust Jamil with my life every day. He's not steering me wrong here and now. I am sure of it.

Holland looks stunned and a little scared. "Of course," she says. "May I send you two away with dinner?" She's already turning to the kitchen.

Jamil lifts his eyebrows—surprising, he says without words,

generous. Then his eyebrows drop, silently signaling we have no time.

"Thank you, Holland, but no," I say. She spins back to me. I lean into her and drop a kiss on her cheek. Then I close my eyes and berate myself for my presumption and lunacy. "Thank you for your hospitality. And please, let's keep the details of this evening's conversation private" —she immediately starts to protest— "for now," I finish. She closes her mouth and nods. Clearly, she can read the gravity of the situation weighing heavily on both my bodyguard and me. "Thank you," I say.

Jamil and I are out the door and taking the stairs two at a time.

"How long?" I ask as we burst out the fire exit, into the alley, and into the backseat of the waiting car.

"I got the call," he looks at his watch, "exactly eleven minutes ago. We'll have you in a helicopter in another seventeen. You should be at his bedside no longer than forty-eight minutes after the call."

Swallowing around an emotion I can't name, I say to my friend, "Thank you." I know he knows how much this means to me. We don't have to say another word.

♡

"Pops," I say to the ashen man looking sunken and nearly swallowed up by the blankets piled on his prone form. My grandfather looks so fragile, so gray, so much like he must already be gone. I wait a full minute before reaching for his hand. Holding it, I pray to all of the gods I've ever known and some I've merely heard of, please let him hear me. If nothing else. Please let him hear these things I must say.

"Son," his paper-thin voice. I exhale my first full breath in more than forty-eight minutes.

"Pops, I love you. I'm so sorry."

"Forgive me, son," my mother's father says so quietly I almost don't catch it. My first instinct is to argue. Forgive you? For what? You've been infallible for my entire existence. You are my rock. I nearly refuse to give him what he asks because I cannot fathom what he is asking for. But my hammering heart and the loss I already feel slow me down enough to see the wisdom of his request.

"Of course, Pops." Of course I absolve this man who, with my father, raised me. My two parents were my father and the father of the woman who birthed me. While I lost my mother thirty-five years ago and my father thirteen weeks ago, when this larger-than-life superhero of a giant of a man goes, I will truly be alone. "I forgive you."

And then without monitors or nurses or a physician to tell me, I know. He's gone. I realize as soon as it's true. I'm holding the hand of my now-deceased grandfather. I close my eyes—his never even opened for me—and I thank all those deities for the moment we had.

Because we are in a hospice, no one rushes me out the door. No one even moves me from my kneeling by the low bed. Whispers around me let me know the professionals in charge of my grandfather's palliative care are fully aware of what has happened. Eventually, I will stand. In a moment, I will talk to these kind and generous carers who have been here all the hours I've had to be away from him. But for this brief time, for these moments when he's still here but no longer here, I hold my grandfather's hand. I'm holding on for something, to something. I'm waiting for one last answer from the man who has always had them. I realize I am trying to divine and absorb the last bits of wisdom from my grandfather.

Because I need him to help me get Holland to stay.

16

Kai is MIA. He's not answering his phone, not responding to messages. I reach out to Naomi and she can't reach him either. I message Zahra, but given the time difference, I'm not really surprised when I don't hear from her.

I pack away dinner. I check my email. I check my phone. I clean the kitchen. I'm not saying I'm worried. I'm just saying that was weird. It finally occurs to me to reach out to Micah. Micah knows everything.

HOLLAND: Hey. Is Kai okay? He left here suddenly.

As usual, as soon as I hit send, I'm second-guessing myself. I set the phone aside so I can further worry and continue to reproach myself when I get a tiny ding.

MICAH: Family emergency. He's very sorry he had to interrupt your evening. He'll reach out tomorrow. He asked me to ask you to expect his call on your office line around noon. I was just about to message you.

My office line. I roll my eyes. Control freak.

But, family emergency, that sounds scary. Empathy wins out over annoyance.

HOLLAND: Sure. Of course. I'll be there. Thank you, Micah.

Trying to remember if I know anything about Kai's family - who might be the subject of the emergency. I realize how much I don't know this man. Falling back on my default, I google it.

Kai's father died recently—my heart clenches. His obituary says he's survived by his only son and his own father-in-law. No mention of Kai's mother in any way. Something about this sets off red flag-high-danger-abort-abort-abort signals which I blindly silence and lock away in my mind. If his father is recently deceased, that must mean—oh, poor Kai. It must be his grandfather. Is he ill? Is he dying? If his grandfather is dying so soon after his father's passing, Kai will be devastated. I never knew any of my grandparents, but I know it must hurt to lose them. I mean, intellectually, I understand it. Ximena loves her grandmother very much. Gosh, are we reaching the age where our friends lose their grandparents? I guess I should reach out to check on Ximena's *abuelita*.

♡

My alarm wakes me just as I've finally closed my eyes. Or at least that's how I feel. On autopilot, I compartmentalize my anger and frustration at Kai and my sympathy for whatever he and his grandfather may be going through. I get ready for work, walk to the bus, head up to the fifth floor on autopilot. The office is eerily subdued. Everyone is moving slowly and speaking in hushed voices. I close my door for the first time since I moved into this space. I settle myself into a seated position on the thick silk rug with my back resting against a chair. With AirPods in and a meditation playing, I stare at nothing and wait for noon.

No, seriously.

I quit this job. The best thing I can do here is not further entrench myself. My peaceful plan lasts about forty-five seconds before my phone rings in my ears. I tell Siri to answer it.

"Naomi," I greet my mother-in-law. I have ice in my voice. I don't realize how livid I remain until just this moment.

"Holland, good morning." She sounds breathless. "Have you heard from Kai?" Oof. I forgot to tell her I'd heard back from Micah.

"Not directly, but he's okay. I hear it's a family emergency," I say. I'm surprised at my monotone and lack of additional information—I'm sure Naomi is hearing it and it's hurting her. Too bad, so sad.

"Oh, it must be Charles," she says quietly.

Well, sugar beets. Now I want to know what she knows.

"Is that his grandfather?" I ask.

"His mother's father, yes. He's like a parent to Kai. Or I mean…" She hears what she's said. I offer her an olive branch.

"I read his father's obituary," I say.

"Yes—I guess he died just recently. I had no idea. Kai and I have missed a lot in each other's lives. We were such good friends for so many years." She sounds heartsick. "We've each experienced so much loss."

"Nomi, did you and Kai–" I can't finish. "Are you and Kai…? Did you ever…?"

"Oh, gosh, no." Naomi doesn't need me to ask the question. "Never. Kai is like a brother to me. He was like a brother to Elias. He's always been family. Never … that." I can't explain why I feel relieved.

"Good," I say. "…to know. Good to know." There's a longish uncomfortable pause.

"I'm glad he's not truly missing," Naomi finally says. I make a noncommittal noise. "You're still mad at me, Holland."

Yup. "I'm still trying to sort through this dilemma, yes," I say. "I gave my two weeks' notice last night. But today, Kai asked me to come to the office. I couldn't refuse given his family emergency situation. But I'm not happy about it."

"You quit your job?" Naomi asks slowly and quietly.

"I did."

"Because of me?" She sounds wounded.

Yup. "Because if I choose to return to work—something I haven't decided for myself yet, by the way—" I know I sound like a surly teenager when I emphasize by the way by drawing it out and lowering my voice—"I want to go to work where no one knows me or Aidan—or you, for that matter." Naomi makes a noncommittal sound this time. "I gotta go. I'm expecting a call from Kai any minute now," I lie.

"Okay, Holland," Naomi says softly. "I'm so sorry I put you in this position. Please forgive me for interfering." Oh fudgesicle. Why did she have to go and do that? Don't ask for forgiveness, darnit.

I take a deep breath. "I forgive you," I say, sounding even surlier and drawn out and lower-pitched than before. This is not a shining moment for me. "And I reserve the right to remain angry about it for a while."

"Of course." She's trying to hide a smile, I can hear it in her voice.

"I really do have to get off the phone, Nomi." I sound slightly less grouchy. "Oh, wait," I interrupt myself, "How's Ximena's grandmother?"

"She's fine. I just spoke to the whole family on Zoom this weekend."

"Okay, good." I am genuinely relieved.

"Have a great day at work, dear," she says as though it's any other Thursday morning. I shake my head, roll my eyes, and end the call. And I immediately go back to meditating. It is my hope to have my head on straight, my anger in check, and a new plan in place before Kai calls in three hours. Deep breaths, Holland. Deep calming breaths.

There's a gentle knock on my door. So much for calm. "Come in," I say.

"Holland, hey." Micah comes in and sits on the floor facing me as though it's the most natural thing for colleagues to sit criss-cross-applesauce on the rug. "Kai isn't coming in today, so I want to run a couple things by you." He opens the file he has in his hands and starts to ask me about projections for next quarter. As though I agreed. As though I still work here.

Sigh. Oh, okay. Let's just put a pin in my quitting until Kai returns, I guess. I give Micah my full attention and start mentally crunching the numbers he's showing me. Oh, this is good stuff. "Wait, look at this," I point to an anomaly. "Where did this come from?" And so it begins.

17

Kai looks rough. Dark circles, nearly bruises, under his eyes. Unkempt beard. The poor man even has stubble growing on his normally clean-shaven head.

"Hey, Kai," I say softly as I enter his dim apartment. No answer. I look back at Micah who has accompanied me up the elevator. He shoos me forward.

"Kai?" I try again. The big man grunts. "Kai, it's Holland. How are you?" I know my voice is getting higher each time I say his name. I must sound ridiculous.

"Holland?" He sounds gravelly like he just woke up. It's four in the afternoon. "Micah, what the hell?" He scowls past me. Like he knows Micah must be back there.

"Hey, boss. See y'all later," Micah squeaks as he steps back and lets the elevator doors close. Coward.

"Kai, may I turn on some lights?" I ask. The lights glow slightly brighter—he must have controls on his phone. The shades let in a bit more light as well. Fancy. "Thanks. That's better, right?" No response. "Are you thirsty? May I get you a water?" In response, Kai sits up and picks up the glass of whatever-it-is-it-isn't-water next to him and downs it.

"Whiskey," he says as he holds out the glass for me to take.

Ah. I see. I go into the kitchen, locate a clean glass, fill it with water from the refrigerator. "Try this first," I offer. He takes the water reluctantly. Then downs it in one go. "Better?" I ask, full of hope. Another grunt. "Kai, do you want to talk about what's going on?"

"Not even a little bit." He sounds twelve years old.

"Do you want to talk about work?" I offer.

"Less," he says and then he lies down on the couch again. As though this brief exchange has exhausted him.

"I get it. I've been there," I say.

Hellebore, I'd be there right this second if it weren't for Naomi and Ximena. And Kai, actually.

"Want to go for a walk? Let's walk." I pick up his discarded shoes from the floor and slide them on his feet. "Come on. You can't sit in here any longer. You need sunlight." He groans, but he sits up, then stands. The image is exactly what I imagine it's like to watch a bear come out of hibernation. From curled up and cuddly to huge and groggy—and I can only imagine how very grumpy. He stretches and yawns, only adding to the effect.

"Where?" He's giving me single syllables, but I view it as progress. I suddenly realize the gross disadvantage of a live-work space. We can't just "go for a walk" anywhere—not if he wants any privacy.

"Want to go to the beach?" I ask.

"Nope." And he sits back down.

Too ambitious, Holland, dial it back. "Let's try this. Let's take the elevator down to the garage. We can head out the back to the running trails. Avoid well-wishers, if you'd like." He grunts his approval and stands.

We ride in silence down the elevator. We walk in silence out the emergency exit to the open land behind the building. Kai winces, visibly pained by the bright afternoon sun. I hand him his aviators— what? They were on the table in the foyer. And the ball cap I also grabbed. He accepts them. I ignore the sparks at our touch and curse the butterflies in my stomach.

There's not much green space left in this part of Los Angeles, so I value this trail through what is most likely soon-to-be-developed land. Kai and I stroll toward the shade of the trees. We are definitely strolling—there's no other way to describe this snail's pace. This feels so different from a normal, healthy Kai.

"Why are you here?" he asks quietly. He doesn't look at me or change our pace.

"Micah thought I might be able to help you…" How do I say this? Micah thought I might be able to help you snap out of it? That'd be an awful thing to say. Micah thought a widow might be the best person to empathize with you? Too emotionally sticky for both of us. I decide to leave it at that. Micah thought I might be able to help you. I nod.

"Are you still quitting?" He sounds resigned. Or pouty. Are those the same thing? Do we just say adults are resigned? When we know it's really pouty-ness? Maybe not. Maybe they're two different things.

"Yes, Kai—" I start. He stops with a huff, turns to stop me.

"Not okay, Holland," he growls.

18

"You earned the position you're in at IPU, Holland," I begin, pouring all the meaning I can into the word *earned* as I hold her gaze. "Every reference I contacted sings your praises. Your professional reputation is that you are a problem-solver who thinks strategically." I prepared this little speech, rehearsing it over and over the last few days.

Yes, we're still on campus, on the running trail I built when we bought this property. But I can't worry about this any longer. I can't let this woman quit. Pops would not have wanted it. No one at IPU would want it. I cannot even fathom her leaving.

"My references?" she asks.

Don't be an ass, Ipu, please do not scare her off.

But, yes, her references. When Naomi sent me Holland's resume, I called every reference listed, plus people Holland hadn't included. I moved beyond vetting her—I thoroughly cyberstalked her. "Your former employers told me about your attention to detail and obsession with researching best practices and tenable solutions." I reviewed everything I could find—from Holland's thesis on co-mentoring to her recent piece in HBR. Hell, Micah even found a video she made for a high school marketing project. She was the cutest teenager with her long honey-colored ponytail and her Mt.

Carmel High School Track & Field t-shirt. Her earnest effort to sell the hell out of her fourth-wave-feminism-pre-Black-Lives-Matter project to educate her peers on gender equity and anti-racism through school sports genuinely impressed me. I plan to ask her about it and throw as much money as she'll let me at the effort… if she is still down for it.

"Every published piece of your writing is insightful, elegantly communicated, exquisitely illustrated with anecdotes which protect the privacy of your subjects while still feeling intimate to the reader." I want her to know I value how well she presents herself in writing. I also had Micah pull together every piece of media he could find that even mentions Holland Siobhan Amster Gallagher. The New York Times wedding announcement with a stunning photograph of what looked like a heart-wrenchingly happy couple stung. A piece in a North Carolina business magazine about the Gallagher family, complete with a photo of Holland and Ximena on horseback, made me stare for far too long. Stay on target, I warn myself. "You know this business backwards and forwards—your time with our staunchest competitor bears that out," I say. The only truly shocking bit of information Micah dug up was a brief stint Holland had working for a rival strategy consultancy—the job she had when Aidan died. She hadn't listed it on her resume and Micah had to dig deep to find out why. Turns out my competitor's shady business practices horrified her and drove her away. Another disgruntled former employee remembered working with Holland. "She was too good for those fuckers," the guy said to me on the phone. I was enormously proud of Holland when I heard that.

"I'm daily impressed with your observations of our industry's best practices, worst problems, and most creative solutions," I say. "To be honest, if Naomi hadn't mentioned you were looking for work, I would have poached you from your next position, anyway." How 'bout them apples? One thing I know to be true: the longer I knew this woman, the more I would've needed her in my life. I mean, in my office. Oh, who am I kidding, I mean in my bed.

"You're the best listener I know," I say to her vividly intent and intensely gorgeous eyes—locked on me, proving my point. "You are the smartest person I know. You're a gifted leader with the confidence to give clear direction. My team tells me that your follow-up and follow-through are pushing them to make improvements long after you have moved on to your next task," I say.

Our HR director sent me a note just this morning, in fact, detailing new policies for recruitment, which were inspired by a conversation he'd had with Holland during her onboarding meeting. (Yes, I'm checking my email. I'm depressed, not dead.) The twenty-five-year professional was filling out forms with her, chatting while he walked her through the offer when Holland said something that made him rethink his diversity, equity, and inclusion practices, he told me in his note. Holland forwarded him a relevant journal article the next day, gently prompted him to commit in writing what he wanted to change and offered to help him proofread his new policies a week later. "I had no intention of dropping the ball on this update, Boss," the director wrote, "but if I'd had any reservations or hesitations, Holland's unflagging commitment to doing the right thing would've put my head right. You got a good one there, Ipu. Let's keep her."

I continue to tell Holland to her perfect face in this quiet space, "The priority list I gave Micah for your first one hundred days was complete before the end of your first month. And you've accomplished each consultation while looking breezy and beautiful" —shit shit shit—don't make it about her alluring appearance, you asshat, I clear my throat, "beautifully poised."

I pause. Take a deep breath. Wait to see if she will respond. Her gorgeous gray-green eyes on me are penetrating. She has been listening (silently)—it shouldn't surprise me, but her silence does, in fact, shock me. We all know I would have been interrupting her constantly, pushing my own points, or making her prove each of her arguments. She leans forward barely an inch while watching me intently with a look of serious concentration. I take advantage of her silence and attempt to find an eloquent way to end my soliloquy and invite her to respond.

"With all due respect, I do not accept your resignation, Holland. In fact, I am prepared to talk about your next steps at Innovated." I'm ready to offer her more money, a job title of her choosing. I'll give her my office if she wants it. I will give her anything. Anything for her, anything in my power, anything in the world.

"I sincerely regret that Naomi had to ask me to offer you a job because I should've thought of it myself after meeting you." I look away from her for the first time since the conversation started— surprised to find myself outdoors, I take in the gorgeous day and the lovely trees. And mentally kick myself yet again for waiting for

Naomi to bring it up. Why didn't I think of that? Because I was smitten with her from the first. Because her heartbreak broke my heart. Because I was thinking with the wrong head that night. I look into her eyes again.

"Holland, you are exactly who we would have looked for if I'd been smart enough to realize we should be looking. Perhaps we were resting on our laurels. Regardless, you bring this company—" a bright and shining light, rainbows and puppies, all the good feelings in the world... "a second wind," I say. "We were running a great race and your insights are the shot in the arm we needed to re-energize our efforts." I struggle to soften my tone. I feel my internal intensity meter moving into the glaring red settle-down-man-you-might-scare-people zone. "Please stay. In fact, I don't just want you to stay. I need you to double down. Join us on the executive team. Let's make this official." That's right. That feels right. She could be my Chief Culture Officer, Chief Knowledge Officer, Chief Joy Officer (turns out that's a real thing, I was just reading about it last week and the article instantly made me think of Holland). Hell, I'll make her Chief Unicorn if she stays. I watch her carefully.

She takes a deep breath and steps away from me. "Let's head back. I'm hungry," she says. Then she turns around and starts walking back to my building.

I can't think of a damned thing to do but follow her.

19

He went from single syllable answers to a Dickens novel's worth of words. *I need time to think. Everything about this has knocked me off my mental feet.* I was still wrapping my head around a grieving Kai when he shed that vulnerability and turned into this verbose advocate of all things me.

So I buy time. We head upstairs the same way we came down. Micah has overseen delivery of an early dinner, which is probably Kai's first healthful meal in days. The table is set, the food looks delicious, there's water poured, and even a bottle of wine.

"Steak salad," I say when I realize he has followed me into the kitchen. I drizzle the lemon-thyme salad dressing over the medium-rare ribeye and crispy vegetables. "The bread's still warm," I say as I hand the basket to him. "Take this out to the dining table?"

"I'd much rather eat in here," he says, pulling out a barstool.

"Really? Eat in the kitchen?" I ask, looking around. It really is a nice kitchen.

"Yes, please." He sits at the island. "How may I help?"

"Well, if we're eating in here, I guess the only thing left to do is open the wine." Without wondering if he can handle a glass of wine, much less the task, I hand him the opener and a bottle of a South African Cabernet Sauvignon. He opens it expertly, pours each of us a glass. Kai is so tall he can reach everything on the island without standing. I appreciate how comfortable he looks (it's clear he's coming out of his earlier fog) and how the entire room seems to revolve around him—like he is gravity itself. Everything pulls to him. He's a force of nature.

My head and heart war with themselves. Because this feels good. This feels like dinner at home should feel. Wait, why did Micah and I plan a meal? This visit should be over—my role here was to get Kai to go for a walk. Why am I still here?

I clear my throat and my head. Just be present, Holland. Just be here.

"Thank you." I accept the wine he hands me. The electricity that accompanies our touch makes the butterflies I've been trying to ignore all afternoon dance. Settle down in there, you, I scold them silently. This is not a date, you stupid *Papilionidea.*

"To you." He offers the simplest and sweetest toast I've ever heard.

"To us," I respond before my brain catches up with my mouth. Really, Holland?! I scold myself this time. How are you going to tap dance your way out of this one?! He tips his glass to mine and sips and I see his lips pull to the side in a barely there smile that has my winged friends aflutter. Settle, I tell them and press my free hand to my belly. With little effort, Kai picks up the enormous white serving platter of salad. He serves me first and then himself.

"This looks great," he says as he starts in on his steak. "Thank you for dinner."

"I had help. Micah and I are excellent orderers," I quip as I take a delicate bite of the greens, too nervous to risk anything more while I try to calm myself after *to us.* Sheesh.

"Not a cook, then?" he asks.

"I love to cook, and I'm very good at it. Like I'm good at nearly everything I do." It's not bragging because it's true. If I do something, I do it well. "There is rarely enough time to show off my skills, however."

"You are excellent at every single thing you do, it seems to me," he says. It could be a throwaway comment, but he sounds so sincere. Maybe it's the subdued mood because he's still so raw over the loss of his grandfather. I'm flattered and flummoxed and determined not to show either.

I have just taken a bite when Kai says something I don't catch.

"Mmm?" I ask without opening my mouth.

"Do you believe in soulmates?" he asks. And I instantly thank dog I have a mouth full of food, so I have a minute to think.

"Mmmm…" I hum. I take a sip of wine. "Soulmates?"

"Naomi and Eli were obviously meant for each other," Kai says. "I noticed she still wears her wedding rings." Out of reflex, I run my left thumb over my own wedding rings. "Do you think they're—they were?—soulmates?" Okay. Non sequitur. But he's not flirting, so that's good. I can answer this question. Right?

I have always believed in soulmates. Growing up without a father, I was completely sure my mother was fully to blame—for my father's absence and for everything else that went wrong in our lives. When I was little, I was sure my father had been a prince enchanted by the wicked witch. Therefore, I was obviously a princess in hiding. Can't say any of that, though, can I?

"I watched way too many Disney movies, I'm afraid," I finally settle on saying aloud. I used to tell myself that my father had escaped the evil witch to find his own true love. It was in this way I could (One) forgive my father for leaving before I was born, (Two) hate my mother for every moment since I was born, and (Three) still believe in fairy tales.

"Say more words," Kai insists. Like we're in a business meeting, he's prompting me to go on. Okay. Here we go.

"As a connoisseur of all things True Love, I used to believe that finding a soulmate was something one could achieve—like good grades, science fair blue ribbons, or first place on the track," I tell him. Why? Why am I telling him this?

"Fascinating," he says. And he really does look interested. It's nice to see him interested after seeing him despondent earlier. "Go on."

So I do, "As early as middle school and right up until I met Aidan, I treated each encounter with a potential suitor as a job interview."

Kai laughs sadly. Is that a thing? A sad laugh? "I wish it were that easy," he says. "Interview a candidate, find a good fit, then bring on a girlfriend for a ninety-day trial period? With a contract? That would be efficient," he scoffs. "Tell me more. Middle school…"

The first boy to show me any serious interest was Jeremy. In eighth grade, he declared himself my boyfriend. I told him, "not so fast—let's get a few things straightened out first."

On the deserted jungle gym in the tiny neighborhood park each weekend, I peppered him with questions while dodging his attempts to kiss me or even hold my hand. "What's your favorite food? Kanye or Drake? Do you collect anything? How many [vinyl records, it turned out] do you have? What do you want to be when you grow up? Where do you want to go to college?" On and on.

I subjected each suitor following Jeremy to the same intense scrutiny. Asher the artsy collected Stephen King novels. Brody the tall collected vinyl records. Finn the feckless collected broken hearts (but not mine, thank goodness). Archer the atheist collected comic books. Tyler the thoughtful collected baseball cards. Miles, who was on my track team, collected the panties of his conquests (again, not mine—hallelujah). My experimental college girlfriend Nadia collected vintage Barbies. Brent, a very tall guy in my major, collected reptiles as pets (creepy). They were a motley crew and I still have a fond little place for each of them in my heart. If pressed, I might have to confess that I collect exes. In my defense, the story did say I'd have to kiss a lot of frogs…

And if a potential suitor passed my tests, they got to hold my hand, confess their undying devotion to me, chastely kiss me good-night… and go home from each date unsatisfied. For despite my reputation as a fast-mover and (whispered among the girls who actually *were* fast movers) a slut, I remained a virgin until I met—and married—Aidan Gallagher.

But I don't tell Kai any of this. I keep it simple.

"Jeremy, eighth grade," I tell him. "He passed all my tests, interviewed well." I smile, thinking of it that way. "He took me to the Valentine's Day dance. Not a bad First Love situation, really." Kai smiles, and it reaches his eyes this time.

"What happened to young Jeremy?" he asks.

"Alas, Jeremy was not my soulmate," I say. My brows stitch together. "But I guess the fact that we were so happy so young only deepened my conviction that finding my soulmate was possible." Huh. I guess I never thought of it that way. Who is this guy getting me to tell him all this? "What about you, Kai Ipu? Do you believe in soulmates?" I ask him as I take a sip of wine.

"I want to know where Jeremy is now," Kai says.

"He moved away at the end of eighth grade," I say. The last thing he did before driving off with his folks was to ask my mother if he could move in with us, instead of moving away. Sweet boy. Of course, the horrible witch said no. True love thwarted by her shriveled black heart.

"Where was this? Where did you grow up?" Kai asks.

"This was in Mary Esther, Florida," I say. "My mother moved us, too, that summer. San Francisco. Talk about culture shock."

"And you met your soulmate there?" Kai asks.

"No. I met Aidan in college," I say. Kai's face is unreadable. I've shocked him? Or confused him? Oh, he's hurting. We've stumbled back to loss. Poor Kai.

20

I have to get up from my seat.

Her warmth radiates down my entire side, she's sitting so close. Sitting together like this was exactly why I suggested eating at the bar instead of the table-for-six in the next room. I feared she would sit too far away from me in there. Here, her only choices were to sit next to me or to stand. It was both a genius idea and the stupidest move I could've made. I can smell her hair—floral, woody, green. It isn't healthy for me to be able to smell her. Earlier today I was unable to get off the couch and now I'm fantasizing about this woman, this widow. Had I known what grief on grief feels like, I might've had more empathy for Holland (and Naomi) earlier.

I now know—after losing the two men closest to me just over a year apart—grief comes and goes as it pleases. It takes what it wants and leaves nothing but shit in its wake.

My father (who didn't drink, didn't smoke, spent his life as an engineer safely driving a desk) died at only sixty of inexplicable and excruciating pancreatic cancer. My grandfather who drank daily, smoked Cubans often, spent his life driving fast cars and making dicey deals died relatively peacefully and not unexpectedly at the well-lived age of ninety-eight.

The pain of losing my heroes and mentors—the two men whose

blood and wisdom flow through me—grinds down on me anew.

My grandfather was a larger-than-life former NFL wide-receiver-turned-hedge-fund-manager whose daughter married the equally huge Samoan software developer. The two men could not have been more different in temperament. Yet they were best friends. My fondest memories are of the two Brobdingnagian men grilling steaks and shooting the shit on my grandfather's back porch or my dad's balcony every Sunday of my early life.

Without a mother, I divided my time between my grandfather's ranch and my father's tiny Beverly Hills condo. Ranching made my body strong, and the academically demanding private schools my father sent me to fed my hungry brain.

"May I?" I ask if she's ready for me to clear her plate. What I'd rather ask is to wrap my arms around her, comfort her, take comfort in her. Sighing, I resolve to take care of the dishes if I can't take care of her.

"Oh, no, I can do that," she protests. The rejection, the dejection I feel must show on my face because she says, "I mean, yes. Please and thank you." I clear our places, rinse the dishes, load them in the dishwasher. The mundane task settles my nerves slightly. I am just putting the last of the serving utensils in the machine when she walks up next to me to bring me the wine glasses. She feels good—and I'm not even touching her. She is radiating at me again. Without even looking her way, I can feel her smile. "I didn't bring the champagne," she says. My heart feels like it might explode. "But I feel a little like celebrating." She shows me the Compartés box of handmade hand-painted local chocolate truffles I bought her the day my grandfather died. I groan.

"Unless you'd rather not?" She sounds panicked.

"Yes, please," I say, berating myself for vocalizing the lust and joy and regret and frustration that hit me like a lightning bolt.

"Okay." She grins at me but sounds a little like a schoolteacher handling an unruly kid. Or a dog trainer backing off a rabid hound. "Let's take your peace offering to the living room." Her smile now looks mischievous. I am completely transparent to her, I realize. She knew all along the champagne and dessert were my way of sweetening my apology for being an ass—dodging meetings and phone calls with her. That night seems so long ago.

Again, I find myself following her. Anywhere, anytime, to do anything—my new mantra.

"What are we celebrating?" I ask as she opens the chocolates, selects one she likes, then hands the tiny artworks to me.

Holland holds her painted chocolate up to mine like we're toasting champagne flutes and says, "To doubling down."

Then, as if she hasn't just said the sexiest thing I've ever heard in all my days, she increases my torture when she bites slowly into the treat, rolls her eyes back, and moans with pleasure.

21

Four weeks later, I try to settle down in the buttery leather seat.

"Are you excited?" Zahra asks from the seat facing mine. "You look like you're anticipating Santa's imminent arrival." Her smile is teasing but warm.

I smile back. "This is my first trip out of the country in more than a year." My smile slips away as the enormity of my statement grips my heart. "And the first time I get to visit my sister in her new office." I try to smile again but feel my chin start to quiver. "Sister-*in-law*, you know, Ximena." Zahra smiles and nods. My mind drifts back and down, back and down—is that why they call it spiraling?

♡

Ximena and I haunted Naomi's ancestral home for weeks. Unspoken and unplanned, we moved in the night we got the news. Ximena locked herself in Ethan's childhood bedroom for two days. I cried myself sick on the porch swing where Aidan proposed. Naomi sat at the piano, not playing it, for hours at a time. Each of us was lost in our own misery—collectively we were a disaster film.

We were wreckage strewn about the house.

Nearly a month into the madness, we found ourselves in the kitchen together at four o'clock in the morning. We brewed tea and Naomi got serious. "This is unsustainable, my loves." Her voice was thick with empathy and affection. "I, for one, cannot do this much longer. I love you, but I have to send you both home." Ximena and I looked at each other. We looked at Naomi. "You've taken such good care of me, my daughters, Lord knows," Naomi continued. "But you should go home. Go back to work. Life, I am heartbroken to say, must go on." Ximena and I said nothing, but I felt my head involuntarily shaking no. I had no interest in leaving this house. I had no intention of leaving Naomi. There was no scenario in which I'd be okay without Ximena by my side. After the silence stretched out for many minutes, Naomi finally said, "I'm going back to Los Angeles. This doesn't feel like home anymore. Everything and everyone I loved here is gone."

My response was visceral and immediate, "Me too, then."

Ximena started speaking at the same time I did, "I want to move home to Mexico."

We looked at each other, my sister and I. I grabbed the leg of her kitchen chair and pulled her close to me, threw my arms around her neck and hugged her tight. She hugged back fiercely.

"Sorry for manhandling you," I said into her thick black locks. She snort-laugh-sobbed in response.

"What will you do?" Ximena whispered.

"Where she goes, I'll go." And I squeezed her tighter.

"Yeah, I can see that." My sister-in-law squeezed me back.

♡

Sitting here on Innovated's luxurious jet, I feel it all roll over me in a wave once again.

"Holland," Zahra leans forward, her beautiful mouth turns down with concern. "Are you okay?"

"I will be, Zee." I sigh. And smile. "I'm feeling all the feels today." I try to laugh but it comes out more of a cough or a sob.

"I can only imagine," Zahra says. And then to herself, she adds quietly, "I cannot even imagine."

I take the opportunity afforded by my friend's introspection to pick up my book. We make eye contact and Zahra takes the hint.

♡

Late last week, the three of us met in North Carolina for the one-year anniversary of Aidan and Ethan's tragic deaths. Naomi, Ximena, and I visited the meadow where we buried the boys without caskets—just tulip trees, goldenrod, Joe-Pye weed (*Eupatorium maculatum*, if you must know), and Indigo Buntings. The stones we selected and engraved were nestled deep in the late summer growth. We each opened a can of Mullinax Stout to toast our dearly departed with their favorite local brew. After visiting long enough to tell all our favorite stories and see a red-shouldered hawk (*Buteo lineatus*, Aidan would have wanted to hear me say), we drove our rental car to the spa.

Between facials and massages and body scrubs, we drowned our sorrows in fruit-infused water and tears. The staff were so kind and generous with us, bringing tissues and tea when they walked onto the terrace to find three widows engaged in a full-swing pity party.

We spent that night and the next in the penthouse suite watching tearjerker films (*Terms of Endearment, Call Me By Your Name, Lion, Marley and Me*, all the best ugly cry movies) on the television above the fireplace and videos of family vacations on each other's phones. We drank all the booze and slept three-to-a-king.

Snuggled between my mother-in-law and my sister-in-law, I slept through the night (both nights!) for the first time in a year. I loved the mini-break and the companionship, and I hated to leave.

After three days of robes and room service, I returned to work more exhausted than I'd felt in forever. Grief has a way of robbing me of my precious positive energy. I felt with painful clarity each moment I spent with my husband and every second I have survived without him—simultaneously.

♡

Presently, Zahra and I sit in companionable silence until she excuses herself to freshen up. I look at my watch. How have the hours passed so quickly? I realize I haven't read a word, rather stared at the pages of my Simon Sinek book, unfocused. I must have fallen asleep. "Grief sucks," I say aloud.

"Indeed," the deep delicious voice across from me says. I jump. I hadn't noticed Kai take Zahra's seat. In fact, I'd completely forgotten he was on this plane.

"You scared me, Kai." I smile though my heart is aching.

"I get that a lot," the big beautiful bronze man in a bespoke black suit says with a lopsided grin. I laugh. It's a genuine laugh. It feels amazing.

22

I love Holland's laugh. I've been watching her emotional roller coaster all morning. And this is the highlight, the pinnacle.

She was visibly vibrating with excitement when she first arrived at the airport. It's obvious she loves to travel, and she looks like she was born for it. Stunning in a sheer (damn, it's practically invisible) pale pink blouse with a silk suit vest over it; she had a thin leather belt at her waist I could imagine hooking my thumbs into and pulling her close. Heels the exact color of her sumptuous-looking skin made her long legs look like they went on forever paired with the perfectly tailored ankle-baring black pants.

I could not take my eyes off her—she was airy and easy, from how she dressed to how she packed (one small wheeled case for a trip to two international cities including a formal event? Damn.)

I was still watching her when her mood took a nosedive after we boarded—I know enough about Holland by now to understand this trip is bittersweet for her. Her first trip without her husband is obviously taking its toll. Of course, I also know how much she's looking forward to the work ahead, plus seeing her sister-in-law, and then Naomi's gala before we head to Santiago.

Maybe I've over-scheduled us. I should have been more aware of the timing. She's just observed the one-year anniversary of the

Gallagher men's deaths. Dammit, I should be taking better care of her. She deserves some time. God knows she has supported me and my time to grieve.

When Holland finally settled down, I watched her from my seat on the opposite side of the plane. My own shoulders relaxed as she fell peacefully asleep.

I need to get her some noise-canceling headphones. No one should sleep on a plane without them.

Our not-a-date at my apartment last month ended shortly after our chocolate toast. She made excuses and nearly ran out the door—before she could tempt me any further with her double entendres (all of which were probably in my head, of course) and the intimate toasts ("to us" nearly killed me, "doubling down" had my mouth watering). It was all too much. She assured me she'd stay at IPU. And ran.

The following week—before taking off for her girls' trip—Holland accepted the position of Chief Strategy Officer. She turned down Chief Unicorn which disappointed me greatly. Since our face-to-gorgeous-face meeting, I have tried to be less obvious about avoiding her. Which probably just makes me seem even creepier since it means observing her from doorways until she notices me. Or accidentally-on-purpose bumping into her in hallways. Watching her sleep is a new low, I have to admit.

"We'll land soon," I say to her. I see Zahra coming back from the lav. We make eye contact, she nods, finds another seat, and seamlessly starts a conversation with our colleagues. I should probably give Zahra a raise.

"I should freshen up." Holland leans around her seat to see if the lavatory is free.

"You look perfect," I say before I can stop myself. Her head whips back around to look at me. The blush I didn't realize I have been longing to see again creeps up her neck. Perfect, I iterate silently.

"Thank you," she says shyly. "I think I fell asleep." She runs her fingers under her beautiful gray-green eyes. "I must look a mess."

"Nope. Not a mess," I say. "You slept for about two hours."

Her face is blank. "I'll be back," she says and grabs her ridiculously large black quilted leather bag. Maybe that's how she can travel with such a small case, I surmise. As soon as she walks up the aisle, I miss her. I had just gotten her attention, dammit.

"Ipu." Zahra says as she slides into Holland's recently vacated seat. "How's it going?"

"Zahra. What?" I bark.

"Don't snap at me, you bear," she says, her eyes lighting up with amusement.

"What is it?" I snarl. This time I'm teasing her—she's good at making me take myself far less seriously.

"Not a thing," she says cheekily. I growl at her in earnest. She throws her head back and laughs. "That's exactly what I thought," she says cryptically.

What the ever-loving fuck was that all about? Even though I know exactly what the crazy non-conversation meant. Well, shit. She knows me all too well. I stand, shove my hands in my pants pockets, and move back to my original seat.

23

The blistering heat of the Mexican sun beats down on the tarmac as I alight from the plane. My sister launches herself at me as though we haven't seen each other in years. "I can't believe you're actually here!" Ximena shouts in my ear.

"'Mena, I'll need that ear." I mock-scold her even as I squeeze back. "I can't believe it either. I'm so glad to see you."

"You look amazing," Ximena says, stepping back to take in my outfit, bag, hair, makeup. I know exactly what Ximena is inventorying, appraising, and complimenting—and in what order. She wolf-whistles at me.

"Hush you." I grin. "You look gorgeous as always, sis. Come meet my friends." I pull Ximena by the hand toward the cars. When we get to the row of SUVs, only Kai's has room for us—I was last off the plane and my sister held me up.

"Gallaghers, may I offer you a ride?" he smiles at us. "Ximena, it's nice to meet you." He stretches out his massive hand. Ximena is in a mood apparently because she launches herself into his arms and hugs him fiercely. Little green bubbles of envy percolate in my heart. I've never hugged him. She's so bold. Ballsy. Darn her. "Oh, hello." Kai hugs Ximena back. "We're hugging," he says awkwardly. Awkward Kai is my new favorite Kai.

"Kai, my mother-in-law will not shut up about you," Ximena says. I watch his face closely. Warmth instantly replaces any awkwardness. He truly loves Naomi as much as we do. "She thinks you're just the best."

"She's been a good friend for a long time," he says. "We're all lucky to know Naomi." The two of them continue to chat as Kai helps both of us into the huge vehicle, then climbs in himself. Kai and Ximena talk about Mexico City, the Gallagher office and Naomi's foundation, a new investment Ximena is considering, a new protein powder Kai is experimenting with. I watch the Ciudad through the window and just listen to my sister effervesce at Kai the entire drive. I love the sound of their voices in contrast to each other: Ximena's almost-too-high-pitched feminine tones and Kai's deep baritone trade back and forth. Not until Ximena says my name do I realize the two of them have code-switched. *Manita, ¿en qué estás pensando?"* Ximena asks.

"I was enjoying your conversation," I respond in English. "And I was watching the view." I nod my head to the window. Just as the car pulls into an underground garage. "Wait! I really was," I protest as the new besties laugh at me. Hmph. Great.

♡

The rest of the day flies by in a rush. We tour Innovated's offices on Av. Jesús del Monte and meet about a dozen people—each one friendlier and more welcoming than the last. In prepping for this visit, I studied all the materials about our Mexico operations Micah gave me, plus a ton of research I did on my own. As expected, I find everyone to be brilliant and inquisitive, a pairing of traits I value greatly. Digging in to work tomorrow will be fun.

But first, my sister is giving me (and Kai, who invited himself to join us on our side trip—something I find both delightful and perplexing) a tour of the Gallagher office. "This is where the mathmagic happens," Ximena quips as we reach the CFO's suite. "My home away from home." She plops down in her desk chair and looks more like take-your-daughter-to-work-day than executive-in-charge-of-millions.

"Mathmagicland," Kai chuckles (a new and charming laugh I

catalog with the others), walking over to check out the view from Ximena's eleventh-floor windows.

"You know it," Ximena says. "What do you think, *manita*? Nice, right? We're still just renting, but I really think I want to stay in this *torre*."

"You should. It suits you," I say. It's obvious this is Ximena's space. Her meticulously organized desk has neat stacks of folders in a full spectrum of bright colors. Her pen cup (not to be confused with her cup full of highlighters) is an oversized coffee mug that says **EASY AS** followed by as many digits of pi as can fit. The whole room smells like bubblegum—a feat I cannot understand as nothing visible is pink or chewable. The walls not covered in charts and maps are covered in family photos—black-and-white images of her family, our family, the two of us. It's joyful, controlled chaos and I love it almost as much as I love her.

The first time we spent together, just the two of us, was shortly after the Christmas we met. Aidan and Ethan were golfing, so Ximena and I planned a get-to-know-you brunch. We sat at that table for hours. Ximena was wearing a pleated floor length skirt and plain white t-shirt topped with a thick tiger-stripe plush coat. I couldn't stop telling her how cute she looked. She gushed equally over my cozy oversized cable-knit sweater with shorts and tights and ankle boots. Aidan and Ethan would later coin the term So-Cutes, as in, "Holland is here for her So-Cutes, honey" or "We need to leave early enough for the girls to give their So-Cutes". Har har. At that brunch we found we shared a love of good wine, clean comedy, and each other.

Since becoming simultaneous widows, my love and affection for this woman has only grown deeper. She is my ride-or-die, my person. She is far and away the stronger of us—her timely return to work and her I'm-taking-the-office-with-me move to Mexico are evidence of how together she is.

Ximena's chair flop was extra playful. She likes Kai... I wonder what variety of *like* that might be... I immediately stop myself. Ximena isn't interested in Kai the way I am. The what?! Suddenly, my lepidopterans go native and start singing Mariachi love songs at the top of their tiny lungs. *Shut up, in there,* I press my hand to my stomach.

"Well, if I'm hungry, you two must be starving," Ximena says. "And I could use a drink—it's definitely tequila o'clock. Shall we head to my mom's house for dinner?"

"I'll let you ladies take the car," Kai says. "I'm going to head to the hotel and grab a bite there."

"Nonsense," Ximena says, gathering her purse and laptop. "My mother would never forgive me for letting a gorgeous, tall, Spanish-speaking, gainfully-employed, single man eat alone."

I catch myself snarling.

24

Absolutely unable to unwind, I'm in the hotel gym at nearly midnight, adding weight to the chest press "system" wishing I had a real bench press with plates so I could slam them. Much more satisfying than the tiny beep I get for each kilo of the up arrow.

What an endless day. I can't count the miles we've traveled, the hands I've shaken, the tortillas I've eaten. At least I stopped drinking booze as soon as Ximena's mom served dinner.

Despite our protestations a traditional light dinner would be fine, Señora Hernández piled the table with *consomé*, salad, rice, beans, mole with chicken, chiles rellenos, and a *tortillero* filled with a bottomless supply of warm handmade corn tortillas. The hacienda brimmed over with what I calculated as five generations from Ximena's great-grandmother to the tiny cousin someone placed into my giant ham-hands when the baby's young mother got up to help bring out dessert, coffee, hot chocolate, and more alcohol. While I was grateful for an excuse to skip the entire last course, the shock and wonder of holding a life so little overwhelmed me.

Don't get me wrong, I want kids. A family is part of my five-year plan, after all. But this charming baby girl who could barely wrap her tiny hand around my smallest finger is the youngest person I've ever seen in person, much less held in my arms.

Truth be told, I have been exceedingly cautious about not bringing any babies into the world, thank you very much. Pops kept a big bowl of condoms always full and on display in my bathroom from the time I was twelve. My dad gave me an updated version of the birds and the bees every year on my birthday, starting even younger. I hated both those things at the time, of course. What I wouldn't give now to hear my father tell me to keep it in my pants or Pops yell at me to wrap that banana. No time to dwell in the past, Ipu. Fuck that.

All that effort to avoid becoming a father. And now all I can think about is spending the rest of my life making babies with an angel. Holding the tiny, cooing pink package, I looked up at the object of my obsession. Holland was enchanting to watch as she made easy conversation with Ximena's family. All the young cousins running around making a ruckus had her in giggles. It was a fucking blast to watch her watch them. My eyes on Holland while holding that precious infant girl was more intoxicating than the *vampiros* before dinner had been.

Speaking of intoxication, the Gallagher girls were quite sloppy when I finally extricated Holland from her sister's grip.

"Holland," —my heart, I choked on the loving words I heard Naomi use—before I said them out loud. Thank fuck. "Holland, kid. Let's go, friend. It's late and we have an early start tomorrow." Grinding my teeth with how much I wanted to touch her, it was all I could do to keep myself from throwing her over my shoulder and absconding with her to the nearest private space I could find.

She finally started speaking Spanish after her second tequila cocktail at the hacienda. Her fluency was obvious; however, she spent the day responding to everyone in English. I couldn't decide if it was timid or rude or appropriate or adorable. Then, in Ximena's family home, when she started a story in English and finished in flawless *Norteño*-accented *español*, I decided. It was fucking adorable.

Long after dessert, I finally got her into the SUV with the help of our driver and one of Ximena's *tios*.

"Kai Ipu," she slurred as soon as the door was closed, and I got a seatbelt secured around her. "Kai Ipu, you are so very glorious, gorgeous, desirable, handsome, magnetic, tempting, stunning, attractive…" she trailed off, apparently running out of synonyms. Dammit.

"Holland, you're drunk," I said.

"You hugged Ximena." She pouted. Goddammit, that pout. I wanted to kiss it right off her perfect lips. "You never hugged me." Because I'd never be able to let you go, I did not say out loud. "And you held a baby," she slurred. "So sexy holding a baby…" Thank all that was holy and unholy, she finally passed out halfway to the hotel. I was pretty sure I would have run completely out of willpower if she'd kept talking like that.

When the car stopped at the front of the hotel, Micah met us at the door with Holland's room keys, a bottle of water, another of Tylenol, and a sympathetic look.

"Her sister's house?" my assistant asked.

"Yup." I fireman-carried her—this is not the throw-her-over-my-shoulder I meant, dear Universe!—grateful she was wearing pants. "Grab her bag."

Together we got her up to her room, out of her shoes, and under the covers.

"Holland, honey," Micah said, kneeling by her head. Why exactly does *he* get to call her a pet name? I growled. Micah plugged in Holland's phone to charge. "There's water and medicine right here. And a bucket, just in case. You'll be okay. I'll call you in the morning."

"You'll come to collect her," I corrected him.

"Holland, sugar," Micah said gently. "I'll come get you at seven-thirty, okay?" Why was he asking a barely conscious drunk girl a question? Dumbass.

"Nine o'clock," I corrected him again. "Let her sleep."

"You heard the boss, baby," Micah said. I really hoped I was not hearing him call her baby. I growled again. "We'll let you sleep a little. I'm taking your spare room key." He stood and turned to me. I can only imagine Micah saw what I was trying to portray: a wall of impenetrable steel prepared to cock block his cheeky ass. "Just in case," he squeaked when he met my eye.

"Yup." I didn't move until Micah was out the door. "Sleep well, sweet girl," I said to her sleeping form.

Presently, I slam an imaginary ten more kilograms onto the virtual bar as I remember my most-trusted lieutenant calling my girl those tender endearments. I'll have to think of an appropriate revenge for his taking such liberties with Holland.

♡

Dripping in sweat after two a.m., I take the elevator to my floor of the hotel. And find Holland waiting when the doors slide open.

"Kai," she exclaims. And puts both her hands to her head. "You scared me."

"I get that a lot," I quip out of reflex. She laughs despite her obvious pain.

"I think I'm still drunk," she says groggily.

"I'll bet."

"I was headed down to get some water." She gestures to the elevator I'm still half-in.

Wait. Am I on her floor? I look at the light indicating that, yes, indeed, I punched her floor by mistake.

"Micah left a bottle for you by your bed," I rumble.

"Yeah, I drank that."

"C'mon, let's get you hydrated." I clench my fists on my towel so as not to (gently!) grab her by her shoulders and turn her bodily around. I walk toward her room.

"Where are you going?" She hasn't moved.

"Your minibar."

"Oh good goddess, those waters are so expensive," she protests.

I turn around to glare at her but catch her eyes on my tattoos. I struggle not to flex. What a fucking peacock.

"Okay, okay." She drags her sneakered feet. She has changed into shorts and the Mt. Carmel High School Track & Field t-shirt I recognize from the video I've watched at least a dozen times. Goddammit, she is cuter now than she was a decade ago. I can't help myself. I must do it.

I snag her hand, pull her close, and kiss her as gently as I can manage, given the torrent of lust and guilt and desire and need coursing through my veins. She feels amazing. Her lips are as soft as I've imagined them. She smells so clean and sweet and summery. I stop myself before I lose my PG rating. But not before marveling at the feel of her warmth so close, the way she raises up on her tiptoes to meet my kiss… *Keep your tongue to yourself, Ipu.* She's still feeling the effects of all that alcohol and I cannot take advantage. And I know one taste of her will pull me right over the edge. I'd never be able to stop. I pull back.

"Thank you." I blink. I'm absolutely positive this is not what I mean to say.

"Oh, no, thank you." Holland also blinks. I'm still holding her hand in mine, so I lead her to her door, watch her key in, and wait until she locks up.

"Drink all the water in the fridge," I say through the door. I see her shadow watch me through her peephole. "Good night, Holland–" my heart.

As I walk back to the elevator cursing myself, my language would definitely earn me above and beyond a PG-13 rating—I'm berating myself for being so bold. But I'm high-fiving myself—she kissed me back. And I'm dying inside that she might never want to kiss me again. Mostly, I am exceedingly proud of my self-restraint. I deserve a medal for almost keeping my hands to myself.

25

What a nice kiss.

Grabbing one of the prohibitively pricey bottles of water from the bar in my room, I drain it. I reach for a second one and decide to sip it as my stomach lurches and I realize guzzling isn't doing me any favors.

What did I drink? Well, I am quite aware of what I drank. How much? That's a far more appropriate question. I hope Ximena feels as awful as I do.

I catch my reflection in the mirror as I stumble to bed. Oh, gosh, Kai saw me like this? And he kissed me like this? In my tattered track shirt and sleep shorts, no makeup, wet hair, red nose, and no bra. Well, if you thought you were decent enough for the lobby, Holland, you were decent enough for your boss. To kiss you. I groan.

He looked and smelled amazing. When the elevator doors opened to reveal a gargantuan sex god walking out, I was sure I was imagining him. He hadn't scared me so much as made me jump out of my skin. He was coming from the gym or a run. His copper skin was shiny with sweat and I could smell his intoxicatingly creamy vanilla, cocoa, wood, warm, spicy Kai smell. Don't most men stink after working out? He smelled like sex and candy. He looked and felt magnetic. That was the best first kiss in the history of first kisses.

Replaying every detail of the kiss and every nerve-ending of the feel of him, I crawl back into bed. And fall instantly asleep.

♡

"Holland." Micah's voice. "Hon."

"Go away," I grouse.

"Holland, baby." He's more forceful this time. "It's time to get up. I let you sleep in, honey. It's nearly eight."

"What?! Wait. What time is it?" I'm up and out of bed in an instant. "Micah! We were supposed to be at the office by eight! Why did you let me sleep?"

"Just kidding," he laughs, the rat. "It's seven-fifteen. Here's your phone. And a triple latte."

"You are the best thing that has ever happened to me." I take the warm ceramic mug. "I mean it, personally and professionally, you are a gift to me."

He laughs. "You flew out of that bed. I wish I'd been filming it."

I smack his arm. "Jackal," I snark with a smile to prove I don't mean it. "Thank you for coming to collect me. Glory, but I drank all the tequila last night. I'm going to make my stupid little sister pay for that." I know full well it isn't Ximena's fault in the slightest. No one to blame but me.

"I gathered," my buddy says as he opens his own phone to review the agenda for the day. "I think you need another shower. Your hair exploded."

"Oh no." I move to the mirror and groan in horror. "I should never sleep with it wet. Give me five minutes." I don't even let the water heat up. A cold shower will do me good. I was dreaming about candy and coffee and, for some reason, bodybuilding competitions.

I open the bathroom door as soon as I am wrapped in a towel, "Talk to me, Goose," I yell to Micah.

From his seat at the desk in my room, he reviews our plans for the day. Meetings, meals, transportation. He wraps up, "Jamil should be downstairs with the car by now. Are you ready?" he asks, looking up for the first time. Trying to protect my dignity, what a mensch.

I decided to braid my unruly mop of chocolate-colored waves instead of trying to get it wet and dry before I was too late to meet the team. "Just shoes," I say as I pull the summer-weight suit coat on over the strapless cotton dress that was—thank Micah and his machinations—freshly pressed yesterday.

"Damn, girl," he says. "Your hangover is completely undetectable. You look fantastic."

"Why thank you," I say as I dip my feet into deliciously soft yellow leather slides. I go to grab my purse and start to freak out. "I cannot carry this behemoth all day," I whine.

"I got you," Micah says. He's at the door of the room holding out my favorite mustard-colored crossbody bag. "Your wallet, room key, phone, and passport are in here."

"I couldn't love you more if you were my own." I kiss him on the cheek. "Thank you, Micah, I don't know what I did before I stole you from Kai," I say to him over my shoulder as I run for the elevator. "Oh wait." Something stops me in the hallway. I freeze. Something… is tickling my brain. A memory…

"Another coffee and your laptop," he says from directly behind me. Distracted, I gratefully accept the silver tumbler and my computer sleeve from my new best friend.

"I don't deserve you." I sip the fourth, fifth, and sixth shots of espresso with piping hot milk and just a hint of cinnamon. He loads me into the elevator, leans in to push the lobby-level button, and waves to me.

"Go get 'em, tiger." He grins as the doors slide closed.

26

Call it the time difference, the sleep of the dead I enjoyed after a late-night workout, the unexpected kiss… call it my overwhelming desire to see Holland again today… whatever you call it, I don't mind getting an early start to the day.

I watch the news while I eat a room-service-delivered huitlacoche omelet and these decadent souffle pancakes I may have to order again, more goddam tortillas (I skipped), fruit, coffee, and a tall glass of horchata. Then I start on my email. Reminded of something I keep meaning to get to, I write a quick note to Holland.

FROM: Kai Ipu, CEO
TO: Holland Gallagher, CSO
RE: Start strong, finish stronger
Tuesday, 7:02 a.m.
Holland,
While doing some research, Micah came across some information about an initiative you spearheaded a few years ago to educate high school students about gender equity and anti-racism through school sports. Well done, my friend.
In his research, Micah couldn't find any current info about the

project. If this is something you're still working on—or if it's something you're still interested in working on—Innovated would like to back you.

I'd like to offer my personal support as my participation on my high school football, basketball, and baseball teams improved my physical and mental health. From my coaches and teammates, I learned the interpersonal skills I still lean on today. And I learned to fail forward.

Use any IPU resources you need—perhaps legal can help you establish a 501(c)3. Or we can help you with marketing, web development, whatever you need.

And please let me know when and how I can pitch in.

Looking forward to working on this together—dare I say, doubling down?

KAI

By the time I get downstairs to meet Jamil, I have solved all the world's problems and found a new way to ask the woman of my dreams to spend more time with me. Okay, maybe not all the world's— *Stop the presses. Who is that? Vicki Vale?*

Holland is an angelic vision in a white skirt suit with an unimaginably sheer scarf (what is it with this woman and her nearly invisible clothes?) and deliciously lemon-yellow shoes. When did yellow become my favorite color? I shove my hands in my pants pockets.

Her hair is in complicated braids wrapped around the top of her head like a goddamn halo. I have actually died, and this is actual heaven.

"Good morning, Kai," she says brightly.

"I—I'm surprised to see you, Holland," I stutter. "We said nine o'clock for you."

"Oh gosh, the day's half over by nine," she says with a dazzling smile. "Did you get coffee? Do you need anything? Jamil is ready for us."

"Oh, okay, yeah." I trip over my tongue again. "I'm good. Let's go." I place my hand at the base of her spine and walk with her out to the car.

When Jamil offers his hand to the bright light of brunette beauty, I snarl. Jamil smiles and his shoulders shake with silent laughter as he steps back to allow me to help Holland into the car. Cocky bastard.

"I'm not sure what you have planned today," Holland says as she slides gracefully into the SUV despite her heels and skirt. Magic. "Let me give you a quick rundown of what I'll be up to." My head is still reeling from her yellow-and-white glow and her I-swear-to-God-she-actually-smells-like-lemons scent in the close quarters of the car. Did this car shrink overnight? I swear she wasn't this close when she was slurring her praises to me last night. I shake my head to clear it.

"No? That's not a good idea?" she asks, thinking I was responding to her question. "Okay, we can skip lunch together." She looks only about half as disappointed as I feel. Of course I want to have lunch with her. But now I'm stuck. I'll have to call an audible as soon as the opportunity presents itself. "So, I'll just meet you in the Gallagher lobby at seven tonight, sound good?" she asks.

I missed it. I missed her entire breakdown of her day. Fuck me. At that thought, the fourteen-year-old version of myself snickers. Yes, please, the sex-crazed adolescent who occupies most of my brain says. I grin despite myself.

"Good. It's settled then," she says with finality.

"Wait, what?" I really feel like we are on different planets this morning. I mean, I'm on Planet Kiss Holland Again, but where the hell is she? Oh. That's right. The real one. Earth. Got it.

"Have you heard a single word I've said, Kai Ipu?" she manages to look perplexed, pissed off, and perfect all at the same time.

"Of course," I say, placing a gentle hand on her knee. "You're spending the day in meetings with the Mexico IT team and Zahra, having lunch with me at one o'clock, getting ready for the gala at your sister's office, and then we'll pick you up at the Gallagher building at seven sharp." Ha. See? I heard her.

She raises one exceptional eyebrow and I withdraw my hand. Because I made my point, of course. Or because if I don't move my hand away now, I may never. Or because of the eyebrow.

"Okay then," she says. "We're on for lunch." She turns her lovely face away, but I can still see her smile.

27

Taking a break from an energizing meeting with Zahra and the local IT team, I launch my email. And find a tempting treat waiting for me: Kai sent me the rekindling of a dream. I send him a quick note of thanks.

FROM: Holland Gallager, CSO
TO: Kai Ipu, CEO
RE: Success isn't given, it's earned.
Tuesday, 9:22 a.m.
Kai,
While I'm a little creeped out that you and Micah were cyberstalking me, I'm over the moon at the thought of picking up where my *high school* teammates and I left off. Our initiative was school-wide, so we called it Aces United (after our mascot, the Silver Aces). We may have to come up with a better name in order to live up to your expectations.

I'm overwhelmed with gratitude. You never cease to amaze me.

My first resource request is for Micah to become my

assistant—I'll definitely need his help on this. Thanks in advance—he's the best.

H.

Kai responds almost immediately. I'm giggling as I read it.

FROM: Kai Ipu, CEO
TO: Holland Gallagher, CSO
RE: Losing is a temporary location, winning is an unending journey.
Tuesday, 9:26 a.m.
H,
Nope. Go get your own assistant. But *I* will be at your beck and call in all things Aces United.
Put me in, Coach,
KAI

Every time I close my eyes, I see the look on Kai's face when he came into the lobby this morning. He looked like he'd just stumbled into a candy store and I was all the tasty treats he wanted to savor. I'm trying really hard not to blush all over again just remembering. He started at my hemline, moved his eyes up to my neck, slowly back down my legs to pause for a heartbeat on my feet. I had to force myself not to wiggle my toes at him. His gaze, nearly a tangible thing, swept back up my body—skipping eye contact completely—to my hair. It was all I could do not reach up to check my braids weren't falling out of the complicated twist. His eyes on me felt somehow both hungry and reverent.

Just now, the room is silent, and I realize Zahra has asked me a question. Jeez'm Pete, pay attention, Holland.

"I absolutely agree," I say—ha! I was listening after all. "We should implement those changes right away."

We break at one o'clock when most of the team leaves for lunch and Kai arrives. It reminds me of my first day at Innovated. Like that day, it's just the three of us catching up on the day's progress over—this time—excellent Mexican food. Kai ordered from a nearby restaurant: Amberjack ceviche, eggplant relleno, grilled octopus, a refreshing cool jamaica, and strawberry flan. Who knew flan could be fruity?! As we're seating ourselves around a conference table to eat, I slip off my suit jacket to reveal the strapless white cotton dress. I catch Kai squinting at me—like he would at the sun. I like it.

While we eat, we talk. Kai asks how it's going, and Zahra and I brief him. Of course, he interrupts to ask insightful questions and to praise us both for finding solutions. Something is different about Kai today. I can't put my finger on it. He's as confident and competent as always, but he seems… somehow both shyer and more forward than he's ever been.

Since our Big Talks—dinner at my place, interrupted by his heartbreaking loss, then dinner at his place while he was still in the throes of his grief—he has stopped avoiding me. Now that I know him better, I am confident that's what he was doing. This isn't that. This is next level. He is—wait, there it is again! He's touching me. I realize in a rush that in all our interactions, we have never touched more than in quick, professional, necessary ways. Today, he's had his hands on me from the first. It seems so natural, I didn't even notice before now. Now that his knee rests firmly against mine under the conference table. Now that he has his huge warm hand on my arm to emphasize a point. How had I not noticed? When did this start?

We wrap up lunch, and Kai excuses himself to return to his afternoon docket of meetings. On his way out, he plants a quick kiss on Zahra's cheek and a sweet and lingering kiss on mine. Then, cool as a summer breeze, he sticks his hands in his pockets and saunters out of the room.

Zahra raised a single eyebrow when Kai kissed her, then both her eyebrows shot up when he kissed me. "Well, that's new," she says, now we're alone.

"Mm-hmm," I respond. I'm still holding my cheek where he just had his soft, warm lips.

Zahra laughs lightly and turns me toward the door. "Let's get back to work," she says, still giggling.

♡

The rest of the week in Mexico City is a whirlwind. Meetings with various departments, quick lunches at my temporary desk, late night dinners with Ximena. I hardly ever see Kai unless it's on our commute to work in the morning. But those commutes are priceless to me.

Honestly, this time with Kai is exactly why I decided to keep my job (double-down, as Kai put it). It's clear he values my input—that speech in the woods, y'all, I could've swooned! —and the work is simply fascinating. How many other CEOs would give me so much autonomy so quickly? How many other CEOs are going to invite me to tell them how to run their businesses? I've always joked that if they would let me tell them how to do it, the world would be a better place. Ha! Aidan used to say, "Nothing wrong with your sense of self-worth, Holly!" Oof. Oh, Aidan. The twisted mystery of all this is that Aidan would have adored Kai. Aidan would have loved this job for me. I shake my head to clear it.

So, our mornings spent crawling through CDMX traffic are the only time I see Kai all week. We stuff a lot into that time together, though. Discussions of Aces United, our goals for Innovated and how to reach them, telling funny stories, and working through our challenges at the office together.

Oh, yeah, and we email each other.

FROM: Holland Gallagher, CSO
TO: Kai Ipu, CEO
RE Goodness gracious.
Friday, 8:11 a.m.
Kai,
For the record, I'm at Innovated for good.
And I mean that in the sense that "for good" means permanence and that it means "for the better".
H.

FROM: Kai Ipu, CEO
TO: Holland Gallagher, CSO
RE: Lightbulb emoji
Friday, 9:09 a.m.
Holland,
Everything about you is brilliant.
KAI

FROM: Holland Gallagher, CSO
TO: Kai Ipu, CEO
RE: Take note.
Friday, 9:32 a.m.
Kai,
All I really want in the world is
- To launch this crazy charity idea with you
- To be the best CSO I can be for Innovated and its fearless leader
- An official Red Ryder carbine action two-hundred shot range model air rifle with a compass in the stock and this thing that tells time
- Micah to be my assistant

H.

FROM: Kai Ipu, CEO
TO: Holland Gallagher, CSO
RE: Watch it.
Friday, 10:11 a.m.
Holland,
From "smart" to "smart ass" in just under 30 minutes. Well done!
KAI

Thursday is particularly traffic-jammed, so we spend the hour plus breaking down Aces United season by season: back-to-school sportsmanship seminars to kick off the fall, toy drives and warm clothes drives organized by athletes playing winter sports, inviting elementary and middle school students to cheer on and learn from spring athletes. It is energizing.

FROM: Kai Ipu, CEO
TO: Holland Gallagher, CSO
RE: Are we stuck in a rut?
Thursday, 9:17 a.m.
Holland,
I know we have so much more to discuss than Aces United,

and it seems lately those two words occupy the bulk of our conversations. Thank you for being a fantastic coach and thank you for letting me take an active role in something that has become important to me.

You are one of the most wonderful women I know. You have a power over people that makes them feel important, confident, and intelligent, and I only hope you never lose sight of those qualities in yourself.

With gratitude,

KAI

Swoon.

FROM: Holland Gallagher, CSO
TO: Kai Ipu, CEO
RE: Know what I like about you?
Thursday, 10:43 a.m.
Kai,
Lots.
It seems more than okay for our conversations to be monopolized by dreaming of a better world for students.
You are the best.
H.

I bumped (figuratively, thank goodness!) into Kai on my way to meet my sister for dinner. After a brief and exceptionally pleasant conversation in the hallway, we had this exchange.

FROM: Kai Ipu, CEO
TO: Holland Gallagher, CSO
RE: Goodness. Gracious.
Thursday, 8:08 p.m.
Holland,
I value our friendship immensely. It makes me happy to hear you do, as well. Thank you for your faith in me, for your support and confidence in me. I appreciate you.

It seems to me, you and I bring out the best in each other.
KAI

I mean, c'mon. What do you do with someone like this? Sigh.

♡

"I'm happy to have you all to myself this morning, Nomi," I say to my mother-in-law over Friday breakfast in the hotel dining room.

"I'm glad your boss could spare you for a bit." Naomi laughs lightly. We both know Kai was happy to let me take some time this morning to spend with her before the gala this evening. "Plus, I'll spend all day with Ximena. I wanted one-on-one time with you, sweet girl." She smiles. Then, in a quick change of tone, "Holland, I need to discuss something with you."

"Of course. You have my undivided attention as always, Nomi," I say sincerely.

"Holland, now that you've come out of your shell and found work that so obviously fulfills and excites you, I want you to seek love again," Naomi says, calm and collected, even blasé—as though she were describing what is on her breakfast plate.

"Nomi, no," I protest. My throat is closing up. I look around the restaurant. This is not a conversation I want Kai—or anyone else I work with—to overhear.

"Listen to me, my darling girl." Naomi holds my shaking hand in hers. "My son would not have wanted you to be alone. Aidan's first and only priority was your happiness. It would break his heart that you are not being adored in the way you deserve." I feel a single tear slide down my face.

"Nomi..." I can't even think of what to say.

"Kai is a dear friend of mine." Naomi goes on. "He is obviously smitten with you. I've known him for a long time and never have I seen him look at a woman the way he looked at you the night you met. Never have I heard him talk about a woman the way he talks about you."

"How did he look at me? Wait. How does he talk about me?" I ask—then realizing what I've said and how I've said it, I start over. "Nomi, no. I cannot—I'm still in love with my husband."

"Holland, I've been a widow much longer than you have, so believe me when I say—you will always be in love with Aidan." She squeezes my hands gently. "That love is frozen in time and will forever feel both fresh and far away." Naomi sounds melancholy but still firm. "You are not only allowed, but hereby officially encouraged, to let Kai love you. My son would have wanted nothing less than this man for you. He's ideal for you. I dare say he might even be a better match for you than Aidan was."

"Don't say that." I spit the words out, indignant and destroyed and confused and hopeful. "Aidan and I were perfect for each other."

"Aidan was still a boy in many ways." Naomi looks and sounds almost frustrated. "I love my sons fiercely and I ache for them every day, but I know their faults. I always feared you would someday outgrow my playful puppy of a son." We both smile. "Kai is your intellectual peer, shares your ambition, challenges you, and supports you." Naomi gives my hands a final squeeze, pulls hers back into her lap. "Just think about it. Open your heart just a little bit to Kai."

"Nomi, you're nuts," I say with an involuntary shiver. "I mean, I do find him charming. He's magnetic—it's like he's a force of nature."

"Oh, I can see that." Naomi smiles broadly at me. "But I think you're the sun in this scenario. He's obviously caught in your orbit, my bright and shining girl."

I feel myself blush with the truth of it.

28

It's disconcerting how much I miss my commute-mate this morning. I've gotten used to having Holland with me every morning. All week, I found myself hoping for traffic as I got ready for work. What a chump. Today, I knew not to expect her, but I still wish she were here.

"What're you up to today, Jamil?" I ask. *Good thinking, Ipu.* This is how my normal morning routine would go. Check in with security. Act as if I don't crave Holland.

"Besides sitting in this traffic?" my driver asks. "We're sweeping the venue for tonight's shindig. Looks like security won't be a problem. My Mexico team is top notch, dude."

"Good to know," I say. "Not surprised, though. You're the best. I can imagine you attract talent."

"Thanks, boss." Jamil looks at me in the rearview mirror. "And fuck you."

I laugh. "What's that for?"

"I don't know, man." Jamil is grinning now. "It felt all sincere and shit in here."

"Shut up," I say as I pull out my phone and pretend I have something important to do. Great, now I'm being all schmoopy with Jamil?

There's a note from Holland in my inbox. I launch into action before we've even reached the office.

FROM: Holland Gallagher, CSO
TO: Kai Ipu, CEO
RE: Ack. Help!
Friday, 7:52 a.m.
Kai,
I had a lovely breakfast with your friend Naomi this morning. She sends her love.
...And then I got a call from Rebecca Smythe. I know you abhor any dealings with The Company Who Shall Not Be Named. And I hate to ask you this, but will you please call her? Her contact info is below. She's trying to poach me from Innovated. I explained I'm in a committed worklationship but she won't hear it. I know she'll shut up if you shut her up.
Hating myself for asking,
H.

FROM: Kai Ipu, CEO
TO: Holland Gallagher, CSO
RE: You owe me one.
Friday, 8:15 a.m.
H,
On the phone with Smythe now. Never doubt my devotion to you.
KAI

Holland formally resigned from her most recent position via email before she accepted the CSO post from me. But they've been extra shady in their attempts to retain her—or maybe to reacquire her. She tells me when they reach out (maybe four contacts from three different executives, so far) but this is the first time she's asked for my help. I'm thrilled to be able to tell Smythe or anyone in her organization that Holland is off the market. It is my privilege to have her on my team, and I'm happy to tell Smythe to back the fuck off. Best day ever.

FROM: Holland Gallagher, CSO
TO: Kai Ipu, CEO
RE: Bless you.
Friday, 8:20 a.m.
Kai,
Thank you. I'm sorry your sacrifice was so great.
H.

FROM: Kai Ipu, CEO
TO: Holland Gallagher, CSO
RE: It's done.
Friday, 9:23 a.m.
H,
Anything. Anytime.
KAI

And of course, I know it is true.

29

This evening after work, I try to remain calm as Jamil navigates the horrific traffic—but it is neither his driving nor the congestion on the streets around us that is making my butterflies hold a cotillion in my belly.

My anticipation (dare I say anxiety) about tonight is making them recreate the ballroom scenes of every Jane Austen-based movie I've ever loved. I snarl at them, pressing my hand to my middle. I know I would not have been this nervous if I hadn't had that conversation with Naomi this morning—about being open to Kai, I mean, open to the possibility of Kai. But thinking of tonight as an opportunity, I'm all aflutter.

When I arrive at my sister-in-law's office, I am whisked away to an impromptu salon in the CFO's suite. Of all the days to skip washing my mop.

Little worry, though—I am transformed by the team who handle my unruly hair, paint my face, update my mani/pedi in delicate nude colors, and generally make me feel girly and giggly.

Ximena and Naomi are within earshot but out of sight, presumably getting the full princess treatment, too. The timing of this trip could not have been better. Naomi's fundraising gala falling on the last night of this work trip with Kai and co.—my first trip abroad since losing Aidan—all converging feels like kismet. It has been overwhelming, of course—but why walk when you can run? Tonight will be the culmination of the first leg of the IPU trip and my good-bye to my family as the team will be back on the plane headed for Chile in the morning. Before my brain can hijack itself into reviewing all the tasks I have to accomplish before meeting my Chilean colleagues, my stylist offers me a mirror to check out my hair and makeup.

With a huge sigh of relief, I am pleased to see that I look like myself—only prettier. "Thank you," I say to the team, making eye contact and smiling at each person. "I love it." My unmanageable mane is swept up high off my neck but somehow still framing my face as I prefer—all that time in braids and all the magic of the hairstylist has it looking wavy and soft (instead of huge and hassled, less like I put my finger in a light socket). My makeup is completely natural-looking. It is nearly undetectable except for a bold black cat-eye. I love myself with winged eyeliner, but I rarely take the time to achieve it. "I just love it," I repeat with gratitude to the team.

"You look beautiful," Naomi says, stepping into my line of sight. I gasp. Naomi always looks put-together and naturally beautiful, but this—this Hope for Flowers sugar-colored maxi halter dress with swirling black geometric designs and drawstrings that cross and tie at her neck with wood beads and thread tassels at the ends—this is breathtaking. If Naomi isn't wearing vintage, it's vintage-inspired—as well as sustainably-made and usually by a Black-owned dressmaker.

"It has pockets." Naomi beams and spins. Her gorgeous auburn hair hangs loosely around her shoulders, her makeup is subtle and flattering.

"You look like Miami in the Roaring Twenties, Nomi. Like a starlet. On vacation." I bounce my eyebrows at her. "I want to see Ximena, too." I get up and turn around just as my sister sweeps into the room (because sweep is what one does in a floor-length Stella Jean dress with a huge full skirt and embroidered puffy sleeves). "Holy perfect-for-you, Batman!"

"I know, right?" Ximena preens. The deep (deep!) V of the jet-black dress shows off acres of Ximena's beautiful warm brown skin. Her shiny black hair is in a low bun made up of dozens of tiny twists on either side. "You look like Frida Kahlo would have looked if she had a team of stylists," I say. The techs packing up their brushes and tools all snort with the effort not to laugh out loud at me. Ximena and Naomi don't even try to stop themselves—they're howling. "I mean it." I try to sound sincere.

"We know, *manita*," Ximena says, wiping at laugh-tears. "That's what makes it so funny."

Whatever.

"What am I wearing?" I ask my mother-in-law.

Naomi sends me into an office they were using as a changing room. Grateful for solitude and a locked door for a moment, I take a cleansing breath. And then I see the stunning gown the Gallagher girls have picked out for me. Oh, I can do this. Instantly in a sweeter state of mind, I slip out of my suit-slash-dress and into the white denim Christopher John Rogers bustier with rainbow topstitching that highlights how amazing my breasts look in this perfectly fitted piece. My favorite part of the top is the utilitarian straps—almost like my comfy Sunday overalls. Next, I step into the floor-sweeping silk-faille skirt with bold chevron stripes in yellow, orange, pink, turquoise, black, white, blue—happy colors that made me feel like dancing. With Kai? I hope. It fits slim through my waist and hips then kicks out to a voluminous skirt complete with a train. I might never take this off.

I call in my in-laws to make sure I am zipped and hooked in all the right places. Both Gallaghers squee when they see me.

"I knew this would be perfect for you!" Naomi trills.

"I just about died when I saw it on the hangers," Ximena says, "on your perfect body, it's killer!"

The women circle me several times, admiring and adjusting and chattering constantly. There is no mirror in the office, so I have to trust how amazing the dress—is it a dress if it's in two pieces and my midriff is bare?—feels. And I must trust how ecstatic my girlfriends are. I realize they didn't have the benefit of a mirror in here either, so I return their praises. Naomi's dress is flattering and elegant. Ximena's is exotic and sexy while still being tasteful. Suddenly—as I heap praise on my friends—I feel half-naked and self-conscious.

"Am I underdressed?" I ask as I tug at my overall straps.

"Absolutely not." Naomi swats at my fidgeting hands. "Relax. You look stunning. Perfect for this event. Perfect for the hot weather."

"You look amazing," Ximena says, raising one eyebrow and giving me her best faux-smolder.

"I trust you both. But I feel exposed." I continue to fuss with my clothes.

"Don't think of it as exposed." Naomi gives my arm a gently reassuring squeeze. "Think of it as open to possibility."

With this thought in mind, I straighten my spine and the three of us finish getting ready for the party. Open to possibility. I can manage that.

30

Why am I so nervous? I blame the fact that I am changing out of a very nice suit and into an even nicer suit. After a long day at the office thinking about Holland—I mean, working—I'd much rather be in jeans. I button the blue linen jacket—sometimes, always, never, as I leave the third button undone—and adjust the cuffs of my white linen shirt. If a cold shower followed by linen on linen doesn't keep me cool this evening, it's because of the weather. Obviously not the woman. No woman has ever had me tied up in knots like this one.

I had close calls with falling before—my high school sweetheart was fun and funny, and we parted as friends after graduation. My only other long-ish-term relationship was with a cheerleader I dated for just over a year in college. That was fun in more explicit ways, but also ended after graduation. Since then, I have not even come close. Dating is time-consuming and I've had no trouble satisfying my needs with the women who simply seem to appear ready-and-willing at whatever bar or club I wander into on my travels. I am meticulously safe (thanks, dad; thanks, Pops) and get tested regularly. I never promise a woman anything, I never break hearts. So I got from college to forty with no strings attached. And I have loved it. Until now. Until Holland.

The last month before this trip, I found myself wandering by her office—she refused to take my office off my hands even when I nearly begged—just to catch a glimpse of her. After living worry-free in my penthouse for more than a year, my apartment "above the store" now feels empty when I commute up three flights of stairs each night. Opening a bottle of wine by myself has me wishing I could pour her a glass, just so we could toast "to us" again. I have not entertained a guest—ahem—since I met Holland. I have two (count them, two!) sky blue vintage Mercedes coupes, but Holland has me thinking of sensible vehicles with child safe car seat tethers. What the perpetual fuck?

And here I am getting ready for this event with no one to check my tie. "Fuck it," I say as I throw the tie on the bed.

"Fuck what, boss?" Micah asks, appearing suddenly.

"Fuck this tie, Micah," I gruff.

"You look perfectly appropriate without a tie," Micah says even as he adjusts his own. "But... are you sure I can't talk you out of Converse?" I growl. "Got it. You look great." Micah puts on his best humoring-the-boss smile. "Jamil is ready when you are. He's lined up a second car going directly to Museo Hacienda de Santa Mónica for Zahra, et al. I assume you want to pick up the Gallaghers yourself."

"Yes," is my sole response, but my heart does that triple-step.

"Excellent." Micah grins.

♡

The steps of the building where the Gallaghers rent office space have nothing architectural to recommend them. However, when Jamil pulls the SUV to a stop in front of them, they are graced by three celestial beings—maybe they are muses?—arranged artfully upon them. Blown away by these women, I surreptitiously grab my phone and snap a picture of them in the evening light. Naomi is on the top step with her hand resting gracefully on the rail. Ximena is halfway down the stairs but far to the right of her mother-in-law, looking back over her shoulder, laughing at something Naomi must have said. Holland is—I swallow but my mouth feels suddenly dry— almost to the bottom of the stairs in the very middle of them in an out-of-this-world brightly colorful and gorgeous-on-her gown that leaves her arms and middle bare and makes my fingertips tingle.

"They look like they're about to drop their debut album," Jamil quips over his shoulder. I snarl at him. Jamil laughs as he gets out of the car to help the ladies in. I beat my driver-slash-security-detail-slash-friend-slash-mock-rival to the punch. I am at Holland's side with one hand at the small of her back as my other lifts her knuckles to my lips before Jamil has even circled the vehicle.

"Holland, let me help you on these stairs," I say. And then only for her, I say quietly, "You look stunning." Okay, she actually looks a little overwhelmed by my rushing to her. I silently scold myself for scaring her.

"Kai, thank you, I'm fine. I've been walking down stairs most of my life," she says even as she squeezes my hand holding hers and leans slightly into my arm. If I apply even the slightest pressure, I have the feeling she'd spin in my arms and we'd be dancing. Note to self: I have to get her on the dancefloor this evening.

"Mrs. Gallagher." I nod to Naomi. "Mrs. Gallagher." I nod to Ximena. "You look lovely this evening, both of you."

"Thank you, Kai." Naomi beams.

"You too, Kai," Ximena says, slapping my ass as she floats by in an extraordinary black dress. All three Gallagher women laughed hysterically at the shock on my face and the blush I can feel on my cheeks. Did I say muses? Angels? Nah. They're harpies.

31

When the car pulls up to the hacienda-slash-museum, Naomi asks me to stay with her for a moment. Kai keeps a watchful eye on us as he helps the youngest Gallagher out of the SUV. "We'll wait for you," Kai says.

"No worry, we'll catch up." Naomi shoos him away.

"Nomi, what's up? Don't you need to get in there?" I ask impatiently. "This is your event." Plus, I want to get to the party and get to dancing with Kai. I'm excited to see the venue and—of course—support Naomi's charity work. Let's go already.

"Please. The team in charge of this event hasn't needed me since we settled on the date," Naomi says proudly. "Have you thought any more about what we discussed?"

"Sorry, what?" I play dumb. Not a good look. Naomi raises a judgmental eyebrow—a silent admonishment she uses so rarely that I jump a little. "Oh, okay, yes. Of course. That's all I can think about. If I'm honest, Kai is all I can think about." Naomi gives me a knowing smile. "Oh, wipe that look off your face." I roll my eyes. "Of course you were right. You're always right." We both giggle. "I appreciate you helping me see things more clearly." Truth is, the grief and guilt have been bogging me down for so long. "I'm trying to be more open—as you keep reminding me to be."

"I'm proud of you," Naomi says. "We both know moving on will not be easy. I just want you to consider it. Consider Kai. He's the best of men."

"Thank you, Nomi." I hug her. "You mean the world to me. I can't imagine my life without you in it."

Naomi hugs me back. "Let's get in there," she says as she opens the car door. Jamil shows up from nowhere to help her out of the SUV. And Kai magically appears to help me down.

"Hi," I say with my eyes on his lips.

"Hello." His low voice rumbles like distant thunder and my entire body reacts—shivers down my spine, tingles in my toes. "Everything okay?"

"Everything is awesome," I say, giggling at my own giddiness.

"Excellent. Then may I escort you?" he asks, placing his hand on my silk skirt, below the high waist and just above the curve of my ass. Like it belongs there.

"I was hoping you would." I smile up at him.

♡

After making the rounds, introducing ourselves to dozens of Naomi's friends and supporters, Kai and I find ourselves alone on the balcony overlooking the festivities below. The hacienda is a beautiful space made even more so with fifteen huge mother-of-pearl chandeliers suspended above the courtyard—between the dining tables and the night sky. I have three just like these in my kitchen in LA—much smaller, but the same retro-glam look. The tables, the bars, the entire atmosphere seem to glow with soft light, glittering gold accents, and beautiful people.

My hand rests on the balcony rail, nearly touching Kai's, I can feel his warmth with his hand so close to mine. I realize with a start that I'm not wearing my wedding rings. Holy ship, I took them off for my manicure this afternoon and—what?! Not put them back on? I try not to panic. And then I wonder what it means. Is this a sign? I check my clutch, and there they are, neatly tucked into an inner pocket. I run my finger over them, but do not put them back on.

"You okay?" Kai asks, one hand in his pocket, the other on the rail near mine still. "Everything… okay?" He looks cool but concerned—I wonder if he saw the panic on my face. And I wonder if he noticed my naked left hand.

"They're like oversized versions of the lights in my kitchen," I say, directing his attention to the chandeliers and trying to dodge his question.

"A piece of home," Kai muses as he looks back out at the lights and the party below. I look at him. He really is gorgeous. I love looking at his face. His beautiful bronze skin, his perfectly trimmed beard, his nearly black eyes that pull my eyes to them.

"It was so nice having you in my kitchen," he says. He must be remembering the evening we spent together when he asked me to double down at IPU. "I remember thinking that night how much it felt like a home with you in it."

We stare at each other for a long, silent minute. A long, comfortable silence full of possibility.

"Kai, I have a question for you."

"How may I help, Holland—" he hesitates, "my friend."

I raise one eyebrow. Had he started to call me something else? My dear? My heart? My love? Let's find out. "Naomi gave me a lecture about how it's time for me to move on," I say.

Kai stiffens. I feel the anxiety wave off of his enormous frame and I sense every muscle in his body tighten. I speed up my little speech to help allay whatever worries he is clearly having. "She said that I'll always love Aidan and that he would have wanted me to find love again." Kai moves away from me, just half a step but he definitely is putting distance between us. Maybe I've misread him? Okay, now I'm worried. "She said that she's watched me alone long enough and thinks it's time for me to find love again." I rush to finish my sentence.

"I see," Kai says coldly. "Yes, of course. Let me work on that. Please excuse me," he says. And he's gone.

I feel a tough lump rise in my throat.

I was so sure he liked me. Naomi was so sure he liked me. I can't believe how wrong I was. I take a steadying breath and drag myself downstairs and toward the bar. On my way there, I catch my sister's eye and give the universal head-tilt that says meet-me-at-the-booze-I-need-you. Ximena's full skirt arrives a moment before she does, and we giggle at the sound and the feel of our hugely full skirts mingling at our feet. She's got me laughing. Goodness, I love this woman—I feel better already. Ximena gives me a side-hug and orders two tamarind margaritas, doubled, and two cervezas. "You always know exactly what I need, Menita." I toast her with the chile-lime-rimmed margarita.

"You wear your heart on your sleeve, *manita*." Ximena takes a dainty sip of her tequila-spiked tamarindo. "It's never difficult to decipher your thoughts. What's up?" she asks, guiding me to a hightop table in the only quiet-ish part of the courtyard.

"Nomi wants me to start dating." I sigh.

"I had a feeling this was coming." Ximena sounds resolved. "You know she's right. I'm in a completely different place than you are, but I can so clearly see that you need to try, Holly."

"Wait, are you saying that I look like I need a man?" I feel my ire and my color rising.

"Absolutely not," Ximena protests. "You need a man like a knish needs an icicle." I laugh in spite of myself. "You deserve someone who loves you and cares for you and supports your total badassery. There is a huge difference."

"That sounds like a dressed-up way to say I need a man." I pout. "Why do I need a man, but you and Nomi don't? What's the difference?"

Ximena ponders this for a long time and finally says, "I think the difference is Kai."

I snort-laugh and down the rest of my strong margarita. I take a breath, snort-laugh again, and start my beer. Ximena gingerly lowers my beer hand and makes intense eye contact with me.

"Holland, I'm not ready to move on because there isn't a man I've met who could compare to my husband. Ethan and I were best friends in childhood. We were pen pals all the years he lived on the other side of the country. Ethan was my physical, social, spiritual, and intellectual match. My perfect match. I honestly believe he and I were meant for each other." Ximena's voice wavers just a bit. She sips her margarita. She dares to merely sip it, the fiend.

"Because you knew Ethan longer, I didn't love Aidan as much? That's ludicrous. He was my whole life." I'm getting pissed off now.

"Of course not. I know you loved him. Everyone who ever met you two saw your love for each other. I felt it every day you two were together." Ximena is adamant. "My experience and your experience are completely different. I cannot picture myself moving on, but I can sure-as-shit picture you moving on with Kai."

"That's nuts," I argue. "He bolted when I brought it up to him.

He's not into me."

"When? When did that happen?" She's incredulous and it kind of makes me feel better.

"Just now. Upstairs. On the balcony," I say.

"I doubt that. It's so obvious to everyone that he adores you. And you look at him like he's *el bizcocho*." Ximena sighs. "He respects the hell out of you, won't shut up about your work and your brain and your success. And you're the same way—not one sentence comes out of your mouth that isn't about Kai." I start to protest. "Stop. It's so obvious. Don't argue." I stop. "So what happened? You say he bolted. What was that all about?" Ximena asks.

"I have no idea." I feel deflated and frustrated all over again. "I told him that Nomi wanted me to start dating again, and he took off like a rocket." We each mull this over as we stand in silence with our drinks and our thoughts. It sure felt like rejection when he pulled away from me and took off like that—as soon as I brought up the fact that I might be ready to date again.

"*Manita*, let me ask you a question." Ximena is wearing her judgey face. This can't be good. "Did you say to Kai what you *think* you said to Kai?" My jaw drops—loosened by tequila, it really falls open wide.

"Are you accusing me of miscommunicating?" I am incredulous only as long as it takes me to get this sentence out. "About my emotions?" I deliver this second line deadpan. She may have a point.

"I'm accusing you of nothing." She completely sees through me. "I'm simply asking if maybe there is more to the story upstairs."

After pondering this for a nanosecond, I pull my shoulders back, raise my chin, and declare, "If Kai misunderstood my meaning, that's on him. I told him I'm ready to date again. He ran. What more is there for me to do?"

"Throw yourself at him," Ximena proffers. "Confess your love and devotion. Jump his bones. Nomi's right. I say go for it," the traitor wearing my best friend's face says.

"Come again?" I worry maybe Ximena has finally lost it. "What are you talking about? Go for what?"

"Let him love you, Holland." Ximena looks like she thinks I'm out to lunch, too. "And go profess your admiration, obsession, and affection for him. You have absolutely nothing to lose." I snort (again! What's with me tonight?) and make a mental list of all the things I could lose if I take a chance on the man who has captured my heart so thoroughly. If things go poorly, I could lose my job, my nerve, my faith in humanity... Nothing to lose, my aspen. If things go well... well, that isn't going to happen because he clearly rejected me upstairs. He scared off pretty easily for a man who "obviously" adores me. What did I say? Or maybe it was my approach? How did I say it? I really hoped the two of us were going to spend this evening together. Dancing, drinking, dining. And I really hoped tonight he would finally kiss me. Or let me kiss him…

Micah and Zahra stand at the table with cocktails in hand as though they've been here all along. Holy ghosts! Have they been here all along? No, Ximena greets them. Phew, I was sure I was losing it for a second.

"Holland, hon, the boss wants you," Micah says.

"Of course he does," Ximena says into her glass. Micah pauses but doesn't take the bait. Thank goodness. I'd have a tough time explaining my sister's antics to my colleagues.

"He's speaking with the youngest Velasco," Zahra says. "That one is rich as Croesus and hotter than fire. Find out if he's single, straight, and looking." She is a smoke show herself, I notice. Zahra looks striking in a poppy red Sai Sankoh high slit, one-shoulder gown. Goddess bless these friends I've made. I'll do some reconnaissance for her.

"Go talk to Kai," Micah says to Holland with a sly grin. "Zahra and I'll babysit your sister," he says as he inches toward Ximena and loops his free arm around her waist. "How you doin'?" he purrs in his best Joey Tribbiani voice. Ximena laughs as she swats him away. Zahra just shakes her head. My eyes find Kai's almost instantly and I move that way, being careful not to let my double margarita show in the sway of my steps.

"Hi," I say shyly, looking from Kai to his companion and back.

"Holland, I'd like you to meet Victor Velasco," Kai says with ice.

"Not the film director," Victor Velasco says in Los Angeles-meets-Mexico-City-accented English, taking my offered hand to pull me in gently for a firm but dry kiss on the cheek.

"Nice to meet you, Victor Velasco-not-the-film-director," I say with my eyes on Kai, not the man kissing my cheek.

"Kai has told me so much about you, Holland." He pronounces my name Ah-land, as though he's transposed the H and the O. "May I get you a drink?"

"Don't let me keep you," Kai says, stepping away from our trio and disappearing instantly into the crowd.

♡

After dinner at Victor's table, after dancing with Victor and his brothers exclusively, and after having extended conversations with three generations of the Velasco family, I am relieved to find Kai standing cool as moose, hands in his pockets, at my side just as dessert is being served.

"Victor, may I borrow Holland for a moment? We have some business to conduct before the evening concludes," Kai says to the perfectly nice man he pawned me off on early in the evening.

Infuriated, I turn on Kai as soon as we are out of earshot. "How dare you? Ask him permission to borrow me? What am I?" I can't even think of an analogy that suits. "Cattle? Chattel?" What is chattel? I can't remember, I am so mad.

"Wait, wait," Kai says. "That was the culturally appropriate move. I meant nothing by it."
"Culturally appropriate," I hiss. "Was it culturally appropriate to just hand me off to some guy like I'm property?" Oh yeah, I remember, that's what chattel means.

32

I pull Holland away from the crowd, looking for a quiet place to talk. Desperate to be able to hear her and to be heard—and yet not be overheard—I pull her into my arms on the edge of the dance floor. She stiffens at first, but then almost immediately relaxes. I pull her close, start to move with her to the music, try to stop myself from enjoying it, and whisper in her ear.

"Don't be angry, Holland—" *my heart,* I catch myself before I inadvertently declare my devotion to her, just like every other time I've ever said her name "—you and Naomi asked me to find you a boyfriend and there's no one better suited than Vic."

"We asked you what?" Holland sounds defeated. In stark contrast to her lead-weight voice, she feels light as air in my arms as I lead her through the dance. She can really dance. Of course she can, and yet I have to let her go. My heart thump-thump-thumps its disapproval of that idea.

"Holland, upstairs." I press my cheek to her temple as though my touch will help her recall. "You told me that you and your mother-in-law were ready for you to find a—" my throat seizes, I can't say it, can't say partner or husband or even date. "To meet someone." She melts in my arms, so I hold her more firmly. What's the matter with her—is she drunk? Impossible for her to move with me and the music like this if she were. She is grace incarnate. I feel like I've been dancing with her all my life. God bless Elias's insistence the entire team take lessons.

"So you found me the most eligible bachelor in the room," she says.

"And the wealthiest. You'll want for nothing if you—" again I choke on the thought of her marrying anyone—where did that come from? — dating anyone, being with anyone but me. "If you let Vic take care of you."

"That's not true," she says, stopping dead in our tracks, pulling away as far as my iron grip on her will allow. "Let me go, Kai," Holland says icily.

"Wait." I hold onto her arm and reach into my jacket with my free hand. She looks the tiniest bit hopeful. "This is for Naomi. Will you please give it to her?" It is important that the Velasco family sees me transact business with Holland after I'd used that as an excuse to pull her away.

"Of course." She takes the envelope and backs away. Absolutely dumbfounded by her behavior, I find myself alone on the dance floor. Better get used to this, this loneliness, this wanting. I ache with the loss of the feel of her, loss of the sound of her, loss as to what the actual fuck is going on. Suddenly the absence of my family crashes down: I can't pick up the phone and call my Pops. I can't strategize with my dad. With a dark cloud of anger and hurt and grief and shame hanging over my head, I shove my hands into my pockets and head to the bar.

Nothing a good bender can't fix.

33

I half-run to the bathroom, lock myself in a stall, and message my mother-in-law.

HOLLAND: S-O-S. Downstairs bathroom.
NOMI: On my way.

Not five minutes later, Naomi flies in. I hear her lock the door to the entire restroom. She knocks gently on my stall. "What happened, honey?"

I tell my mother-in-law everything Kai said and did—from freezing upstairs to foisting me on some guy to insulting me on the dancefloor (while dancing like he was born to it, sigh)—and I add, "He gave me this donation, like, 'Don't go back to your mother-in-law empty-handed.'" I slide the envelope through the door to Naomi. "That's it and that's all. He doesn't want me." I'm not crying. I'm not.

"Just wait, Holland, hold on," Naomi says gently. "I know this man—Kai's in problem-solving mode, he's trying to fix something for you—he really just wants what's best for you. I'm sorry he's handling this poorly." I can practically *hear* my mother-in-law roll her eyes. "But I promise he will not rest until the matter is settled. Tonight." And then under her breath, I'm sure I hear her say, "and neither will I."

I open the stall door—I've been keeping out of sight, not conducting my business—and fall into Naomi's arms. "It hurts, Nomi."

"I know, my heart." Naomi pats my back sweetly. "Oh, honey, I know it does. Look," she gently takes me by both my shoulders so she can hold my gaze, "I've known Kai a long time. This is how he acts when he thinks he's doing the right thing for the people he loves. Please overlook this"—she rolls her eyes in earnest—"caveman-like behavior and look instead at all the things he has done for you, all the ways he has proven his true feelings. Those true feelings of love he is stupidly hiding." Her small smile looks to be one-part sympathy for me and one-part venom for Kai.

"He's *hiding* his feelings? Sure felt like he was showing them when he told me to marry Victor Velasco," I whine.

"The film director?" Naomi asks.

"No, the one who is here tonight. Some rich guy."

Naomi laughs. "Holland, I just ran into the youngest Velasco brother. He told me how much my daughter-in-law and Kai Ipu make a beautiful couple. I think you have nothing to worry about."

"I hope so. I really hope that's true. Because I'm falling in love with that big dumb beautiful man. Who has absolutely no feelings for me."

"We'll see about that." She sounds like she's hatching a plan. I'm a little scared of her. I guess Ximena isn't the only badass in this family.

34

I take my second double of scotch to sit with the Velasco family.

We chat amiably about business. We talk about Naomi's charity and its work in Mexico City. Victor tells me all about his horses and his ranch. In the fifteen minutes (at least!) I've been with the Velascos, no one has mentioned Holland.

I nod to a waiter to bring me another drink and force myself to bring her up. "Victor, tell me." I try to keep the demand out of my voice, "do you like Holland? Did you ask her out? Will you see her again?"

Victor looks both shocked and amused. "Ask out your woman, Kai? No, thank you," he laughs.

"What do you mean, my woman? You've spent the entire evening with her, dancing, drinking, talking." I'm dumbfounded.

"Yes, because I thought you were having my family and me entertain her while you worked the room," Vic says. "I had no idea you were trying to play matchmaker." Every Velasco at the table laughs. "Do me a favor, Ipu," Vic says. "Next time you set me up, please find me a woman you are not head-over-heels in love with."

Victor's grandmother, who sits on my other side, reaches up and pinches my cheek. *"Sigue los consejos de la abuela,"* she says. "Marry her. And soon."

35

Naomi helps me get freshened up. Cool water, soft tissues, and a mother's touch go a long way to helping me recover my makeup and tidy my hair.

"You're so beautiful, sweetheart," Naomi says, "I wish you could see what I see."

I nearly start sobbing (again... but I was not crying before, okay) because I love Naomi, and I wish she were the only mother I've ever known. My mother was such a narcissist, so angry all the time—drunk when she could afford to be, just pissed off when we were truly broke. I never knew what to expect from my mother.

In the years Naomi and I have been family—not even fifteen percent of my life, I quickly calculate in my head—I have learned exactly what to expect from my mother-in-law: unconditional love. I never understood what a gift it is to know Naomi wants nothing more than my happiness. I didn't know what I was missing until I had it from her—there's no need to earn Naomi's affection, nor do I fear losing her love.

And now that Aidan is gone, I find Naomi's friendship and support, love and especially her affection to be more sustaining than ever. I think of him every day and having this connection with his mother helps me continue to feel connected to him. And it is its own beautiful kinship. She is truly my family.

"I hate to rush you, sweetheart," Naomi says, slightly distracted, and looking at the envelope in her hands. "But I'm supposed to make some remarks from the stage. Come with me?"

"Oh, of course," I say apologetically. "I'm monopolizing you with my drama." I step back to really look at Naomi. "How is it I just cried snot-bubble tears all over you and you look like you just stepped out of the salon?" I ask, amazed at Naomi's put-togetherness yet again.

"Well-made dress, low-maintenance hair, freshly-applied lipstick, and I'm good," Naomi says. We beam at each other a moment longer and then head out to the gathering and the microphone on the tiny stage where a band has been playing most of the evening.

"Break a leg." I whisper as I squeeze Naomi's hand to let go.

"Not so fast." Naomi holds tight to me, "you're breaking your leg with me."

Too loyal and too poised to pitch a fit (out loud!), I dutifully (and perplexedly!) follow Naomi up to the microphone. "Ladies and gentlemen," Naomi says into the microphone. *"Gracias por venir esta noche."* Still holding my hand, Naomi gives a brief impromptu speech in English and Spanish about the Foundation, its mission in Mexico, and some recent wins they've had in the CDMX. I have no idea why I am also on stage until Naomi turns to me while still speaking into the microphone, "To thank our most generous donor of the evening, please welcome my daughter-in-law, Holland Gallagher."

Naomi steps back, hands the envelope I got from Kai back to me, and then this woman I trust so much (eyeroll emoji) shoves me up to the mic. I stare a question back at Naomi, but autonomically open the envelope, look down at it, stare at it, and then turn to the crowd. I am searching both for Kai and for what to say. "My boss, Kai Ipu, Founder and CEO of Innovated Processes Unlimited handed me this envelope earlier this evening," I begin, unable to find Kai in the sea of faces before me. "It's—this is an incredibly generous gift," I stammer, "he's an incredibly generous man. And the Naomi & Elias Gallagher Foundation will be able to fully fund," I math it in my head, "more than eighteen fellows in their social justice reform incubator." The crowd audibly inhales. And then explodes with applause. I am grateful for the delay because my eyes finally find Kai's. "Ladies and gentlemen," I start in English. But then I switch to Spanish because I want to hide from what I'm about to say, just a little. *"El hombre más amable, querido, inteligente, ingenioso y generoso que he conocido donó esta enorme cantidad de dinero a mi mejor amiga y suegra,"* I say (because Kai is the kindest, dearest, most intelligent, resourceful, and generous man) and I look over my shoulder at Naomi. *"No me dijo por qué hizo esta donación, pero no tenía que hacerlo. Dio este dinero porque cree en Naomi, cree en la humanidad, cree en la Ciudad de México. Y sé que él cree en mí,"* I explain that he believes in Naomi, humanity, Mexico City, and me. *"Por favor, ayúdame a agradecer y apreciar a mi jefe, mi amigo, mi..."* I hesitate just a moment and search for the word, and then, oh fuck it, *"mi amor."* I take a deep breath. "Kai, *mi corazón, ¿podrías venir aquí para que podamos agradecerte como es debido?"* He looks surprised for less than a second and then practically flies up to the stage.

He forgoes steps to leap up to me and, as naturally as though we've been doing this forever, he puts his huge hands around my bare waist and slides them around to my back—chills chase his touch everywhere his warm and rough hands are on my skin—and he literally sweeps me off my feet. His soft linen suit coat is luxuriant as I slip my arms around his neck. The vanilla-cocoa-woodsy scent of him envelops me as we embrace. The whole room, the whole world falls away as his warmth and sheer magnitude absorb all my attention. Finally, he dips his head and his warm, full lips are on mine. He kisses me the way I've been dreaming he would kiss me: I feel it in my lips as he tenderly then feverishly explores them, I feel it in my feet dangling inches off the floor, I feel it in my butterflies who sing, "Hallelujah!," at the top of their tiny lepidopterological lungs. His heart pounds where our chests meet, I feel every beat. He tastes like scotch and heaven. I've waited for months—maybe since meeting him that first night at the restaurant with Naomi—I've denied my feelings for so long, this need to kiss Kai. Our lips part and he spins me around in a full circle, puts me lightly on my feet— we are inches from the microphone when he says, "Please go on a date with me, my heart."

And the crowd reminds of us their presence with scattered laughs and applause.

36

What the mortifying fuck? I did not realize the mic was both live and so close. That is not my style. But we're in it now. I turn to Naomi with a questioning glance. Naomi's beaming smile is all the answer I need to the unasked question, "May I escape with her?" She grins her agreement—we smile fiercely at each other for a beat.

Then, with my arm firmly wrapped around Holland's (bare! perfect, soft as silk) waist, I turn us toward the crowd of well-wishers and start making our way to the door. It feels even more amazing to hold her than I ever imagined. When we reach the portico, the look on Jamil's face is priceless—he clearly witnessed the scene on stage even though he somehow also beat us to the car, and has it running. Our getaway driver. Good man.

I hand Holland into the car, then stop to tap elbows with Jamil who looks almost as happy as I feel. "Final-fucking-ly," Jamil says with a laugh as he closes the door of the car. I am pleased to see that my driver, bodyguard, friend, and co-conspirator has raised the privacy screen when pulling the car around.

Holland and I both start talking at once.

"I can't believe you just did that." Holland is glowing.

"I can't believe I just did that," I say at the same time and we laugh, and I catch her as she falls into my arms. It's hard to believe all it took was a gross misunderstanding, a big fat check, and a public gesture of affection, and now I'm finally allowed to put my arms around her. Should've tried this tactic sooner. Ha.

I force myself to take my time, go slow, be gentle. I pull her onto my lap (seatbelts are for single guys).

"I thought you wanted me to date Victor Velasco-not-the-film-director," she says into my neck as I hold her close.

"I was under the impression you and Naomi wanted me to find you someone more suitable than I." Thank all the heavens and earth I was wrong. I am so overwhelmingly grateful I misunderstood.

"Kai, I'm sorry I wasn't more clear on the balcony," Holland says, nuzzling my neck some more. My cock loves it, but I have to think about baseball because I'm taking this slow. *If the player is replaced as a starting pitcher, he can continue as the Designated Hitter, and if the Designated Hitter is replaced, he can continue as the starting pitcher (but can no longer bat for himself).*

"You're who I want. I've known since I met you. I was just trying tonight to let you know I'm ready. To move on. With you," my angel says.

"Please don't apologize." I kiss her hair. "Holland, you are all I think about. I can't get anything done. For weeks, I've wandered around LA on foot—your influence, of course—thinking about you, buying you gifts, wishing you were with me," I say.

I have yet to give her any of the things I have picked out for her. There is a pile of presents for her on my kitchen table—I was thinking I might use the gift-wrapped packages to bribe her to date me. Thank fuck it didn't come to that. I was bold enough to buy her a 1950s pinup dress on La Brea but was too uncertain to give it to her. Same with the eco-friendly hand lotion that smells herbal and sweet like her hair, the fair-trade beach blanket the exact same color as her eyes, the lingerie... so much lingerie. I'll have to shower her with gifts when we get home. Home. With Holland. "I lost interest in my hometown before I met you," I say. "Lately I find myself driving through different LA neighborhoods looking for places to take you to lunch, to dinner, to dance. But it has all been daydreaming until now."

"I had no idea." She sounds amused. "I've been working my buns off, trying to get your attention in the office, and all the while you were out wandering the city," she deadpans. I smile at her, even though I have her tucked under my chin.

"You've had my undivided attention since the first moment I saw you." I pull her tight against my chest. "Even when I'm with you, I'm distracted by you." She giggles. I love her little laughs.

"I really really like you, Kai Ipu." She twists in my lap to look at me. If she doesn't sit still, I'm going to have to do something about this raging hard-on... sooner rather than later.

"I really really like you back, Holland Gallagher." I push her beautiful hair back from her gorgeous face. "I'm blinded by you."

She leans in to kiss me. It starts soft and sweet, but quickly grows hot and frenetic. I can't keep my hands off the soft skin of her bare arms, bare back. Her hands are on me, too, digging her nails into my shoulders and driving me insane with desire. I just know she'll be as delicious in bed as she is in this car. We make out like horny teenagers (who knew kissing could be this good?) until I hear Jamil clear his throat at the open door of the parked SUV in front of our hotel.

37

At the door of my hotel room, Kai presses his lips softly to my cheek, watches me safely inside, and then retires to his own room. I lean against the door and blink for a long time. This feels like high school. A hot and heavy make-out session in the car and then a chaste kiss goodnight. I turn to check for him through the peephole—he is truly gone. I wonder how we mutually agreed to spend this night apart without saying a word. Because that was exactly what I would've co-signed if we had put it to a vote.

My butterflies make their presence known—is that a burlesque fan dance in my belly?—as I imagine the alternative. Spending the night with Kai? That's a terrifying and tantalizing idea. I'm definitely on board, but this evening has already been a whirlwind. I am grateful to Kai for letting me have this space (both figurative and literal) even though I am wistful and already missing his touch. I wash my face (and the eight other steps I do nightly, let's be honest) and brush my teeth (and floss, mouthwash, put in my retainer, c'mon), and get ready to climb into bed. My phone buzzes. It's a message from Kai.

KAI: Hello, for our first date, may I take you to Sicily? How's tomorrow? 7 AM. I'll pick you up. Don't look for Jamil. It'll be me.

I laugh out loud. How cute is that?

HOLLAND: Hello. I would love to go to Italy with you. What will my boss think about my ditching a work trip to Santiago, though?
KAI: I want to talk to you about that.

I wait patiently for him to follow up. In the month or two (is that all?!) we've known each other, I've figured this much out. He's not waiting on me, he's formulating his next sentence. The phone makes me jump by ringing in my hand.

"I'd like to discuss with you our options going forward," is his greeting.

"I'm listening," I say with my butterflies staging a full-fledged ballet. What is making me nervous? My insecurities? Outweighing my excitement? Maybe. For a moment.

"Holland, I've been wanting this since the day we met," Kai says.

I wish I could see his face.

So I hit the video call button on my phone. Ain't technology grand?

He answers right away and is smiling. He is also shirtless, and I think I might die of desire. Can one die of desire? "Well, hello there," I flirt.

"Hi yourself." He is checking me out too, I'm pretty sure, in my skimpy tank top. "Holland, you're captivating. It's very difficult to have this conversation with you looking so delicious in that—can we even call that a shirt?" he raises his sexier-of-the-two-eyebrows. I have rated them, of course. Like ya do.

"I appreciate the sentiment and assure you it is one hundred percent mutual." I stare longingly at my first full view of the tattoos that start at his collarbone, extend over his pectoral muscle, his gorgeous shoulder, and then become a three-quarter sleeve on his right arm. "Your ink is spectacular. I'd love to hear all about it."

"Someday." He flexes, and the intricate interwoven dark black lines dance. I fan myself with my free hand.

"Damn," I say under my breath.

"Please do not allow my foul mouth to teach you bad habits." He raises the second-sexiest-of-the-two eyebrows. They are my obsession, his eyebrows. He delivers entire monologues with them. "I've heard you cuss exactly twice and both times have been this evening."

"I know, it's the worst—Wait, what was the first time?" I don't cuss. Ever.

"You said, 'oh fuck it' on stage, into a microphone, in English no less, just before you called me *mi amor*." He beams at me.

"Out loud?!" I let my hair fall forward. I am mortified.

"Show me your angelic face," he says. I look up and let my hair fall back again.

"Damn." This time it is he who says it. Then he clears his throat. "Listen." I can tell he is trying to be serious again. "I could stay on this call with you all night, but I have already rearranged our plans. We will spend the next fourteen days together, alone." He pauses. He lets that sink in.

"One day for each hour spent on the flight over?" I ask after calculating the distance in my head.

"Goddamn, you're smart. Yes." He grins at me. "I want to get to know you," he says, looking earnest.

This time, I raise one eyebrow. "And you think that'll take fourteen days? That's adorable." I give him my biggest cheerleadery smile to let him know I'm being playful and not reprimanding. He growls. I nearly hang up the phone so I can run to his room.... His growls never scared me. But now, suddenly, they completely turn me on.

"At whom are you growling, Ipu?" I pour all my flirtiness into it even as I experiment with a nickname for the first time.

"If I'm growling, kitten, it's usually at myself," he says. We are both trying out pet names. How sweet. I purr in response to this one. He smolders at me and then clears his throat. "Seriously, though, may I take you on vacation? Tomorrow?"

"I'd be thrilled and honored. Yes, please. But first, may I ask you a very serious question, Kai?" I give him a small crooked smile of my own.

"Mmm?" he asks.

"What are you wearing?" I really want to know if he is in pajama pants or boxers or ...ahem... completely naked.

"Good night, Holland, my heart," he says as he ends the call.

I laugh out loud. Good answer.

38

Holland and I do not go to Chile the next day. I send Micah and the rest of my team to Santiago on commercial flights (business class, I'm not a monster! That's an eight-hour flight). Honestly, there isn't one thing that will come up that Micah can't handle. The man genuinely is my right hand.

When I collect her this morning, Holland answers the door in light gray joggers and a seafoam green sweatshirt that falls off one shoulder—God bless the nineteen-eighties—instead of a suit. "Good morning, Holland." I smile at her.

"Good morning, Kai." She beams back at me.

I slowly run the back of my hand down her bare shoulder as I softly—*gently, damn you, Ipu*—kiss her lips. What I want to do is to *gently* push her back into her hotel room, rip off her clothes, and fuck her brains out for the rest of the day. For the rest of my life.

But that's not how we're going to do this, I promise myself for the millionth time.

"Ready?" I ask.

"For our date?" she asks back.

"Ha. Yes. Our first date."

"Two weeks in Italy. Yeah, I'm ready for that." She giggles a little.

"Let's go." I take her bags and her hand, and escort her first to a

146

hired car and then to my plane.

As soon as we're seated, I bring her legs to my lap and remove her sneakers and socks as the plane takes off. She moans as I massage her sweet little feet (how do they hold up all six feet of her gorgeous body, these pretty little feet of hers?).

"The first time I saw you in a skirt, I thought you had on white stockings," I say to her ankles as I push up the cuffs of her joggers to expose her lower legs. "Then I realized it's your flawless skin." I kiss one ankle. "Creamy." I kiss my way up her calf. "Snow white." I switch to her other leg to kiss the top of her foot. "Perfect," I say.

39

I'm trying not to squirm. Kai's touch, his kisses, his words go straight to my head.

"I have always used both a chemical and a physical sunscreen." I get nerdy to regain my composure. "Plus, all my running clothes are UPF 50." Such a geek. I sigh. "That was some first kiss last night," I say to Kai as he moves from my feet and ankles to kissing my hand, my wrist, my arm.

"*Cara mia,*" he whispers, and I giggle at the Addams Family reference. Goddess, how I do adore this man. "That wasn't our first kiss," he says, pushing up my sleeve to shower my arm with little touches of his lips.

Wait. "What do you mean, that wasn't our first kiss?" I can't make this fit in my brain.

"The hotel? In the hallway? When you went in search of water?" his eyes grow huge and search my face. "Oh, wow. You don't remember?"

And suddenly I do. I was such a mess. I woke up after one in the morning feeling like death. Showered. Took acetaminophen with the water by my bed. Finding I finished the bottle, I stumbled out in search of another. Then the elevator dinged and delivered something better than water... It really felt like a dream. Now, I remember how sweetly he just barely touched my lips with his at first. Then I kissed him back. I arched up to press my lips to his more thoroughly. He was holding my hand...

"I swear to God it was only a kiss." He looks panicked. He backs up as far into his seat as he can get without climbing out on the wing of the plane. "I swear that I did not take advantage of you." I have to stop him from spinning out about this.

"I know that. I remember now." Clicking out of my seatbelt, I slide onto his lap, wrap my arms around his neck, and kiss his face all over. Kiss his cheek, his jaw where his beard is perfectly rough, his perfect ear. "I thought I dreamt it," I whisper. "Such a sweet warm kiss," I say dreamily. He groans.

And I know as he wraps his giant arms around me: He wants me. His hard length beneath my thigh is impossible to ignore, but it's more than that. His reactions to me make me feel cherished, desired, craved. Since we met, Kai has pulled me to him—as undeniably as gravity itself. This is that—but amplified by magnitudes. He is ready for me. We have this whole plane to ourselves (crew excluded, of course). On our way to two weeks of vacation, just the two of us, exploring Italy, exploring each other. It's exhilarating to feel him like this—after weeks of wanting him and all that frustrating denial I want him. Plus, wondering about his feelings and, of course, feeling him now. It's a lot.

Pausing in my tour of kissing his shaved head, his neck, and his throat, I whisper in his ear softly, "I was a virgin when I married Aidan." Record scratch. Did I just say that out loud? I freeze. Now it is my turn to panic. Kai clears his throat. At least he's not growling. I bite my lip.

"Okay... Good to know," he begins. "Does that mean...?"

I can't make him say it. "Yes. It means I've only had sex with one person. In my life." For the second time in two days, I bend my head so my hair covers my face. Feeling suddenly cold, I slide off his lap and into my own seat. In fact, I grab my bag, pull out a pashmina, and cover myself. If I had a pillow, I would cover myself with that too.

"Stop. Stop. Stop," he says as he takes my hand in his. "Don't hide from me." He tucks my hair behind my ear. "This is okay. This is more than okay. This is—well, first of all, this is you. And I want you exactly the way you are," he says so sweetly, holding my hands and bringing them to his lips. "Plus, there's nothing better you can tell a man than that his woman has never been violated by anyone before him."

I snarf. "I don't think that's actually factual," I scoff. "And I know for sure that's not what I said."

He winks at me. "This is good news," he says.

"I don't know about it being good news?" I say as though it were a question. "I guess I just wanted you to know." Feeling like a teenager, I grow more and more embarrassed.

"Hey. Holland." He tilts my face to his with a finger under my chin. "I'm not going anywhere. I'm all in. And I am willing to go as slow—or as fast, just saying—" he teases. I love that he's trying to lighten the mood I brought crashing down with my confession. "Seriously, I'm willing to take this slow and easy." He kisses me sweetly. I get lost in the kiss for a minute. His delicious full lips are just the beginning of his kisses—his whole mouth, his whole face, his tickly scratchy lovely beard kisses me. I can't keep my tongue out of his mouth, he just tastes so deliciously good. So perfect. And then I pull back—my overwhelming need for him conflicts with my mortification.

"I guess that's why I mentioned it." I tuck my hair behind my other ear. Stupid embarrassment. Hold on, Holland. This is not who I am. I'm an executive. I'm a badass. I straighten my spine. "And well, I appreciate your perspective. I just wanted to get all of our cards out on the table." My boardroom voice. Better. "Your turn, Ipu. Whatcha got?"

"Come again?" his eyebrows climb up his forehead.

"Cards. Table. Let's have 'em," I demand. "Mr. I-want-to-get-to-know-you, this only works if we both share."

"Can I get you a drink?" he gets up from his seat.

"Sit," I command. He sits. My eyes grow wide. Wow, that worked? "Spill it."

"You're not thirsty? Let me call for a drink." Before I can stop him, he hits the call button. A flight attendant appears instantly. He orders me a mimosa and a Blanton's neat for himself. I'm not amused. I fold my arms and wait (impatiently) for our drinks. In silence.

After the cocktails and a snack are served and we thank Elaine (of course Kai buys himself time by introducing me to the — okay, very nice and helpful — attendant).

"Look," Kai says. "My life has been very different from yours.

The thing you need to know is that I am all in. I'm here for this, all of you, all of this." I feel my heart soften and my mind trying to turn a blind eye.

"Kai." I feel tears prick my eyes (why does this make me want to cry? is it just embarrassment?), "is that truly the only thing I need to know?"

He takes time to think about it. This isn't stalling. I can tell he is genuinely considering the question. Our hands are entwined and mine look so delicate and feminine holding his huge hand.

"No," he begins, meeting my eyes. "You should also know that I have been meticulously safe—obsessively safe—and that I am disease-free and have no offspring." I feel my eyes grow wide again. He was right to measure his words. This is not even a little what I expected him to say. Not one bit. "And you should know that I will wait for you. We'll do this at your pace. I haven't been with anyone since well before the night I met you—and I plan to not be with anyone but you for as long as you'll put up with me," he says. "That's it. Those are things you should know." He takes a breath. He looks like he's waiting for me to get angry or defensive. Like he is waiting for the other shoe to drop.

"Thank you," I say.

"Thank you." He pulls my hand to his lips, relief on his face. "Come here. Please."

I stand instead and say, "I'm tired. Let's go lie down."

We spend the rest of the flight with very strict Do Not Disturb instructions for the flight crew.

40

We don't make love on the plane. We talk. For hours and hours. Holland asks me about my friendship with Eli and Naomi. I tell her the story of how I helped Elias pick out a puppy for Naomi and Aidan.

"Eli was so excited to have a son," I begin. "He wanted his boy to grow up with a dog, so we headed out to an animal shelter. Naomi's only instruction was to get a little dog. She didn't want to deal with training and feeding and walking a big dog. So there was this litter of chihuahua puppies and Eli was instantly smitten with the only boy dog in the bunch."

"Chihuahuas? How cute! They must be so tiny as pups," Holland says.

"They were pretty small." I laugh. "You're giving away the punchline, though." Holland gives me side eye. "So he adopts this puppy and takes it home to Aidan—"

"How old was Aidan?" Holland asks, her throat catching. My sweet brave woman asking about her dead husband as a boy.

"Oh, not more than two or three," I say. I reach for her hand to hold it, offer comfort, I hope. "He loved that little dog. The puppy's shelter name was Milo and they kept it—a little name for a little dog,

Eli said."

"Wait. I remember stories about Milo—but that dog was huge, a Vizsla or something. Aidan and Milo used to go for runs around the lake together." Holland starts to laugh as she gets the point of the story. "They thought big ol' Milo was a chihuahua when he was a puppy?"

I laugh too. "The animal shelter swore his mama dog was a nine-pound chihuahua. You've never seen anyone as shocked as Naomi. Every Sunday she'd weigh that dog as he just got bigger and bigger. He was at least fifty pounds when he was full grown!"

"I never heard that story." She giggles. "I love it. Milo was gone by the time I showed up, but Aidan loved him enough to tell me stories and show me pictures. How sweet that you helped bring him home," she says. "Tell me more. About college and football and Eli and Nomi."

So I do. Talking about college leads to telling her about starting Innovated in my dorm room.

"I looked at what life would be like after my degree and saw there was very little I couldn't start doing right away," I say. "I built a website one night and started promoting myself as a consultant to financial institutions and individual investors facing hardships during the Great Recession. It never occurred to me to doubt they'd trust my advice," I muse. "It seems so ballsy to me now—but in the moment, it was the right thing to do." She agrees.

Lying side by side, her head on my chest, I'm rubbing lazy circles on her back, we find a natural break in the conversation and, fully clothed, fall asleep for several hours. When we wake, we call in the banished Elaine to request a snack.

Fourteen hours is a very long flight.

As we eat, she asks about my family. She knows about my dad and grandfather—about losing them so recently. "It seems to me that grief doesn't go away," I say. "I read somewhere that grief is like a house and new experiences grow like ivy over the house. It'll still be a house full of all the things you and Aidan built together. As my house is full of things my dad and grandad built with me. But the ivy growing over time will be fresh and green and full of life," I say.

"That's beautiful." She tells me with unshed tears glistening in her eyes.

"Tell me about Aidan," I say quietly. So she does. She talks about dating in college. She addresses the burning question.

"I didn't mean to wait for marriage to have sex," she says shyly. "Not really. No one before Aidan met my incredibly high standards." I laugh quietly at that. "When Aidan and I started to hang out, we were just learning to be friends. I called him after the election. Maybe to rub it in a little, maybe to hit on him." I see her neck and her cheeks light up red. I smile at her, silently encouraging her to go on. "We hung out a few times with friends. We kind of just realized we liked each other and were dating. We'd been seeing each other pretty casually. But when he went home for summer and Thanksgiving, we talked on the phone for hours and hours at a time. If I wasn't at work, we were on the phone. We kind of fell in love long distance while we were apart."

I squeeze her shoulders with one arm and bring her hand to my lips with the other. "Is it too hard to talk about it?" I ask.

"Not at all. Thanks for listening. I want to share with you," she says. "The rest is as much a love story about Nomi and Ximena and Ethan as it is about Aidan and me. He invited me to North Carolina for Christmas. That winter break was so peaceful and full of love. I met the family Christmas and we all just seemed to click."

I'm still curious about the waiting until marriage, but before I can even ask, she says, "Honestly, by the time Aidan and I were ready to have sex, we were already engaged. So we just kind of decided to wait." She looks up at me. "Is that weird?"

"Nope." I run my hands over her hair. "I get it." Then with what I think of as my devilish grin, I say, "Tell me more about these incredibly high standards of yours."

We move back to the bed as she tells me all about her Disney-obsessed visions of frog princes and her absent father's enchantment by a wicked witch. Of course, that leads to trading crappy mother stories.

She tells me a story about mother cleverly disguised as a story about her favorite things: two ceramic rabbits who have followed her everywhere since she was little.

"One is bright orange, one is lemon yellow, and they are the only things I have from growing up," she explains. "My mom and I were on a road trip when I was in third grade. I was missing school because my mom couldn't take 'one more minute in this podunk town,' she'd said."

"Where did you grow up?" I swear I'm not interrupting her, it is a natural question.

"All over. We were living in Dallas at the time." She laughs. "Podunk was a state of mind, I think. We drove up to Tulsa, Oklahoma, because my mom wanted to see where Okies come from. She was crazy. No better place to see a true Okie than at a flea market, she said." Holland pauses for a long moment. Then she looks at me and says, "I have years of practice telling stories about my mom, so they sound whimsical rather than traumatic." She's blinking tears away. "I feel safe telling you the true version."

"I'm glad you do. I hope you do," I say around a painful lump in my throat. She goes on to tell me that this particular trip really was rather fun — regardless of the fact that by nine years old, Holland was already old enough to know that her mom was toxic and that her manic road trips were not doing Holland any favors.

"'Most kids would be thrilled to skip four days of school!' my mom would scream with all the windows down and the car radio blaring. You act like I'm punishing you!' she'd holler as she incessantly honked the car horn and drove way too fast," Holland says. "When I saw these two cookie jars at a junk stall, I begged my mother to get them. They were two enormous cartoon rabbits with knowing looks on their faces and ears pricked to listen to me. I think they were all of twenty-five cents apiece." She tries to giggle at the memory, but I see the sorrow and suffering. "I've moved them to every place I've ever lived. They're the first thing I unpack. They're my signal to myself that I'm home."

"A very wise investment at two bits each," I say solemnly, even as I grin at her.

"No one ever uses 'two bits' correctly." She laughs.

I encourage her to tell me more.

"When I was eleven, I figured out that my mother never remembered what we talked about—much later I understood it was because she was drinking all the time." Holland sounds miserable as she says this. "Anyway, I started writing things down and making her sign them. It worked pretty well for a while." She laughs awkwardly. "She was a mess. She left me in a rented room in Pacoima when I was seventeen. Our landlady told me my mom had paid her for the month but then I'd have to move out—it was April and I was all set to graduate high school the next month. I packed what little I had— just some clothes and books—and lived out of my beat-up VW Jetta until I moved into my dorm that fall."

I'm speechless. At least my crappy mother was kind enough to stay out of my life. I just hug her close to me.

"I have mixed emotions about that time even all these years later," she says as I hold her. "It was a relief to have only myself to worry about and care for. But of course, it was shocking and sad that my mother left without a word."

"Was it scary to live out of your car that summer?" I ask. My heart is breaking for my sweet Holland's seventeen-year-old self. That cute girl in the track t-shirt and her honey ponytail.

"Sure, it was pretty scary." She hesitates. "I've spent enough time in therapy to know I disguise my sadness and anxiety as frustration and anger," she says. "I've spent too many years pissed off at her. I'm working on truly letting her go. Naomi's friendship helps with that."

I hug her closer and say, "I bet it does."

She asks about my mother. I measure what and how to say the ugly truth that now pales in comparison to Holland's story. I tell her that my mother left when I was five, making some excuse about needing to discover what she thought for herself. "All this testosterone," she wailed as she threw some clothes in a bag. "I can't hear myself think. I'm not running away from you, baby," she said as she kissed me on the top of my head. "I'm running toward me." And I haven't heard from her since.

"I imagine she must be dead," I say.

"You've never checked?" Holland tells me she set up a Google alert for her mom's name years ago.

"Nah. No reason to," I say. "She wasn't a parent even when she was around. My dad and her father were the only parents I ever needed."

41

"You are a good man, Kai," I say as I snuggle into his side. I am sad for the five-year-old who watched his mom walk out. And I am proud of this man he's become. He pulls me closer.

"I don't know if that's true. But I want to be a good man. I want to be a good dad, Holland." Something in his serious almost melancholy tone tells me it might be time to lighten the mood. His gravity increases when his mood gets serious; I feel myself pulled more firmly into him. So, I roll on top of him and say in my (I hope) sexiest, most wicked wanting-him voice, "We can work on that..."

He kisses me deeply with the passion I was hoping for. He feels so amazing under me. I move over him until I'm straddling him—he is a mountain and I am more than ready to climb him. He slides his big hands around my waist, looks like he just killed a puppy, and moves me off him and onto the bed. "Soon, sugar," he says. "Let's move." And he actually gets up off the bed.

"We're on a plane." I am incredulous. But he's serious. Out in the main area of the plane, Kai drops to the ground and starts doing push-ups in the aisle. I stretch a little but mostly watch him, trying not to drool.

When we get notice that we're landing soon, we each take a quick shower, and change clothes. I put on a summer dress with fresh socks and sneakers. He puts on a henley I immediately want to rip off of him (he looks so delicious with that thin soft gray cotton pulled across all his muscles), jeans, and boots.

When we disembark at Falcone Borsellino Airport, we agree we're starving. So, we find a place to eat a traditional (tiny!) breakfast in a café —we left our Mexico City hotel before breakfast and arrived in Sicily in time for breakfast. It is surreal that we spent only fourteen hours in flight, but it is truly the next day. Even I have trouble doing the math.

We decide the best course of action to avoid being sucked under by jet lag is to keep moving, so we walk around the city center, hand-in-hand. I'm overwhelmed by this sense of security—holding Kai's hand, I feel both emotionally safe and actually protected. We're in a sizable city I've never visited on a continent far from home, and I should maybe have a little anxiety about all this newness, but he makes me feel perfectly at ease. Just as I feel completely at ease sharing stories and jokes and kisses with Kai. I can't remember the last time I felt this content.

The weather is perfect. I'm tired, for sure, but I truly think I might be able to walk forever with him like this—learning each other and the city—through the heart of Palermo. As we discover outdoor markets, we discuss our favorite foods to cook (Kai says he's a grill guy, like his father and grandfather before him) and to eat. Ducking into Gothic, Arab-Norman, and Baroque churches, we discuss the history of the island (fascinating!) as well as our views on spirituality and religion. Kai believes in a higher power but isn't sure that makes him spiritual or religious—fair enough. And as we explore the many piazzas, I finally get to quiz him with my traditional first-date litany.

I pepper Kai with a million questions—over the years I have learned to disguise my inquiry as fun and flirty "tell me more about yourself"—Kai is a good sport who plays along nicely. "What's your personal mission statement? Coldplay or Radiohead? Do you collect anything? How many [vintage cars, it turns out] do you have? What did you want to be when you were little? What do you want your legacy to be?"

Kai passes each aspect of my test. A vision of social justice guides him (something we share). Coldplay for concerts, Radiohead on vinyl, but he actually prefers country music (I approve!). Four: two identical (seriously?) Mercedes coupes, a restoration-in-process 1962 Chevrolet Corvair Monza Club Coupe, and the little red sports car I saw. A firefighter. He wants IPU to be his legacy, of course, but not just the company, all the people in it and affected by it.

"I want everyone Innovated reaches—employees, clients, employees of clients—to live richer, happier, more generous, and mindful lives because they worked with us," he says. Hearing what he just said, he gives me a crooked grin. "Not asking too much, right?" I assure him it's just enough. And punctuate my assertion with a kiss.

When we come to a little souvenir stand, Kai turns to me and reaches to hold both my hands. "Holland, may I ask you something?" Again, his gravity pulls me closer. It's a phenomenon science should study—how this man's emotional seriousness manifests itself as a force that attracts my body toward his own. "You told me your postcard collection is from your travels with Aidan." I absolutely love it when he makes statements when others would ask a question. I smile, knowing he'll go on. "Would you like to continue that practice? With me?" Back-to-back questions. He's nervous, afraid I'll say no. Bless his sweet, sweet heart.

I give him my biggest, most sincere smile. "I love that idea, Kai." I hug him. "I was not looking forward to mailing postcards to myself — on solo travels." Pulling back so I can see his handsome face, I say, "Keeping this little ritual alive with you is so much better. Thank you for thinking of it."

He locks eyes with me and says in a low, sexy rumble, "You're all I think about, sunshine," and he kisses me sweetly. We choose our favorite cards and I feel my heart swell—it's a small bit of healing and my heart and I need it.

After exploring a bit longer, I am starving. We hunt down a restaurant where Kai orders, in what sounds like fluent Italian (swoon!), roasted marinated eggplant and peppers, bruschetta with sundried tomatoes and olives, fettuccine with fresh fish, cherry tomatoes, and mint—a delicious combination I am instantly obsessed with—then more fish stuffed with breadcrumbs, raisins, and pine nuts. And finally, a not-too-sweet plum cake with whipped cream. Oh, yeah, and lots and lots of wine.

I savor every bite and every moment with this man. We try to make each other laugh with silly puns (fake noodles are *impasta*, ha ha; don't step on a grape or it'll let out a little *whine*) and just enjoy each other's company.

He's so easy to be with.

Jet-lagged, full of good food—and a little tipsy—we walk to our hotel. Before it is even three in the afternoon, we fall onto the bed, fully clothed, and sleep through the night, tangled up together.

42

This waking-up-next-to-the-woman-of-my-dreams thing is really starting to piss me off. Not because she is here. That is magical, and I simply cannot believe my luck. But both on the plane and here in our hotel room, we fell asleep in all our clothes.

It is probably four in the morning and I know I have jeans seams permanently impressed into my legs. I roll off the bed slowly so as not to disturb the softly glowing creature curled up against my side. In the bathroom, I strip off all these ridiculous clothes, relieve myself (we drank so much wine… oh, how I love Italy) and start a cold shower. I hope I don't wake up Holland, but a shower is absolutely necessary. I am covered in soap when I hear her angelic voice.

"Kai?" she asks with the bathroom door just barely cracked open.

"Good morning, sunshine." I stick my head around the shower curtain.

"Hi, um, hello." She blinks several times. "May I pee? So sorry to bug you."

"Of course, I'll hop out and give you some privacy," I say, rinsing as quickly as I can.

"No, no. Just keep the curtain closed. I'm the one disturbing you," she says.

I laugh silently to myself. I guess we'll have to discuss some bathroom-sharing rules. How great is that?! I can't think of anything that makes me this happy. I'm sharing my space with Holland, hot damn!

I get out of the shower, pull on some flannel lounge pants, and slide back into bed next to her.

"You smell good," she says sleepily.

"You feel amazing," I say, wrapping my arms around her. She slipped into a tiny t-shirt and very short shorts when she got up to pee, I guess. So much more skin, I cheer silently.

"I should shower too," she says.

"When you wake up, sugar," I murmur into her hair, which still smells like a summer day, like green grass and mint and sunshine. "No hurry."

"I'm awake," she says just before her breathing evens out and I know she slips back into dreamland. I hold her and thank all the things in the world that led me here.

♡

We wake up at about six a.m. which we figure is a perfectly reasonable time to start our day. Holland suggests we go for a run, so I take her to Favorita Park. I love running with her. She is a specimen in her sports bra and tights—she should be a fitness model. She is probably in better shape than I am, to be honest. I keep up with her, but it becomes apparent after the 5k loop that she can run much longer than I.

"You're a beast," I tell her as we slow to a walk and head down to the water toward our hotel.

"Hardly." She laughs. "Have you seen you?"

"I have a feeling we can teach each other a lot," I say. "You can improve my stamina; I know that for sure." I give her a steamy look to match my smutty double entendre. She winks at me, the little she-devil. My heart triple-beats. God, I like this woman.

"I hate lifting weights, so you'll have to help me learn to love it like you do," she says as she runs a soft, warm hand up my arm. "I don't want muscles like these, but I know strength training would be good for me."

"I don't think this lithe feminine frame would ever develop

muscles like mine." I put my arms all the way around her and swing her up into a hug. She giggles and wraps her arms around my neck and lets me spin her around. When she is back on her feet, she doesn't drop her arms.

"I love touching you," she says. "It's how I wanted it to be with us. My fingertips used to tingle looking at you, wanting to reach over and touch you."

"I know the feeling well," I say. "The same with kissing you." And I demonstrate how happy I am to be able to kiss her anytime I want. Sure, we're on a public street, but I still get to kiss her because we are finally together. I woo-hoo at the top of my lungs.

"Kai!" Holland laughs. "It's not even seven a.m.!"

"Palermo should know how fucking delighted I am to have you all to myself, Holland Siobhan Amster Gallagher." I'm laughing too. "Move in with me."

She gives me her most crooked grin. "I mean, aren't we sharing a room?"

I squeeze her and swing her around again. "You know what I mean! Move into my room above the store. Think of your new commute. Just three flights of stairs. Or, I mean, you can absolutely use the elevator, if you prefer."

She is laughing. "Let me think about it?" she smiles.

"Of course."

"If you say yes, I want to look for a real house right away, though." I take her hand and start walking back to the hotel. "We can't raise our kids in an office building." I turn to wink at her and find her blushing. My new favorite color is Holland's blushing cheeks. What is that? Cherry? I kiss her cheek just to check.

43

For a week, we ignore our phones and lock our laptops in the hotel safe. We run together every morning—along the seafront or through the park, often both. We lift weights in the gym each night—his dedication is infectious. Plus, it is a good chance to work off some of the pizza, pasta, and wine I have been gorging myself on. We hide from everything but Sicily and each other. And the room service staff, of course. We befriended the bringers of our morning coffee and pastries very quickly.

We spend most of our time making plans. I haven't agreed to move into the penthouse with him—sharing a hotel suite with Kai is exhilarating and stressful enough—his plan to live together makes my head swim. But let's be clear, there is nearly nothing at my loft I'm attached to. Including the apartment itself.

One evening as we watch the sunset from a seaside bar with Negronis in hand, Kai turns the conversation to Innovated.

"Check your watch," I say cheekily. "We got to Day Four before the boss brought up work!"

"Har har," he says, "this is important, Holland." He tries to look stern, but it only makes me giggle. We've been enjoying each other's company like this—out of office in the extreme—for days. I've gotten so used to schmoopy, romantic Kai that I kind of forgot CEO

Kai is his default.

"I'm sorry, dear," I say slightly dramatically. "I'm listening."

"I've asked the Board of Directors to name you CEO after I retire." Kai is so matter of fact. I, on the other hand, am speechless. "Holland, I meant what I said about retiring so I can raise a family." I blink. "With you, if you'll have me."

I blink several times more. He does his wait-patiently-for-Holland-to-gather-her-wits thing. I take the moment he offers. This is a big deal. Am I ready? For any of that?

"Kai, I'm delighted," I begin, "and grateful—" and trying to be cool about it even as I suffer from a crippling case of impostor syndrome paired with vertigo from moving way too fast— "can we take those huge statements one at a time?" He laughs his biggest boldest laugh that makes everything (especially my restless butterflies) feel better.

First, his desire to promote me. He's young to be CEO of a company Innovated's size. I'm more than a decade his junior. "What will the rest of the executives think?" I ask him. "What about the Board?"

"They have already endorsed you as CEO, Holland," he says. I am again shocked into speechlessness. "Don't look surprised, sweets, everyone respects the hell out of you. We discussed it before leaving for Mexico. To a person, they cosigned the idea of working for you." He assures me we would take our time. That he'd never be far from me—especially if we're living together "on campus".

We take a few more minutes to talk through the logistics and the timing of moving into the role, and I start to relax. "I'm honored," I say finally, "I will seriously consider your offer to take the helm of your company, Kai. Thank you for asking."

"It will be our honor," he says with a sincerity I can feel like a seismic shift. "When you accept." He winks.

Trying to avoid the "raise a family" part of his big plan, I ask: "What are you going to do all day if I'm in charge at IPU?"

"You mean other than creep in your office and watch you work?" he jokes. Oh, goodness, I hope he's joking. "Just kidding. Mostly." He raises an incredibly sexy eyebrow (I'm too flustered to even know if it is my favorite). Then he explains how much he wants to dive headfirst into philanthropy, especially Aces United. It's fun to daydream about a life of just giving away one time, talent, and treasure. As we settle the bar bill and walk to the restaurant we picked out for dinner, we hold hands and imagine all the possibilities. "It is fun to think of paying forward what I've been so freely given," he says. "Maybe it isn't saving the world, but it's a start."

I'm filled with pride and a sense of wonder. When we are seated in the intimate little bistro and have wine in front of us, I start panicking about the other topic. "Soooo... the second part of your big announcement?" I sip my wine. "Raise a family?" I can feel myself blushing.

"I want at least four kids," he deadpans.

"Oh my." I put my hand to my lips in mock horror. "That's a lot."

But seriously, it isn't nearly as many as I've spent my whole life hoping for. My most closely held secret plan for as long as I can remember is to fill my home—with a partner at my side who wants the same thing—with children. I am desperate to be a foster mom, I want very much to adopt, I think it might be okay to birth children. I want our home to be the home where all of my kids' friends come to hang out.

But how can I explain any of this to Kai?

Before I can decide, he kisses me. My butterflies each hold up tiny Olympic judges' signs rating this kiss a perfect ten-point-zero. I kiss him back.

But I have a sneaking suspicion we are on different timetables. I have a feeling he is going to make me wait.

I am starving for Kai every day—even when we're together, I am absolutely famished for him. Despite all our teasing, both verbal and visceral, Kai is taking things very (very!) slowly. We sleep in the same bed every night (turns out he sleeps in the nude at home but puts on pajama pants out of respect for me; I sleep in my tanks and sleep shorts, and Kai has yet to complain), but we've only ever touched and tasted and kissed and cuddled. I am both frustrated and grateful. Everything with this man is a balance. His brute strength and his gentle touch. His immense desire for me and his restraint. His professionalism and his playful side. I love it all. And I want more.

I grab the lapels of his casual linen jacket and pull him closer. "Kai..." I breathe. He has this way of making me feel wanted, even as he rebuffs my advances. He changes the tone of his kisses, moves his hands from my neck to my hair, pulls away slowly and thoughtfully. I love even this. He always leaves me wanting more.

"Holland, my heart," he says with a soft smile. "Dinner is here."

He nods to the server right behind me. I jump.

"Oh! Hi! *Molte grazie.*" I blush. All three of us laugh.

So we eat the amazingly fresh seafood (no shellfish, because I *like* breathing) and drink the ridiculously good wine.

44

This morning begins like all the others since our arrival in Sicily: I wake up to sweet kisses on my shoulder, my neck, my ear. Kai wraps himself around me. I love it when he is the big spoon, I love the feel of his giant frame. I roll over to kiss him. We slide our hands and mouths all over each other, passion building for each of us (I know I am getting to him as much as he is getting to me), but—just when I am about to offer to get naked and down to business—he kisses my nose, rolls over, and calls room service for coffee and *cornettos*. Sigh.

After adding caffeine and carbs to our systems, we get dressed and go for a run—our new routine. When we get back, Kai showers first while I lay out my sightseeing clothes for the day. Maybe we'll go to Taormina this weekend. When he gets out of the shower, I will ask him. Waiting for my turn to wash off the sweat and salt air from our seaside run, I toe off my trainers and socks. I love how perfectly normal all this feels.

I'm happy, I realize. Over the moon, actually. Nomi and Mena were right—who knew?

My man comes out of the bathroom in a towel and again I marvel at his jaw-dropping body. Almost as a reflex, I start stripping out of my running clothes while he watches.

I smile at him as I take off my sports bra (sports bra removal is probably the least sexy strip tease in history, but I try to make it work for me), then my skin-tight running pants. I stand before him in a thong and nothing else. He takes in every inch of me.

I kick out my right leg (in what I hope is a sexy move) and put my hands to my hair and slowly drag out my hair tie. My hair falls around my shoulders, and he gapes. My effect on him is powerful, heady.

"I guess it's my turn to shower?" I purr as I slip my thumbs into the top of my underwear to pull it off. He swallows. I watch his Adam's apple move. I want a bite of it. He is across the room in a flash, scooping me up like I weigh nothing, covering my salty skin in kisses and nips. He growls ferociously. I giggle with hope for some release. But instead of throwing me on the bed, he puts my feet down on the cool tile of the bathroom floor.

"Yes, my heart, it's your turn to shower. You are the sexiest woman I have ever seen and if you don't stop teasing me, I will have to..." he takes a deep breath. "Holland, I want to wait until we're married." Then he looks sheepish. "If we get married."

I gape.

"We have our whole lives together. I want to save the good stuff. I want to show you on our…hypothetical…wedding night that we are worth the wait," he says, looking serious and intense.

I know this. It's not really news. I kind of figured this is what he was thinking since our flight over here. I have to smile at him. "I understand. That's a lovely sentiment. And I'm going along with it… mostly." I raise a wicked eyebrow at him. "I just really need you to know how much I want you."

He takes my hand in his and presses it firmly against the front of his towel. He is hard as a rock. My mouth waters. "I want you." He pushes my hand harder against his length. "I need you." He takes a breath and moves my hand to his lips, "and I can wait for you."

I sigh. "Thank you?" We both laugh. Then he drops my hand, whips off his towel, revealing his huge smooth gorgeous erect penis, and whips me with the towel. "Now get going." He winks at me. I squeal and jump at the feel of the towel corner on my hip. Or am I squealing and jumping at the thought of his length and girth? A little Column A, a little Column B. "Okay! Okay!" I giggle and turn on the water.

♡

I step out of the shower refreshed (no, I did not masturbate in the shower—although I was sorely tempted). I hear Kai speaking— I listen as I put my hair in a towel, at first because I think he is speaking to me. Then because I realize he isn't.

"Okay, we'll get rid of her after we get back. It's the only way forward, she's just not cutting it," he says. I move closer to the open door of the bathroom so I can hear him better. "No this is ridiculous. We've wasted enough time waiting for her to get her shit together. We brought her in as a favor to her family, and we just can't wait any longer for her to get her feet under her. This is a waste of resources." I can't believe my ears. There is so much wrong with this... first of all, why is he on the phone? Was he working every day? Is he making calls any minute we aren't together? And—*priorities, Holland, sheesh*— is he talking about me? Is he getting ready to fire me? Didn't he just ask me to be CEO? My head is swimming. Wow. He's talking again.

"No, it has to be me. I have to be the one to tell her. Just let me get us back to LA. She's not getting anything done right this minute, anyway. Speaking of which, I gotta go." I back away from the door— the change in his tone indicates he is looking this way. I turn on the faucet to give him the impression I can't hear and haven't been listening. "Stop. I'll handle this. I made this mess. I'll clean it up."

He must end the call because he says, "Holland, my heart." I turn off the water.

"Yup," is all I can get out. My head is swimming even as my heart is breaking. I am humiliated and horrified. How could I have gotten everything so wrong? I've failed. Have I failed only at work, or at my relationship too? I can't catch my breath.

"Are you interested in the archeology museum, or will you let me take you shopping?" He gives me his biggest, most loving smile. I feel sick. "Neither." I need time to think. "I—I'm feeling my introvert right now. I think I need to curl up with a book today—" I can't even say his name, I am terrified and hurt and angry. "You should go." I force my voice to sound lighter. I want him to hear, "you should go on ahead without me" and not what I am really feeling, which is more like, "you should get out of this room right this second".

"Wait, what?" He looks genuinely confused. He walks into the bathroom and reaches for my shoulder. I flinch. "Holland, what's going on?"

"Nothing. I'm fine," I lie. "I just need a day off." Then, employing my fakest positivity, "seriously, I'm okay. Just let me have some alone time. I just need to 'put on my soft clothes and read a book' —" I pull my lips back in what I hope looks like a smile. "That's what I used to tell my mom when I was little and she wouldn't stop to give me time. I'm really fine, Kai. Come back for me so we can go to dinner?" I reach for him this time — it hurts, but I know it will buy me some time.

"Is this because I wouldn't make love to you?" Kai sounds hurt and confused. "I swear, I want you, sugar, I—" but I cut him off.

"No," I say. "I promise. That's not it. I'm just exhausted."

"Okay." He sounds reluctant. "I don't like it, but I guess I get it. I'll grab my laptop and go work for a few hours."

I bet. "I'm not done in here." I am trying to get him out of the bathroom. I feel incredibly vulnerable in only a towel, and I want him out. How quickly things have changed.

"Yeah, sure." He kisses me — on the forehead — then he backs out. He's reading my vibe. "I'll see you in a bit," he says, and he closes the door behind him. I stare in the mirror, not seeing myself. What in heaven's name was that all about?

45

What the actual fuck was that all about?

I am dumbfounded. Holland was like a different woman in there. I run over every moment of the morning. We woke up, made out, had coffee, went for a run. It was just like every other morning since we arrived. Right? What changed? Is this about sex? Is she angry at me? Did she decide in the shower that she wants someone else? Did she decide to leave me? I smack my forehead for being such an ass. That's not it, Ipu. Okay, so what then? I can't think.

I'll give her what she asks for—a few hours, and a little space—and then I'll work out how I might be able to help her.

When I get to the lobby of the hotel, I grab another coffee and a seat. I fire up my laptop for the first time all week. I'll get this useless intern bullshit handled while I have a moment. This is the last time I hire a college buddy's kid.

♡

Holland is still cold as ice when I collect her for dinner. In fact, she is packing. "What's up buttercup?" I keep my tone light, almost singsong. It sounds fake even to me. "Where are we going? Why ya packing?" I move up behind her and—instead of putting my arms around her waist to pull her body against mine like I so very much want to, I stop short and put my hands on her shoulders. She's tense. Way too tense. "Holland, look at me." I gently encourage her to turn around. She is boiling just beneath the surface I can see it.

She gives me a tight smile. "I think two weeks is too long. I'm ready to go home. Aren't you?" She tries to lighten her voice, but I can see the turmoil.

"What's going on, Holland?" I step back and plant my feet. I need answers.

"I'm just tired." She turns back to her packing.

I move to the other side of the bed in an attempt to see her face. "Holland, don't hide from me." She gives me her eyes, but not her face—essentially glaring at me across the king-sized bed. Then, seeing the devastation I am sure is on my face, she finally tilts her chin. "What happened?" I barely keep the demand out of my voice.

Her lip quivers but her voice is steady when she says, "I'm exhausted. I miss my family. I want to go home. You don't have to come, I can book a flight. But I need to get to..." she hesitates. In fact, her hesitation becomes a long, painful pause. But I'll be damned before I put words into her mouth. I hold her gaze and keep my mouth shut. "I need to get back. This is overwhelming. It's too much. I—" she breaks off. "I need another shower." She turns her back on me and locks herself in the bathroom.

I pushed her too far, too fast. Making a scene like that in public, on stage? The first time she gave me any indication at all that she was into me? What the presumptuous fuck?

Flummoxed, numb, self-loathing, and bereft, I follow her to the bathroom door. I lean my fiery forehead on it. "I love you, Holland," I tell the door. Is this the first time I say it? The first time I tell my future wife I love her is through a bathroom door. Whatever. There are bigger issues to contend with. "Whatever you want or need, I'll do." Even as I am talking to the wood, I am again replaying the entire day. Had Holland really compared me to her mother? What was that bit about soft clothes and when her mother wouldn't leave her alone? Fuck, something is seriously wrong. "We can leave first thing in the morning." No response. "Or I guess we could head out tonight—"

She cuts me off. "That would be better," she says curtly.

"Okay." I feel my broken heart crumble into a fine sand and blow away. "I'll call the crew."

"Please do," she says flatly. I press my palms to the door and resist the urge to break it out of its frame. Balling my fists, I give her some space and call my pilot. Goddammit.

46

On the flight home, we spend eighteen hours (why does it take so much longer going home?!) in virtual silence. I am heartbroken. I pretend to sleep most of the time. But I also need to move. I pace the aisle and ignore Kai's worried looks—he is obviously acting worried. Or pretending or whatever. Kai works on his laptop most of the flight, watching me like a hawk and handling me like an injured animal. He orders dinner, breakfast, a snack, lunch—he keeps having Elaine put food in front of me. I ignore it for the most part. But I do let Elaine bring me drinks. Whiskey, water, more whiskey, wine, more water, more wine. I like the buzz and I love the excuse to keep hiding in the lav.

I am officially in problem-solving mode. That's how my brain works best, right? Come across a problem, find a solution. I have been allowing my emotions to rule my thinking for far too long. Peaking when I overheard Kai making plans to end our professional relationship on the phone. That may not have even been an emotional reaction—that might've been flight-fight-or-freeze. Doesn't matter because now I'm in fix-it mode. I shake my head to clear it.

I knew it was a mistake to stay at Innovated after I found out about Naomi and Kai plotting behind my back. Hiring me was some kind of twisted in-law nepotism and I knew it. I hate it. I should've stayed the course when I tried to quit. I should have resigned. No use looking back; it's time to move forward. I have my notebook and a pencil—I don't want to put any notes on the IPU laptop I brought with me. I make list after list. A list of all the times I have been rejected just like this. A list of all the people who have abandoned me just like this. Pros and cons of breaking up with him when he fires me. Pros and cons to quitting on this plane before he can fire me. Pros and cons to throat-punching him right this minute. I scratch out the last one violently.

The most disturbing part of this mess is I know he's right. I fall into an old habit of repeating a childhood mantra: "The world values winners. I must succeed at all costs. I must avoid failure. I am what I do. To earn my place, I must be the best." Clearly, I haven't done enough, accomplished enough. I'm failing to meet my own goals, so I must be failing to meet Kai's. I am raking myself over the coals.

And this stupid vacation. If we'd gone to Santiago I could've... What? Could have what, Holland? I feel the wheels coming off my entire train of thought. Why would he talk to me about promoting me, tapping me as his successor, just to let me go? What changed in just a few days? Maybe we got new reports? I mentally replay the call—he was obviously speaking with the office. Had he been working every day? What, when I showered? I took his word for it that we were taking a true vacation. But he's obviously in touch with LA. So maybe IPU isn't doing well? Then the worst fear of all. Maybe we're not doing well? I hate this.

I return to my notebook and my lists. Pros and cons of falling in love with your boss. I start filling out the cons column first. And then I lock myself in the lav one more time to have a good, long cry.

♡

Zahra and Micah pick us up at the airport. I am genuinely glad to see them, but I dread faking my way through the niceties of having dinner as a foursome.

I pull Zahra into the backseat with me—ostensibly so the men can sit up front, but truly because I want space from Kai. She gives me a what's-up glare. I give her the same look back. She's got to know what's going on with work—if anyone knows about Kai's intention to fire me, it's Zee. And she obviously wants to know what's going on with me and Kai—I mean, I can't stand to look at him and he's acting like I'm made of glass. But neither Zahra nor I want to risk whispering, so we drop it.

When we get to my building, Micah and Kai unload the car, and Zahra and I grab the carefully packed bags holding our meal. The plan was for me to host our welcome-home and so here we are. I'm not at all thrilled about it. Yay, houseguests.

I let us in the lobby, call the elevator. Four silent figures carrying our burdens, we load into the lift—it looks like guys against the girls as Zahra and I stand on the opposite wall from the men. She senses the tension and behaves accordingly—Micah senses it too but chooses to launch into a one-man show. Micah hates silence almost as much as he hates conflict. He tells his hilarious version of the Kai-kissing-me-at-the-microphone-at-the-gala story, and by the time I'm unlocking the door to my loft, we're all laughing (maybe a little awkwardly).

The city is light enough for me to see, so I move immediately to the kitchen to set down our meal. Zahra and Micah move around the space, turning on lamps, opening windows, opening wine. Kai has clearly taken our bags to my bedroom and I wonder if he'll hide in there for a while. I kinda hope he will. I'd like to ask Micah and Zahra what they know about my imminent joblessness. But of course, he's back in an instant. Our eyes meet but I quickly look away. My heart aches—I mean it, really, like a physical pain in my chest—that he is keeping this secret from me. I hate feeling betrayed like this. But I'm good at it. I have felt like this many times before. What I need to decide is what to do about it. If (I mean, when) he fires me, do I break up with him? Where does that leave me? For now, it leaves me in silence.

Filling the void, Micah and Zahra do most of the talking as we set the table and pull out the take-out containers of piping hot, fragrant Thai food. They catch us up about the trip to Santiago. For the week Kai and I were in Italy, it turns out we really didn't miss much. Or maybe it is just that the team is so capable and handled everything perfectly smoothly in our absence. Or I guess in Kai's absence? I mean, I'm apparently superfluous. Or maybe it is because Kai was secretly working the entire time. My blood pressure rises at that thought. Which, of course, makes me feel inadequate and mortified all over again. I'm in a feedback loop of misery.

Pouring red for Kai and himself and rosé for Zahra and me, Micah asks about Palermo—I let Kai do all the talking. I sip my drink—I'm good and drunk (again? still?) at this point. How many hours have I been drinking? Oh, that's right. I don't care. So I drink some more.

Once Kai has the floor, he turns the conversation to work (of course). "So, Micah, I had a day to catch up on work just before we left Italy," Kai says, trying to meet my eye but I am having none of it. I want to laugh in his face. "I let that insipid intern go. I called her dad first. He was not at all surprised. And then I called her," he says.

I nearly choke on my wine. "What happened?" I realize this is the first time I've spoken when all three of them gape at me. I also realize I might have slurred my words the tiniest bit. Playing it back in my head, it sounds more like "wha-ha-happenn?" *Flattering, Holland.* Real nice.

Kai eyes me carefully and answers my question. "We hired this underqualified, overconfident intern because I played football with her dad when I was older than she is now." He rolls his eyes. "We kept throwing resources at her, but she continued to do nothing."

Micah takes over. "I called Kai at the hotel—even though I knew y'all were avoiding your phones—because I didn't think we could let her go without muddying the waters with his buddy." He looks abashed.

I make an effort to close my mouth, but it's still hanging uselessly open.

Mother of pearl. Are you freaking kidding me? A godblessed intern? How badly I misunderstood the situation. How quickly I leapt to the wrong conclusion. What a dumbbell I have made of myself. What a mess I made of our vacation. I put my head in my hands and try very hard not to cry. Kai is at my side in an instant. "Are you okay?" he rubs soothing circles on my back. After staying out of my way for the last twenty-four hours, something about my body language must signal that I'll let him in, let him touch me, comfort me. I feel it too — like I've opened a door and flipped on a light. In fact, I'm dying for his touch.

"Oh, Kai." I look up at him, gently lay both my hands on his handsome face, and start to cry. Then I start to laugh. I am hysterical. "I'm so sorry."

He wraps his huge arms around me. "Don't cry, sugar, don't cry.

Are you crying?" Poor guy is as confused as I am.

Micah and Zahra quietly get up from the table. I notice they take their wine glasses. And both wine bottles.

"Kai, I assumed the worst. I'm so so sorry." I try to calm down. "I ruined our vacation. I was so mad and so hurt and I shut down and I—"

He stops me, "Holland, hush," he soothes, "what happened?" He pulls his chair around the table to sit as close to me as possible. I tell him everything—through sobs and gulps of laughter—it's not funny, but I can't stop giggling—about overhearing his call and assuming he was describing my failures, my waste of resources, preparing to fire me.

He looks as dumbfounded as I feel. He continues to rub his warm hand over my back, clearly struggling to keep his mouth shut (I know he wants to interrupt me; he's being so good). Patiently, he lets me tell him what has been going through my mind for the last day. Has it really only been that long? It feels like an eternity. "Kai, I'm so sorry," I say for the millionth time. I sit up straighter, run my fingers under my eyes, and try to smile. "I should have had more faith in you."

"Holland, you should have had more faith in *you*," he says.

47

I push her hair back from her beautiful face with a tender touch. I want her to feel the weight of my words. "Holland, you should have had more faith in *you*. And you probably should have asked me about the phone call, rather than just assume the worst."

"Of course, Kai—" she starts.

"Sugar, let me finish, please." I look deep into her stormy green eyes. She's such a good listener, I know she's just thrown off her game tonight. Or y'know, for the whole last day. The day that feels like the longest year of my life.

"Holland, you are the farthest from useless or insipid. I am so proud to work with you. Honored to work with you. I wish you believed that." I'm still holding her face with the tips of my fingers in her silky hair. "On top of that, I love you with every fiber of my being." I move my arms around her now and hug her tight. Then I pull back and get stern and serious. "We are a team. And on this team, we face our issues directly from now on."

"Yes, I get it," she says. "I'm so sorry. I can't believe I got it so mixed up. Please know that I trust you. I'm all in. We are a team. We face stuff directly from now on. Together." She kisses me sweetly.

"Excellent." I punctuate the conversation with a knock of my fist on the table, closing the case. Now we can go back to our originally scheduled programming. "Let's eat."

Holland excuses herself to wash her face and I retrieve our friends from the balcony where they were giving us privacy. Holland sits next to me (so much better!) and tells Micah and Zahra the least embarrassing version of the story of our early return from Italy.

"I get it," Zahra says. "Kai for a week? You deserve sainthood for sticking it out as long as you did."

I give her an eyebrow and Micah just grins like he's happy to be out of the line of fire.

The four of us talk long into the night over dessert and coffee. We talk about work—but we also talk about the Dodgers, our reading lists, and our plans for the weekend. Finally, we agree we're exhausted and wrap up the evening.

Zahra and Holland make a date for breakfast on Monday morning. Micah kisses her on the cheek and I hear him whisper, "I'm always on your side, kid." Dammit. I may have to let her steal my assistant after all.

We walk Zahra and Micah down to the car. As soon as they pull away, I turn to Holland.

"I feared I'd lost you," I say.

"Next time I swear I'll ask you instead of just being injured and angry," she says, looking up at me.

"There's not going to be a next time," I say as I slide my fingers into her hair with my thumbs on her jaw. "I think we need to make some changes around here." I reach into my pocket, where I've been carrying this gift for her for ages. Delicately I run my knuckles from her collarbone to my fingertips, she shivers deliciously at my touch. I take her left hand in mine, and—right here on a downtown street in view of all the world, or at least the Arts District—I drop to one knee and say, "You are my heart, Holland." I slip a vintage five-carat round canary yellow diamond set in platinum ring on her finger. Damn, it looks good on her.

She gasps.

"Let's be more than a team. Let's be a family. Please say you'll marry me."

A neighbor walking her tiny yorkie mix dog says, "Awwww…" I drop my head, laughing silently. When I look back up at Holland, she's grinning. And nodding.

"Yes, please."

I stand and scoop her up. The lady claps, the yorkie barks,

Holland and I are laughing. A guy across the street yells, "Honey, if you said no, I was gonna run over and steal him from you." Because, LA.

"Upstairs," I say.

As soon as we're in the deserted lobby and at the elevator, I take both her hands to say what I have been working out in my head over the last day. "I need you to understand why I'm not having sex with you." She tenses. "This isn't about you or your sexy, perfect body or your brilliant brain." It's all about me. I feel like shit for having had sex with so many people. I've been using my restraint with this sexy perfect woman to prove to myself (and to her, let's be real) that our relationship is not about sex. I don't say any of that, though. "Listen, sweets, sex is easy. Intimacy is extremely difficult. At least, it always has been for me." She squints and gives me the slightest nod. "I would hate it if, for one second, you feel unloved or undesired. I truly love you." And moving her hand to my lips where I kiss her palm and follow my kisses with a swipe of my tongue, "and I deeply desire you." Her sharp intake of breath lets me know she feels my meaning as much as she hears my words.

I slowly lower my lips to hers. Then the wildfire starts. My hands run down her arms, squeeze them possessively, and then encircle her waist. I lift her and put her right back down. It's like I can't decide what to do first. It's infuriating. My hands are on her perfect ass, then on her back. And just as I am sure I am going to rip her clothes off, the elevator dings.

"Fuuuuck," I say. I pull her into the elevator after me and put my hands all over her again. This time I'm seeking her silky perfect skin. My hands are under her shirt and hers find the buttons on mine. Game all the way on. And the elevator dings. Again. This time we both laugh.

"C'mon," I say, grabbing her hand again and pulling her toward her front door.

48

We come as close to making love as we have yet to. We touch and taste and tease each other to the brink of insanity. But we still (still!) don't have sex.

We are exceedingly intimate, though. And now I know how much that means to Kai. It's honestly better than sex.

Everything is new—even my apartment. In this white-on-white wonderland, I suddenly see possibility everywhere. As the city glows magic shapes on the wall, I take a deep breath of what smells like home. The constancy of the traffic outside sounds like breaking waves washing in with nostalgia and out with opportunity. The depth and breadth of this room begs to filled with friends and family. I imagine filling the table-for-twelve with my homemade (crustacean-free) paella and bottles of wine, filling the industrial-size loft with good music and bad karaoke. The modern sculpture of a lamp my sister found for me lights the room softly. In this space, I have started to make my own way in the world. And in this room, the man I love has helped me see a future where I will have a family to love. So, maybe it's someone else's blank slate I imagine here. I think it's time to pack up my cookie jars.

"I like my little apartment," *finally*, I don't say out loud. "But I think I would like to move in with you." Kai looks extremely happy about that. But he doesn't say a word. He just scoops me up and kisses me thoroughly. I guess that was the right thing to say.

♡

Jet lag starts nipping at our heels, so we decide it is time to get ready for bed. In the week we shared a hotel suite, I marveled at having Kai all to myself. Tonight is the same—especially because I came so close to ruining everything just over a day ago. I watch him brush his teeth like it's the best show on TV—is that weird? He smiles a toothpaste smile at me, and I swoon just a little.

"Holland, I want to revisit a conversation we had a while ago," he says after he rinses his mouth. I nod. "About your five-year plan." I nod some more. "You said your plan included rising to the top of your field."

"I did," I agree.

"You didn't mention a personal five-year plan." He sounds just the tiniest bit nervous. A little glimpse of shy Kai, one of my favorite versions of him. He pauses. I know he won't say any more than that. And I know it is a question even though he didn't ask. His question, unspoken, was whether he has messed up my five-year plan. By proposing.

I mull it over. We stare at each other for a long moment. He's leaning against the vanity counter, huge and comfortable and sexy as sin. "Kai, I think if I had told you a personal five-year plan when you first asked," I muse, "I would have said something quite different from my current five-year plan. ...I know it wasn't that long ago." I marvel at this fact again. "But my priorities have shifted since I've known you, Kai. And as of earlier this evening, I am pretty sure I agreed to spend not just the next five years, but forever with you. As your partner. Together." Forever.

"I'm glad you say 'partner'," he says with a small, crooked grin. "That's very good to hear. May I ask you another question?"

"All the questions you want," I say.

"This time about my five-year plan," he says, putting his hand on my hip. He's arching that stupidly sexy eyebrow, and my head is spinning with the feel and smell and sight of him. "Is this a good time to open negotiations about kids?"

"We've been engaged for two hours!" I laugh at him.

"That's a yes?" he asks as he puts his lips on my collarbone. "I opened with four. What's your counteroffer?" It's hard to think with his hands and lips on me. Shivers run up and down my spine.

"May I tell you my most closely held secret plan for as long as I can remember?" I ask. He hmms into my neck. "Maybe we don't have to make all those kids... maybe we could open our hearts and our home to foster kids?"

He pulls back from kissing me. The look on his face makes my heart swell.

"Yes." That's all he says.

"That's it? No discussion? No negotiation? Just yes?"

"It's exactly what we should do, Holland. There's no more perfect way to create a family. I can picture us with a house full of kids. Our kids, their friends, strays." We both laugh. "I absolutely want to be a foster parent with you. We can adopt kids. We can make babies together." He raises that amazing eyebrow again in his sexy smoldery way. "Holland, I'm crazy about you and I'm already obsessed with this idea. Love isn't pie—it doesn't get divided up and handed out until it's gone. The more we love, the more capacity we have to love."

More wisdom from this great and good man.

"We can keep adding to our family any way we want for as long as we want," Kai says. "As long as you're their mom, our kids will be amazing. Our family will be… amazing." He swallows hard. He choked himself up, I think.

"I cannot believe how lucky I am. That's as perfect a picture as I could ever have imagined." I turn my happy grin into a slightly wicked one. "When do we start?" I'm not on birth control—and we have already medically confirmed our mutual disease-free status.

"Well," Kai says. "Let's get married and get you in the family way. And we'll see how it goes from there." He gives me a quick smack on the ass and a wink in the mirror.

"I love you so much," I say as I stick my own toothbrush in my mouth. I freeze—is this the first time I've told him that? I've thought it so many times. I look up at him, toothbrush and all, and smile. He gives me his sweetest grin and kisses me on the top of my head.

"I knew it," he says. I giggle at his back.

I finish getting ready for bed and am in cute pajamas I found in a little shop in Italy. I head into my dark, cool bedroom. And... Kai is sound asleep. Poor baby. I quietly climb in next to my mountainous man and curl up against his side.

And I lay in bed next to my big beautiful boyfriend—ack! fiancé! —wide awake. All night. I replay the last thirty-six hours in my head. I rake myself over the coals for nearly ruining everything. What am I afraid of? Why did I assume I had failed? Why did I assume Kai was abandoning me? I can't calm my racing thoughts. I feel sad and scared and hopeful and guilty.

Finally, just as the sun is peeking into the room, I have an epiphany. As soon as it comes into my mind, I take a deep, cleansing breath. And fall fast asleep.

49

When I wake up next to my woman, I am overwhelmed with gratitude. I really thought I'd lost her for a second there. In the big scheme of things, that will be a blip on our radar. Our engagement, on the other hand, is monumental.

I watch Holland sleep. Is it less creepy now than it was on the flight to Mexico? Maybe. She looks like such an angel, so relaxed and peaceful. I am just so damned glad to have her back. That was too close for comfort back there. I feel a lingering fear travel down my spine. I kiss her on her forehead and try to move out of bed without waking her.

"Kai?" she murmurs.

I abandon my effort to get out of bed and wrap my arms around her. "Hi, I was going to let you sleep," I whisper.

"Call your mother, Kai," she says groggily. And then she rolls over and starts to snore softly. I'm glad she can't see the abject horror on my face. Call my who? She's having a nightmare. Call my mother? After thirty-five years. I don't think so. I roll out of bed and head for the gym closest to her place. Put all thoughts of that crazy bullshit out of my mind.

A couple hours later, as the icy water of the shower beats down on my head and shoulders, I am still turning "call your mother, Kai" over and over in my mind. Maybe I heard her wrong. Or maybe she meant Naomi? Call her mother-in-law, maybe she meant. But the two of them talk every day. (I mean, every damn day. Even when she wasn't speaking to me, Holland was talking to Naomi.)

Call my mother? As if.

I turn off the water and grab a towel, still thinking over the absolute insanity it would mean if I even tried to find my mother. If my mother isn't dead, why hasn't she reached out to me? She's the parent. I'm just the kid. And then it hits me. I'm not a kid anymore. My mother left a five-year-old but now I am a grown ass man. The founder and CEO of a big fancy ass corporation. And I am going to marry this beautiful, brilliant, broken woman. Of course.

We both have to find our mothers.

"Fuck me," I say into the mirror. Fuck those abandoning bitches and, fuck all fuck, we have to find them. Goddammit.

50

My lack of sleep (and maybe the aftereffects of all that drinking? Was that just yesterday? Holy ravioli.) is beating me over the head with a baseball bat when I wake up mid-afternoon. I need water and aspirin and a shower and probably a few more hours of sleep. "I feel like dog doo-doo," I say aloud.

"You look adorable," Kai says from the chair across the room. "Good morning."

I nearly jump out of my skin. Was he watching me sleep? I'm one part flattered, one part worried. Does he think he has to watch me?

He rises from the chair and pours me a cup of coffee from the insulated carafe on a tray at the foot of the big bed. "Bless you, coffee." I breathe into the cup. Kai laughs my favorite whole-body laugh.

"The coffee gets blessed? What do I get?" he asks.

"Kisses," I say as I put down the cup, roll up onto my knees, and throw my arms around his neck. I cover his gorgeous face and freshly shaved head with kisses. "You smell delicious," I say as I sniff and kiss him all over.

"Much better than blessings," he says as he leans into my affection. "God, I love you, Holland." I feel his big arms move around my waist, then he runs one hand up under my tank top and the other down over my butt. "You feel so good, sugar," he says, kissing my neck. I feel my butterflies get very restless. I change the nature of my attention from giggly good-morning kisses to let's-get-it-on teasing and touching and tasting.

"Kai." I start to say something—anything—to beg him to make love to me...

"I think we should find our moms," he says into my hair.

We both freeze.

And we both start to laugh hysterically. He falls onto the bed, pulling me down with him. When I catch my breath from laughing so hard at the non sequitur (which, of course, reminds us both of my virginity confession on the plane), I finally say, "What the what?" Which only makes Kai laugh harder.

"Sweet, sexy girl, you are so fun," he says between kisses on my cheek, my temple, my hair. He pulls back just a bit to make eye contact with me. "I heard what you said this morning, I think I should try to reach my mom."

"I said that?" I am bewildered. I fell asleep thinking that. But I don't remember saying it at all.

"Yes, but you may have been talking in your sleep." He smiles softly at me. "I'm beginning to think you are your most unguarded and honest when you're tired. Or tipsy. And definitely when you're both." I'm trying to decide if that is a good thing or a bad thing when he says, "It's adorable."

"Well, I had a very hard time falling asleep last night," I say. "I was wrestling with my horrible reaction to hearing that phone call between you and Micah." Kai groans like I've punched him in the gut. "I'm still so very sorry, baby," I say petting the side of his face. He leans his head into my palm. Like a big cat. I love it. "What I mean to say is that I fell asleep thinking about your mother and mine. So I guess it makes sense I said something to you about it the first chance I had?" My voice pitches up like it is a question.

"You threw me for a loop," he says with a wink. He's not mad, so that's good. "But I mulled it over and I think you're right."

"I hate being right about this." I curl my lip like something is stinky. "One more thing, Kai," I say. My whole body shakes with anxiety about this but I know it is the right next step. "I'd like to do some premarital couple's counseling. I think I'm pretty screwed up. And I want us to get this right."

The look on his face is priceless. Like I've just offered him chocolate cake. "Hell yes!" he says. "I love that idea. Thank you." He stands up and brings me with him. "Fuck, woman, you are a genius." He squeezes me with my feet not touching the ground. I laugh. And hug him back. And wonder why I was so scared. I guess we both probably have some abandonment issues. And I shiver again.

51

Back at the office on Monday morning, I call a private investigator I've used a few times over the years.

"Kai Ipu, good to hear from you," Savannah says in her deceptively sweet and innocent voice. "I hope all is well in your world. But if you're calling me..." she trails off.

I laugh a short and mirthless bark. "A hazard of your profession, I imagine, Van."

"Sad but true." She sighs into the phone. "How may I help you? Or is this one of those calls where we need to meet in person to even get the ball rolling?"

"Nothing so cloak-and-dagger as that." I smile at her even though she obviously can't see me. "The good news is, I'm getting married."

Savannah snarfs on her end of the line. "Fuck, Ipu, I nearly spit my coffee across the room." She laughs out loud this time. "Married? You? Huh. Shit, I never thought I'd hear it."

"You're hilarious, Van," I say. "You kiss your wife with that foul mouth of yours?"

"And she loves it," she quips back. "So, this wife-to-be of yours, you don't trust her?"

"What? Of course I trust her. I'm marrying her, aren't I?" I dig this banter with her. Of the very few people I actually trust, Savannah is near the top of the list. I knew the moment I met her she'd keep my secrets even as she helped me ferret out the secrets of others. "Nah, it's not Holland I'm worried about. We both have good-for-fuck-all mothers. And we'd like you to hunt them down."

Savannah whistles long and low into the phone. "Not a fun one, Kai," she says. "Why you gotta pick at old wounds, dude?"

"I don't really have an answer for you on that one, Van," I say. "We just feel like we will be more prepared to get hitched if we have some insight into the women who left us high and dry in our youth. Shit, you're right. This sounds like a terrible idea."

"No, man, I get it," the investigator says with sincerity this time. "It's actually very healthy of you both. Tell me where to start digging."

So I give her all the information I can about my mother, when she left, where she said she was headed. Then I tell her all the details Holland jotted down for me over the weekend about her mother. "I know I don't need to say this out loud, Van, but while money is no object, discretion is," I say.

"Yeah, if I speak to anyone, I'll say I'm helping them inherit money or something. You and your girl get to determine if and when there's any contact," Savannah says. "Give me a couple of days to get digging. I'll call as soon as I have any details."

We say our thanks and our good-byes. I end the call and holler for Micah.

"Jeebus." Micah races into the room, "What, boss?" he asks.

"Sorry to scare you, dude." I run a hand over my head. "I'm in a mood. Would you please—" I emphasize the please both to apologize to my bud and to emphasize my desperation "—please get me some Alka-Seltzer?"

Micah laughs like it is the best joke he's heard in ages. "Are you kidding? Oh, shit, you're serious. Yeah, of course. I think I might have to run to the drugstore. I'm confident we don't have any here. But, yeah, I'll go now." He says as he hustles right back out the door he just came in. I put my head on my desk. And then I bang it there. At least two or three times.

52

On Monday morning, Zahra and I sit outside the IPU café with our coffees and breakfast burritos. "Okay, so tell me the good stuff," Zahra says as we settle in.

"About?" I feign innocence. "Italy, of course," Zahra says as she unwraps just the top of her eggs-beans-and-cheese burrito—expert burritoing, as I've come to learn now that I'm an Angeleno. "We ran every day we were away," I say just before I bite into my eggs-potatoes-and-bacon burrito. I chew and swallow (also known as delaying the inevitable), and say, "And Kai taught me how to lift weights."

"Nice! Do you like it?" Zahra asks. Perhaps I won't have to talk about this after all.

"Nope, it's the worst!" We both laugh. "I'm half-kidding. It's excruciating, but it can also be pretty fun with a partner as knowledgeable and enjoyable as Kai is." I mentally smack my forehead as I realize how suggestive that sounds.

"I'll bet." Zahra winks at me. I don't take the bait. We all work together after all—and while Zahra and I have become friends, *some* boundaries might be a good idea. "But seriously, Italy was spectacular until—you know, until it wasn't." I giggle-slash-groan.

"Look, it seems to me you two are stronger for that little mishap.

I mean, look at this ring!" she pulls my left hand into hers to let the light sparkle on it. "Engaged. I'm so happy for you both. Although, he is clearly getting the better end of the deal," she delivers this line straight-faced, but I laugh anyway.

"Why, thank you." I overact with a seated bow and a flourish of my imaginary top hat. My goofiness is a feeble attempt to disguise how much her friendship means to me.

"How's the wedding planning coming along?" Zahra asks.

"Well, as you may have heard." I roll my eyes at myself, "I threw a bit of a monkey wrench in our courtship. So, we're trying to focus on being together, being present, working on ourselves for a minute. But Kai moved my stuff from my loft into the penthouse. So that's a start."

I tell Zahra the story. On Sunday morning, Micah picked me up at my apartment so we could go to brunch—or so I thought anyway. We were in Santa Monica having pomegranate mimosas when he handed me a huge beautifully wrapped gift box he'd been hiding somewhere.

"What's this?" I love to give gifts, but I am supremely awkward at receiving them.

"A gesture of my devotion to you and my gratitude for making the Boss happy." He winked. Now I was not just awkward, I was genuinely scared. Imagining the worst (a giant box of lingerie would have been the creepiest), I opened my gift to find my cookie jar rabbits. What magic was this?! "How'd you do that?" I demanded, looking around for the key to the trick.

"As of eight minutes ago," he said, looking at his watch, "Kai and a team have you all moved out of the NoHo flat. A little birdie told me you'd like to take these guys to your new pad yourself." Now *that's* a gift! Moving without lifting a finger? It was a dream come true.

Zahra smiles knowingly but doesn't say a word. She was in on it, I see.

"You might also have heard, we haven't been engaged very long," I deadpan with a shrug. We crack up at that. And then we both go back to admiring my ring for another minute. It's that lovely. I don't know how Kai knew I'd want something vintage and conflict-free (he had the jeweler research and document its provenance, the saint) and unique.

"Holland, you couldn't be more perfect for Kai if he custom-built you himself," Zahra says with great affection. "What you need to focus on is figuring out if he's as perfect for you. You deserve a great love." The unspoken sadness of "a second great love" hangs between us for a moment.

"You're so sweet." I give my friend's arm a squeeze. "He is perfect for me. I knew it the night we met. He's my rock."

"Hard-headed, you mean?" Zahra teases.

"Ha! Maybe a little. I just mean, he's solid. He's a strong foundation in a world I thought I'd be lost in forever." I feel tears prick my eyes, but I am absolutely done with crying. "I had no idea I would ever fall in love again, but here I am."

"That's amazing, Holland. I'm so happy for you. For you both," Zahra says. "And only just a tiny bit jealous." She winks.

"Okay, so tell me, Zee, how do we find you a great love of your life? What are you looking for?" I turn more fully to my friend, ready to listen and leap into action. Everyone should feel as happy as I feel. Even when it's hard, loving Kai is the only thing I want to do.

53

Savannah calls me midweek to request a meeting. We agree to coffee in Grand Park. It's crowded enough that we'll be anonymous and large enough we won't be overheard. I spot the tiny blonde in her little summer dress, way too much blood-red lipstick, and her hair in space buns. Hiding in plain sight, this detective. Last time we met, she was in jeans and a hoodie.

"Kai, you know I shoot straight," Savannah says when we're seated on one of the bright pink benches in the park. I raise an eyebrow at her. "Fuck, man, you know what I mean. I'm not going to candy coat this for you."

"I know what you mean." I smile at her. My teasing her is an obvious and childish defense mechanism. I could tell on the phone: she does not have good news.

"Shut up, dude. I have shitty news," she confirms as she puts a firm, feminine hand on mine. It must really be bad if she's trying to comfort me. "Kai, your mother died shortly after she left you and your dad," Savannah says quietly. I listen silently, staring at my coffee cup, while she tells me what she's discovered. Not even a month after storming out, my beautiful, vibrant, brilliant, fucked-up mother was in a fatal one-car crash on Mulholland Drive. She never even left Los Angeles. "Listen, it didn't take me long to find this out," she says softly. "I spent more time trying to get you details surrounding her death than confirming it happened." She doesn't say it, but I know what she is getting at.

"My father knew she was dead," I say without looking up.

"All signs point to yes, my friend," she says, this time with her hand on my shoulder. "They had life insurance. Bank accounts. A mortgage. He must've known."

"And my grandfather," I say. The truth of it hits me like a ton of bricks.

"That has to be a yes, too," she says sadly. "I'm confident after reading the police report that both your dad and grandfather were informed of her death."

"Thanks, Van," I say into my coffee cup. "Anything else?"

"Not yet. I'll pick up the search for Holland's mom now. I just — I didn't want to sit on this info for you, y'know?"

"Yeah, I appreciate that, Van." I finally look at her. I'm sure she can see the dark cloud of confusion and resentment that has just settled over me.

"Of course, boss." She gets up to leave. "Need anything before I go?"

"Nah, I'm gonna sit here a minute," I say.

"Your best-man-to-be is circling the block if you need him," Savannah says. That makes me laugh bitterly.

"How the hell?" I look at her again.

"It's my job, dude," she says as she slips away into the midmorning crowd.

54

That night after work, I walk up three flights of stairs to my new home and see my fiancé. In an apron. In the kitchen. Preparing dinner.

My mouth is watering—but it's the man and not the meal. Scratch that, it's the domesticity of the man.

"Well, actually," he confesses, "I hired a chef. Marcus—from the restaurant where we met?"

I smile widely and nod. "I remember Marcus!"

Kai explains he hired Marcus as both our personal chef and as executive chef for the cafe downstairs. "Turns out Marcus grew up watching his single mother cook in her tiny Chinese restaurant," Kai says as he tosses the pasta and sauce. "When he and I talked, he said he was done waiting tables and really wanted to cook."

"This is so nice," I say as I sit down at the table which is already set for dinner. I pour us each a glass of wine as Kai brings our plates to the table. "Lambo wants me to tell you—" Kai starts.

"Who's Lambo?" I ask.

"Ha! That's what I call Marcus. Don't ask." He winks. "He wants me to tell you—" he pulls out his phone "—to enjoy this artisan chickpea pasta coated with arugula and green pea pesto, tossed with crunchy quinoa croutons and creamy vegan cashew cheese."

We each pull a face. Then we each take a bite. And we both moan. "This is amazing," I say. "How can something that sounds so awful taste so good?"

"That kid is magic, I swear," Kai says.

"Can we keep him?" I ask as I try not to inhale my plate full of food.

"Absolutely," he says as he takes another bite.

After dinner, we clean up and sit on the huge white couch together, in front of the fire.

"Holland," Kai says quietly. I look over at him, his tone worries me. "I talked to Savannah today."

"Oh, wow." My eyebrows shoot up. "Already. Yours or mine? Or both?"

"Mine, sugar," he says. I hold his hand while he tells me what he learned. "I think this must be why my grandfather asked me to forgive him," he says with absolute anguish on his face. "I didn't understand when those were his last words. But now I do." Then I hold his head in my lap while he silently cries. I run what I hope is a soothing hand up and down his arm as his shoulders shake. My heart breaks for him. After a long while, I realize he's fallen asleep in my lap. I will all the love in my heart into his sleeping form. As I watch him rest, I try not to worry about what Savannah might dig up about my mother.

♡

I don't have to wait long to find out. On Monday, I get a message from Kai in the middle of the workday.

KAI: We have a meeting with Savannah this afternoon. Jamil will pick us up downstairs at 3 PM.
HOLLAND: Of course. Good news or bad?
KAI: Don't know. She wants to talk to us in person. Together.

I sigh. I get it—Savannah setting an appointment for this afternoon is professional and thoughtful. But I am nauseated at the thought of having to wait four more hours. I pick up the phone and dial Kai. He answers on the first ring. "Holland, are you okay?" he asks with just a hint of panic in his voice.

"Are you free now?" I ask.

"Yes, but Van isn't. She can't meet us until later."

"Want to go for a run?" I ask him.

"Fuck yes," he says. He sounds relieved. "Meet you out back in twenty minutes. Let me wrap up a couple things."

"Okie doke," I say, dreading even those twenty minutes alone.

I run upstairs to change and put my hair in a ponytail. I sing Dear Evan Hansen songs to keep my mind occupied. Nothing like the world's most heartbreaking show tunes to distract myself. I run back down the entire building's stairs, and I am well warmed up by the time Kai meets me at the trailhead behind our office.

"Ready?" I ask, hoping to get going before he can ask any questions—or I think of any to ask him.

"Yes'm," he says as we take off together.

In my haste to get the fudge out of the building and my head, I forgot water. But my always prepared and ever thoughtful fiancé hands me a cool steel bottle about twenty minutes into our run. I drink it gratefully. He takes it back and returns it to the belt I didn't even notice he had on when we met up. I am so lucky.

We are so lucky—but that merely means we have so much to lose. I tilt my head back to look up through the trees, willing myself not to worry. There is no need to borrow trouble. I have absolutely no idea what Savannah will tell us. Reminding myself to be present on this beautiful trail with this extraordinary man, I look over at him—he is watching me. I wink at him and take off again, picking up my pace. He matches me step-for-step for the next ten miles.

55

After our exhausting run, we race up all twenty-one flights to our apartment. This woman might actually be the death of me. But I have to admit it feels amazing to run together. I love her athleticism. I cannot wait to test that amazing endurance in bed. Cold shower, Ipu. "I'll use the kids' shower," I say as I fill a water bottle from the fridge door and turn to hand it to her.

"What did you say?" her grin is blinding. I can't remember. I have to play it back in my head. Oh. I said that out loud, huh. "The kids' shower..." I repeat. The next thing I know, she launches herself at me. She wraps her legs around my waist and I am granite hard before my brain catches up with our bodies.

"You've already" kiss "started" kiss kiss "thinking of it" kiss kiss "as the kids'" kiss "room" she rubs that hot body all over me. She is sweaty and salty under my lips and I fucking love it.

"I guess I have," I say, smiling and kissing her at the same time.

"Kai," she says in that tone I know means she is going to test my patience. I want this woman so fucking much. I'm starting to think with the wrong head.

"Holland, my heart." I try to engage my big brain. "Honey." I take a deep breath of her skin. "We've got to go, sugar," I remind us both. She freezes. Oh, sweetheart, I'm sorry to pull the plug on you like that, I silently send her. What I say out loud is, "We have an appointment." She slides down my body like she's melting.

"Yeah, of course, I know," she says. "Sorry."

"Hey." I grab her hand before she can walk away. "Never apologize for your affection. I'm sorry we always have such crappy timing." I wink at her and put a loving hand on her jaw.

"I'm pretty sure," she says, running her hand over my chest, then down my abs, then over the length of my erection through my shorts, "that our timing is going to be great someday." She dances her eyebrows at me, turns on her heel, and marches out of the kitchen. I pour her entire bottle of ice-cold water over my head.

♡

Holland's super sad music is still at top volume in the bathroom when I carefully approach the door to check on her. She's been in there a really long time. I'm dressed and ready to go, but she is singing about missing dads and shitty moms at the top of her lungs, and the water is still running. I open the bathroom door just a crack. "Holland?"

She tells Siri to stop the music. "Hi!" she shuts off the water too.

"You almost ready?" I ask. "If we hustle, we can grab lunch on our way to meet Van."

"Yes," she says cheerfully as she pulls on the door handle. I nearly fall into the room with her.

"Hi," I say, regaining my feet. She is fully dressed with her makeup and hair done. "I thought you were still in the shower."

"Nope. I was..." I see her looking for something in her head. "I was just running the water so I couldn't hear myself think."

"Oh, Holland." I try to pull her into a hug.

"No. No. No, don't be nice to me, please," she says as she pushes me away. "Let's go eat. Did you call Jamil?" She asks Siri to call Jamil.

"I called him.".

She stops Siri. "Sweet. Let's get out of here," she says as she marches right on out of the bathroom, the bedroom, and if I don't stop her, down all twenty-one flights of stairs. I call the elevator and hold tightly onto her hand.

"I won't shower for a week," she says quietly.

"What, honey?" I turn to her.

"I feel super guilty for running the shower all that time. I'll take whore's baths all week to save water."

The look on her face is heartbreaking. But I can't help but laugh at her. "I think California will forgive you just this once for choosing mental health over water conservation, my sweet girl." I give her a quick kiss.

♡

After eating Burgerlords takeout in the backseat of the SUV (Marcus's valiant efforts have me ordering vegan burgers now), Holland hands me a wet wipe from what I've heard her call her post-pandemic-pack in her purse. Wipes, hand sanitizer, a tiny bottle of pure rubbing alcohol, face masks, nitrile gloves, and Fauci-only-knows what else.

"Thanks, love," I say as I wipe the Brainburger off my hands.

"Any time," she says. "I feel so much better, Kai. I think I was hangry. Is there a word for hungry sad? Instead of hungry angry?"

"That song you play is tough," I say with a twitching eyebrow.

"Sungry?" she offers. "It's Ben Platt. I love him. That song makes me feel better."

"I'll take your word for it." I give her a small smile.

We pull to a stop on the edge of The Strand. "Thanks, Jay. This might take a minute."

"No worries, boss," Jamil says to the rearview mirror. "I've got a burger and fries up here. Take your time."

We walk out into the golden afternoon, and Savannah appears out of nowhere. "Kai. Mrs. Kai. Nice to see you," she says in her sweetly melodic voice. She wins Holland over in a heartbeat. Mrs. Kai, nice touch.

"Savannah, hello." Holland thrusts a hand at her to shake, then changes her mind and pulls the shorter woman into a hug. "It's so nice to meet you. Kai thinks the world of you and your work."

Oh, she's regretting being cute now. Savannah hates hugs.

"Yes, well, thanks." She awkwardly pats Holland on the back.

I offer what I hope is a rescue. "Want to walk, Van? Or should we find a place to sit?"

Savannah eyes Holland and decides on the walk-and-talk option. "Let's keep moving," my investigator says. "Holland, my report is for you, but since we have never met, I thought you might like to have the boss around," Savannah says.

"Thank you for that, Savannah." Holland sounds already choked up. I feel my own throat tighten. My heart aches for her. We reach for each other's hands simultaneously.

"Holland, is this your mother?" Savannah pulls out an eight-by-ten photo of a woman who looks so much like Holland, it could be her in a wig. Holland gasps and stops in her tracks, swaying a bit.

"Maybe we should find somewhere to sit after all," I insist. We find a bench. I let the women sit side-by-side, and I stand behind Holland, bracing her with my knees. If she is going to pass out, I'm going to lower her gently to the ground. I one-thumb text Jamil to park and come find us, but to stay out of Holland's line of sight. No need to panic her, but I want backup on hand. Savannah slipped the photo back into her bag while we walked over here.

Now she pulls out the file again and hands the whole thing to Holland. Smart, give her something to focus on, something to do with her hands.

"Holland, if that is your mother." Savannah pauses long enough for Holland to nod. "She's currently living in a residential re-entry facility in San Diego."

"She was in prison?" Holland asks. Her voice actually sounds steadier. I can only imagine that having a definitive answer to where her mother has been for nearly ten years feels reassuring. But prison. Damn.

"Yes, more than once." Savannah starts to break down the details. One of the things I like best about working with her is Van's narrative style. She tells Holland the story starting with Pacoima just before Holland graduated high school. I feel my blood pressure climb with each new trip to rehab, each jail sentence served, each hospitalization, and finally a prison sentence followed by this halfway house in San Diego. It's not a short story—I'm troubled by how much this woman has fit into the last decade. I am grateful and glad the person Van describes left my sweet Holland alone, sparing her of all that turmoil.

Holland takes a breath. "Sounds like I dodged a bullet, huh?" Holland echoes my thoughts. This woman. She is a pillar of strength all of a sudden. God, I love her so much.

"I think so," Savannah says. "There's more." Holland turns her attention back to the detective. "She seems to know all about you," Savannah says. "She talks to her housemates about her successful daughter. Brags about your work. Knows you're living in Los Angeles."

Holland's hand meets mine as I put it on her shoulder. "How? I've been here only a couple months. Does she know? Or is she just making things up?" Holland is as much talking to herself as she is asking Savannah.

"I asked those questions of the housemates I could talk to," Van says. "It's hard to tell. I think some of it comes from the internet— you're by no means unknown, Mrs. Gallagher." Holland nods. "And I think you might be right that some of it is in your mother's head. Here's what I do know." Savannah pulls a sheet of paper out of the stack in the file on Holland's lap. "I'm not saying I violated any HIPAA laws, but I am saying your mother is a very ill person."

Holland summarizes the document aloud. "Schizoaffective disorder, bipolar type. Episodes of mania and major depression. Paranoia. Delusions of persecution."

"That sounds like half the DSM-5," I say under my breath. Holland looks up at me with heartbreak all over her face.

"I had no idea," Holland says. Then she shakes her head like she's shaking away a thought. "Well, that's not true. I always knew. But I didn't have any proof." She holds up the paper. "Is this proof, Savannah?"

"Yes," the investigator says definitively.

Holland closes the file and hands it back to Savannah. "Thank you. This has been illuminating. Is there anything else you think I should know before we leave?"

"I think we covered everything," Savannah says. "This is your copy of this file. Do you want to keep it?"

"No, I don't need it. Thanks, though," my woman says brightly. "You've done a ton of work. I really appreciate it." Holland stands. "Ready, Kai?" She smiles at me and I nearly believe the cheer she puts on her face and in her voice. I turn my head slightly to make eye contact with Jamil. I give him the sign to pull the car around to pick us up. Jamil nods and disappears.

"Yeah, of course," I say, nodding but watching her eyes intently. She turns to put her arm around my waist, so I let her drop my gaze. I turn my attention to Savannah. "Seriously, Van, thank you for being thorough. We'll be in touch."

The investigator and I have a silent exchange that goes something like this.

Kai: Send me that file ASAP.

Van: Of course.

Kai: Anything you left out?

Van: Her crimes were ...unpleasant.

Kai: They're in there?

Van: Yup.

Kai: Think Holland saw them?

Van: No. She would've reacted.

Kai: I owe you.

Van: Oh, you'll get my invoice.

Finally, out loud, Savannah says, "You know how to reach me." And she disappears into the crowd of families and joggers and bikers and skaters on the beach trail.

"She's very nice," Holland says, as though we just bumped into a neighbor.

"Yeah, she's top notch." I guide her toward the car as Jamil pulls up. "Ready to head home?"

"Yes. I'm kind of tired," she says. Those are her words, at least. What I hear behind them is a ticking fucking time bomb.

56

I wash my face and brush my teeth, take two antihistamines, close the blackout curtains, and crawl into bed as soon as we get home from the beach.

Kai brings me a cup of tea shortly after I fluff all the pillows and then throw half of them on the floor.

"Hi," he says as he perches on the edge of the bed.

I take the tea from him and breathe it in. It smells herbal and earthy. His presence and the chamomile help me feel a bit calmer. "Hi," I finally reply.

"You're ready for bed?" he asks.

"Yeah, I'm emotionally and physically exhausted. We ran like fifteen miles today. And I found out my mom is alive and very very sick," I say as matter-of-factly as I can manage.

"That's a lot, I know." He puts his huge warm hand on my thigh over the duvet. "Want to talk about it?"

"No, I really want to sleep on it," I say. "Do we have any melatonin?"

He brings me the bottle and a glass of water.

"Kai, we haven't talked about your mom yet. And now we have this hanging over us. Are you okay?" I ask.

"Yes, sugar, I'm okay." Kai leans over to kiss me sweetly on the lips. "Drink your tea. Get some rest. I'll be out in the living room if you need me."

"You're not coming to bed?" I look at the clock. It is not even seven in the evening yet. "Oh. Ha!"

"I'm definitely going to sleep with you in my arms, Holland." He winks at me. "Just not yet. I have some work to catch up on."

"Thank you for the tea. Thank you for taking care of me," I say.

"My pleasure," he says. He pats my leg, kisses me on the top of the head, and leaves the door cracked just a bit when he leaves the room. I take one more sip of my tea, then snuggle down into the covers and let the exhaustion and the sleep-aids take me under.

57

Reading the file Savannah built on Holland's mother is like watching a DARE video in middle school. The dangers of getting involved in drugs. Intellectually, I know her nonviolent crimes were all forms of self-harm and self-medicating. But picturing a person this ill, this irresponsible that close to my Holland enrages me and breaks my heart. I'm reading the final part of Van's report when—"NOOOOooooooooo!" I hear Holland scream.

A new appreciation for the phrase "screams bloody murder" floods my senses. Adrenaline has me nearly throwing my laptop across the room. I am at her side before I even register what is happening.

"Holland." I hold her shoulders, looking her over by the light spilling in from the hallway. "Are you okay? What happened?"

She's as white as the sheets. "Not sure," she gasps through sobs. "Nightmare?"

"Oh, honey." I pull her to my chest. "My poor girl, I'm sorry. How do you feel now? Are you okay?"

"No, I'm okay." She is boneless in my arms. She's starting to calm down, gulping air as the sobs subside. "I mean, I'm not okay at all. But I'm fine. I don't really remember the dream. Just the feeling."

"I'm so sorry, sugar, try to let it go," I say, rubbing her back.

"I wish I could let it go." Her voice is rough with sleep and screaming and tears. "I was hoping sleep would help, but I actually feel worse. She's so sick, Kai. How can I hate her when she's such a mess? I'm angry and hurt and confused and feel guilty as sin."

"I'm sure. It's a lot." I run my hands down her silky-smooth hair. "Here. Let me hold you. Tomorrow we'll look at all this with fresh eyes. Okay?" I slide down next to her and wrap my arms around her. It's still only about ten o'clock and I am not really ready for bed. But I'll hold Holland for the rest of the night if she needs me to. "Do you think you can go back to sleep?"

"If you stay?" she asks.

"Of course. I'm not going anywhere."

"Thank you, Kai," she says into my shirt.

"My pleasure," I say into her hair. She curls up against me and her breathing starts to even out. It takes a long time, but I breathe a sigh of relief as soon as she is asleep. And I drift off not long after she does, still holding her in my arms. My dreams are of her screams.

♡

Holland wakes with a start this morning. (At least it wasn't another scream. That shit aged me a decade.) I pull her close and breathe in her delicious sweetness. "You're okay," I whisper. I slept fitfully and fully dressed with her wrapped up where I knew she was safe. "How are you feeling? You slept better."

"Yeah, good morning." She nuzzles deeper into my embrace. "You feel good."

"Mmm-hmm," is all I can manage.

"Let's go for a short run," she proposes. "Let's get back into our Italy routine?" Maybe it's overcompensating, but she sounds pretty good. Pretty well put-together for someone so close to falling apart last night.

"Good thinking," I say without making a move to get up.

"Kai." She smiles. "I can't get up when you hold me like that."

I am smiling too. "I can't get up when I hold you like this," I say. "Well, I mean, parts of me can..." I don't finish the thought because she is laughing. I love her laugh. I love making her laugh. She wriggles out of my arms and the feel of her body moving against mine like this is proving my point. We either need to get married soon or I need to rethink this no-sex plan.

We go for a run (not fifteen miles today—that was brutal) and she lets me use the elevator to get back upstairs. By the time we shower and dress, I can see that she is feeling so much better.

"You look lighter."

"I feel lighter," she says. "I was in shock yesterday. Today I have a little more perspective."

I let Micah know neither of us will be in the office today. We have some things to work out.

For someone who did not want to think about what's going on, Holland has a solid plan. She has decided to reach out to her mother. She wants to speak with her, see her. Today.

I am not a fan of the idea, but I completely understand her desire to confront her mom. I just hope it is in search of finality—and not the start of a long, painful decline into her dark, ugly world. Trusting Holland knows best, I leave this unsaid and throw all my effort into helping her.

We reach out to the Federal Bureau of Prisons and arrange to head down to San Diego later this morning. After talking to the BOP, we agree to ask our lawyers downstairs to help us find an attorney to deal with the legal aspects of Holland's mother's next steps after the halfway house. We also make appointments with a marriage counselor who specializes in grief and a psychiatrist to answer some of Holland's questions about her mother's diagnoses. She's worried that she might be at risk of having those same issues, I fear. I can't blame her. The little bit of reading I did last night was scary. I try not to let sympathy for Holland's mother seep into my heart, but there it is.

Holland must be on the same page because she says, "It's hard to be angry at someone who's so ill."

"I was just thinking the same thing. We'll do everything we can to get her the help she needs, Holland." I put all the love I have for this woman into my light touch on her arm.

"Yes, and…" she pauses to gather her thoughts. "I don't want to bog our life down in her drama. Maybe that sounds harsh, but I got here—" she gestures around us and to me "to you, to Innovated, to us" she puts her lovely hand over mine "because she cut me loose. I don't want to lose sight of that."

"Yeah," is all I can manage to say. I look at her gorgeous sea-green eyes, amazed at how she must be reading my mind.

58

Ximena calls while Kai and I are waiting for our train. I pick up on the first ring.

"How did it go?"

"Overwhelming," I say. On our way south, I let Ximena know the plan. We agreed to talk after I saw my mother. Giving her the details of my visit feels right—I know she'll tell Naomi the parts worth sharing. I don't think I have it in me to talk to Naomi about this yet. It's not even *her* feelings I'm worried about. I'm afraid I'd just wail useless tears into the phone if it were Naomi calling me.

Plus, debriefing with my sister is a good opportunity to iron out everything my mother and I talked about. I'm still processing. It was a lot. I rough in the details of arriving at the halfway house, checking in, all that. It felt so clinical when I was speaking to the receptionist (nurse? officer? person checking me in), and then there she was. Her always so curly brown hair was sprayed and scrunched and sprayed some more, the way I remember it. She was wearing enough makeup for a red carpet event—but that's how she always wore it. One of her great disappointments in me was my lack of interest in the latest makeup trends. Her goal always seems to be "look at me and my makeup" and my goal has always been to wear only enough makeup to look natural. Her teeth were a wreck—quite a few are missing and the rest are dark. This twists the knife a little—she loved her teeth and taught me to love mine. I have zero cavities and my dentists have always commented on how well I take care of them. I thought it was good genes, but… well, can't make any assumptions. Maybe alcohol isn't her only vice now. She was wearing a floral t-shirt and blue shorts—a plain and conservative outfit for my mom. Maybe she didn't have much choice. It dawned on me this outfit must be clothes provided for her somehow. Of course.

"The worst part of the entire day was our greeting, I think," I tell Ximena. You remember how Ximena tends to greet me, right? She launches herself at me even if we've only been apart for a day or two. How do I explain to *her* that my mother and I tried to hug, but it felt so cold and distant? "It was just so obvious that we don't know a thing about each other anymore." That's not quite it. It was more like we knew way too much and didn't want to remember any of it. Uncomfortable in the extreme.

"That sounds rough, *manita*. I'm sorry," she says. "What did you two talk about?"

We talked about logistics at first. My mother wanted to sit outside, so we negotiated that. I was relieved to sit in the front of the building so I could see Kai—he visibly relaxed when he saw me. He was leaning against a tree on the far edge of the property—I imagined he had a view of every means of egress from there, and that is how he'd describe it. It made me smile.

"We sat on a blanket outside in the shade of a big tree," I tell Ximena. "It's actually a nice property. I don't even want to know what it's costing the San Diego taxpayers to keep my mother comfortable while she transitions to life after prison." We both groan at that thought. And we both know that my everyone-deserves-a-second-chance heart doesn't believe my cynical words at all. "She seemed pretty coherent—but given her illness, it's hard to know what's true."

"I get that," Ximena said. "But we can fact-check anything you really need clarified."

"Yes. You're right."

"So, given you haven't confirmed anything yet. What did you two discuss?" She's being logical with me, and thereby inviting me to be logical.

"We talked about her living arrangements and her job. She is required to work full time, so she's doing landscaping and greenhouse gardening. It actually sounds perfect for her. She seems to like the work."

"What about Kai? Did he meet your mom?" Ximena asks.

Kai was a gem. He was present and strong. "At the end of my visit with her, yeah. He came over to meet her." I introduced him as my fiancé—it made me giddy in the moment, and I still feel my butterflies in my stomach. *Fiancé*. Sigh. "I forget how intimidatingly large he is until I see someone else meet him for the first time. It was almost funny to watch her watch him walk up," I say. "She was a little overwhelmed, I think." Overwhelmed not only by his size, but also his charm, his good looks, his obvious wealth. The mother I knew would have tried to charm him right back. This person just looked hungry. I started to worry she might want money and favors from Kai... and how he would handle that. What a horrible tightrope for him. I need to work out how to avoid all of that.

"What did he think of her? Does he hate your mom?" Ximena does not sound the least bit embarrassed by her bold question. My sister. Gotta love her.

"I don't think he hates her." I look over at him. He's pretending to read the paper while I stand just out of earshot while I'm on the phone. He's obviously watching me and listening. But he's giving me the illusion of privacy. I couldn't love him more. Honestly, if he were hovering over me, I'd hate it. And if he were giving me too much space, I'd feel adrift. He's perfectly protective of me. "I think he sees her as a problem in need of a fix. His questions for her were about the home and her meals and her meds."

"You got a good one," Ximena says. And we both hear the silent end of that sentence: again. My heart aches for Mena—we both have lost so much. Every day I miss Aidan, and I know she longs for Ethan just as much, just as profoundly. And, yet, I've found a partner and true love, a second chance at a happily ever after. And my poor friend is still alone. Before I can fall too deeply down that grief-filled rabbit hole, she asks, "What else did you talk about?"

I tell Ximena that my mother—after nearly thirty years of dodging the question—finally told me how my father died before I was born. He was a soldier, killed in action in Afghanistan. My mother did not scare him away. He died a hero. "My mom didn't understand or didn't realize—or didn't care—that even though they were never married, I might've had benefits from the Army," I tell my sister.

♡

I'm back on the lawn of the halfway house with my mother. "Why didn't you tell me any of that?" I don't have the patience to sugar coat anything for her.

"I always feared you would like him better than me," she says. Ridiculous.

It's mind-boggling how she abandoned me more than a decade ago and yet here she sits, so familiar. She's aged, don't misunderstand. She looks like she's been through the wringer. But, in many ways, she has not changed at all.

My mother continues, "and then later, I thought you would be better off without either of us."

I will deal with my emotions about all of that very soon in therapy, but in this moment, I have to get something off my chest. "You made me feel rejected. By him. By you." Maybe she's too sick to understand any of this, but I have to say it. "My fiancé, this perfect man I've fallen in love with, has to suffer the consequences of your choices all the time. I nearly ruined everything at the mere suggestion of his rejecting me. That's on you. Can you see that?" My voice is calm. I'm not mad. I just want to know if she understands what she did to me. However, because karma is a cold-hearted witch, the moment I confront my mother, I realize she might be right. My mother cut me free—and with that freedom, I went to college, found Aidan, found Naomi, and my sister—and eventually Kai.

♡

"Do you think you'll be able to forgive your mother?" Ximena quietly asks, reading my mind.

I think for a long moment before I answer. "Yes. I think I already do forgive her." A weight lifts off my shoulders as I say this aloud. "More importantly, I think I'm ready to forgive myself."

"Oh, honey, what makes you say that?" Ximena asks.

"For so long, I have blamed myself for all of this. For my father's absence. For my mother leaving…" I have gone so far as to blame myself for Aidan and Ethan's fatal crash—but I can't finish the thought aloud because I don't want to hurt Ximena. All of these things—and so much more—have been my responsibility for so long. "Confronting my mother wasn't actually about her at all. I had to go to talk to her to find some resolution for myself. I needed it to realize I can only be responsible for me."

"Manita," she says. "I'm so proud of you. Happy for you. My heart breaks for you but is also full of love for you. This is big stuff." The station bells ding to alert us that the train arrives soon. Kai folds his newspaper, stands, and turns my way. I smile at my gorgeous, gregarious, generous man.

"Te quiero, Ximena," I say, already walking to hold his hand. "Thanks for calling. Thanks for listening. I love you so much."

"Always," she says, and we disconnect our call.

On the train back from San Diego, I rest my head on Kai's shoulder. I watch the California coastline zip by and try to organize my thoughts. Suddenly inspired, I pull out my notebook and pens. I start to list questions for my new doctor, questions for our couple's counselor… I feel Kai's attention turn to me and my notes. He taps the page.

"We should ask about residential psychiatric care options for your mother. Your doc can help us with referrals." I am so comforted by his interest that I have to stop writing to turn and stare at him. How did I get this lucky? I sigh and write down his suggestion, smiling.

59

Six weeks later, on a chilly fall morning, I stand in front of the mirror of my Malibu hotel room and run my hands down the half sleeves of my pale ivory lace boatneck top.

"You look like you're hugging yourself," Ximena says. "Let me do the hugging." She wraps her arms around me, careful not to muss me or my dress.

"You're the sweetest. I was just admiring how it feels," I say. The top falls just below my rib cage and looks like it was custom-made for me—even though I found it in a consignment shop. The vintage floor-length ivory chiffon skirt also fits like a dream, which is a miracle in itself. It's not easy finding floor-length anything when you're five-foot-eleven-and-change. "I've tried on all these clothes before," I say to my sister-in-law's reflection, "but today everything is so different. So bridal."

"You look divine." Naomi beams. I turn to my mother-in-law and we three widows find ourselves in a loving, sweet, delicate-to-protect-our-hair-dresses-and-makeup group hug.

"Nomi, Ximena." I turn to say to my two best friends, "I am so thankful to you both. So grateful for you both."

"Holland, my heart." Naomi's eyes glisten with tears. "We don't need your thanks. We just love seeing you happy."

"*Manita*, this is exactly how it should be." Ximena steps away to admire me some more. "Plus, you are the hottest bride I've ever seen. Damn, girl."

I feel myself blushing even as I silently accept Ximena's compliment—I look and feel amazingly beautiful. This two-piece dress reminds me of what I wore to Naomi's gala, what feels like years ago. I know Kai will love it—maybe almost as much as I do.

Naomi picks up my bouquet of palest yellow peonies. Their soft color sets off the vivid yellow of my engagement ring on my right hand, leaving room for the wedding band soon to be placed on my left. She hands me the flowers and says, "If you're ready, it's time for me to walk you down to beach—to the best guy I know." Naomi smiles her sweet smile, her eyes shining. What a gift it is to hear her describe Kai this way. The three of us still fervently love our Gallagher men—and because love isn't pie, we all three love Kai just as much. Or, in my case, maybe I love him even a little bit more. (Don't tell Aidan I said that.) Well, actually, I sat down last night with Aidan's and my wedding album and I told him everything (in absentia, of course). He gets it, I think. I believe his mother is right— he always wanted the best for me. And Kai is the very best.

I reflect on her unasked question for a long moment.

I am hugely, intensely, insanely ready to marry Kai.

We have spent the months since Italy baring our souls to each other. First, in premarital counseling, which has been super useful in helping us (okay, mostly me, let's be honest) let go of the anxiety and fear of losing each other so we can just be present and together. And things got eye-openingly real, real fast when we started our work with LA County to become foster parents. Preparing to foster has been thrilling and scary and an adventure I love sharing with Kai— soon we'll be fully vetted, trained, and inspected, and ready to welcome home a child (or a dozen!) in need. We've developed a new circle of friends in our support group for foster parents. I'm sure we have learned more about parenting in an hour with that group than we have in any three hours of the county training course.

After I filled out mental health inventory forms like it was my job, my psychiatrist assured me that my mother's diagnosis is not a guarantee that I will develop the same. When all my screenings came back negative, I finally started to relax. "At your age, you most likely would have seen symptoms by now. I think your moods and anxieties are all well within the normal range of someone with an upbringing like yours, Holland," Dr. Roarty said at our most recent appointment. "I'm happy to help you get your mother placed in a residential facility—and after that, I don't think you and I will need to meet unless you feel differently. We can set up an annual check-in appointment." What a relief.

Dr. Roarty referred me to an ACT therapist I've been seeing weekly. I feel more centered and fully myself than I have in years—well, actually, I am more centered and more myself than I ever have been. Acceptance and Commitment Therapy is new to me—my favorite part is that unlike other types of therapy I've tested over the years, ACT starts with the present. My therapist (who feels more like a mindfulness and meditation coach than a shrink) told me we don't have to look back at my childhood or adolescence. (To be clear, though, we have spent a whole ton of time talking about my unhinged reaction to Kai's phone call in Italy.)

"We can accept who we are and where we come from without having to relive the past," Ivy said. "The work now is to learn to be in the moment and commit to actions which will help you live a life consistent with your values." I nearly cried with relief, but I was actually too excited about moving forward to waste those tears. To help me identify my values, Ivy did this amazing exercise with a stack of cards with words on them like Honesty, Beauty, Duty, Fitness—principles and morals and such. I had to winnow down to a handful of words that meant the most to me. Then down to three, and ultimately to one word. My final three were Justice, Connection, and Intellect. I chose Connection as my top value. The goal now is to make all my decisions, to fully live my life, with my values at the center. It's been enlightening. I wrote my words on the mirror in the bathroom and I have sticky notes in my office, my planner, my wallet. I think it's helping not just me, but also, it's helping my relationships with Kai, Naomi and Ximena, my colleagues.

And my mother. If I want to live a life centered on justice as well as connection, those values must shape how I interact with her. So, for now, that means most of my dealings with her are through my lawyer. In fact, when I left my contact information with the residential re-entry facility, and with my mother, it was Elise's number I gave—my lawyer and I hadn't even met in person yet but we instantly connected on the phone. She's like a lawyer-version of Ximena—ridiculously intelligent, deeply committed to her work, and wildly entertaining. I feel much more comfortable having my caring yet badass attorney acting as a buffer between me and all of my mother's drama. What I have with my mother never was, is not now, and never will be a perfect relationship. And that's okay. We'll see how things improve when she has consistent psychological and psychiatric care in a supportive group home environment. I'm starting to learn not everything in life is perfect nor can everything be resolved. Sigh.

Every night after work, I walk up to our apartment to find Kai in an apron plating the dinner Marcus made for us. My training to take over as CEO plus keeping up with my Chief Strategy Officer responsibilities often keep me at my desk much later than Kai. (I filed a complaint with management, but all I got in response from the current CEO was kisses. It was awesome.) Over dinner, we talk about everything — no holds barred, nothing held back, all cards on the table. We have officially turned the guest rooms into kids' rooms even as we look for a house to buy or to build. Several nights a week, Kai invites key players to dinner to discuss Aces United—athletes he played with, philanthropists he knows, educators he admires—and we've made great strides in revitalizing the organization we're still trying to rename. (Kai likes it the way it is, but it seems like a marketing nightmare to me. We'll figure it out—we always do.) We are partners in every sense of the word, and I feel more than ready to marry him… make it official… double down on this family.

"Nomi, I fell in love with Kai the moment you introduced us," I say, remembering how he felt magnetic, like a force of nature, even that first night. I couldn't take my eyes off him and, while I had mixed emotions about how instantly I felt attracted to him, it was like electricity was sparking between us—even across the table. "Of all the blessings I'm counting this morning, that is what I am most grateful for. Thank you for bringing him into my life."

"My pleasure," Naomi's smile says volumes more than just this simple sentiment. We haven't discussed it since Naomi's job interview confession, but I know beyond the shadow of a doubt that she orchestrated our love connection from the very beginning.

"Mine, too." I wink.

We giggle and hug again, and as a trio, we head down to the water's edge.

♡

Kai and I are married barefoot on the sand with only our closest friends: Ximena is by my side, Jamil stands with Kai. Zahra plays her mandolin (who knew?) and sings a stunning performance of Leonard Cohen's "Hallelujah"—even the groom wipes a tear at that. And Micah, ever the most helpful, performs the ceremony.

"Holland and Kai, do you, with these friends as your witnesses, present yourselves willingly and of your own accord to be joined in marriage?" Micah asks.

"We do," we reply in unison.

"Will you promise to care for each other in the joys and sorrows of life, come what may, and to share the responsibility for growth and enrichment of your life together?" our oh-so- serious officiant asks.

"We will," we say.

Kai's vows say everything. "Holland, my heart—" he turns to smile warmly at Naomi to acknowledge he straight-up stole this endearment from her "—the moment I saw you with candlelight in your eyes and twinkle lights reflected on your hair, I fell in love with you. Whatever life throws at us, it is my job to keep you safe so you can continue to light any room you enter. We have feared the worst—when I thought you wanted me to find you a husband." Our friends snicker at that. "When you thought I wanted to fire you from your job." Our friends laugh out loud. "And we have fared well. I promise to love, honor, and protect you. I promise to put you first, even when our home is full of children." Several of our friends gape at this. He's going to start rumors. How fun is that? "These people who surround us now." He looks around to make eye contact with our closest friends. "We are, all of us, a team. And with their help, this marriage will last forever. I promise."

I'm giddy to share the vows I wrote for Kai (I didn't write my own vows the first time around and I'm just so happy that I get to speak from my heart now). "I adore you, Kai," I start. "From the moment Naomi introduced us." I also look at her with warmth and love, "my heart was ready to love again. It just took a while for my head to hear that." I giggle a little and Kai laughs his big hearty, happy laugh. "We have hit some breathtaking peaks and a handful of manageable valleys—" (I pause for giggles and they arrive, thank goodness) "—and now we know we can weather anything. I join my life with yours. Wherever you go, I will go. You are my rock, my shelter, my foundation. I vow to not only listen, but also to share." He gives me a most-knowing grin at that. "I promise to hold onto you and to hold you up. I promise to be my best—for myself, for us, and for our future together." We both know I mean our future filled with kids. But I don't spill any of the beans like Mr. Can't-Keep-A-Secret over there. "I promise to deal with things directly, be they better, worse, richer, poorer, in sickness, and in health. Forever," I say. He smiles and squeezes my hands.

Micah sets us up for our exchange of rings. "Wedding rings are made precious by wearing them. Your rings say that even in your individuality, you have chosen to be bound together. Let these rings also be a sign that love has substance as well as soul, a present as well as a past, and that, despite its occasional sorrows, love is a circle of happiness, wonder, and delight. May these rings remind you always of the vows you have taken here today." I mean, can you believe this is Micah? Such a beautiful sentiment.

"I give you this ring as a symbol of my love and my faith in us. As I place it on your finger." Kai slips a simple platinum band on my finger. "I commit my heart and soul to you." I say the same as I place a titanium and koa ring on his finger.

"You may now kiss the hot-as-fuck bride," Micah says at the end.

The thirty or so guests laugh and then cheer as Kai pulls me in, dips me low, and kisses me thoroughly. When he rights us, he mock-growls over his shoulder at his friend. Everyone is smiling and laughing as they step up to congratulate us and offer their best wishes. I love how casual and comfortable the short-and-sweet ceremony feels. No chairs, no fuss, just a circle of friends celebrating a cosmic and colossal love.

Naomi wraps me in a faux fur shawl and ties the long ribbons for me. Ximena hands me my flowers, but I can't take my eyes off the groom in his zip-front cream-colored sweater with a single daisy pinned on his broad and beautiful chest—we agreed the simple flower was a perfect reminder of our first non-date—and an open-ended ti leaf lei. His bespoke ecru jeans (turns out there really is such a thing as custom denim) fit him in a way that makes my mouth water. I could not be prouder to be his wife. *His wife.* Swoon.

We gather around a blazing bonfire for brunch on the beach. Naomi and Ximena have outdone themselves, planning a perfect morning picnic complete with champagne mimosas to toast and individual picnic baskets loaded with way too much deliciousness—details planned all the way down to s'mores kits to take full advantage of the fire.

Before I lose my nerve, I hand Naomi my wrap and cue Micah to play the music my (secret!) Samoan dance teacher helped me choose for my Siva Samoa bride's first dance. I know my favorite photo of the day will be of Kai's look of surprised awe as he hears the music, realizes what it is, and sees me mo'e mo'e into the center of the circle of our friends.

It's the best party I've even been to, and I can't wait to leave.

Finally, after I have run completely out of patience to be alone with Kai, our guests send us off with well wishes and a shower of bubbles blown by all our friends making kissy faces. Can't wait to see those photos, too.

60

We decided to honeymoon close to home, so I fire up the red sports car—you know, the one that failed to impress my wife on our first date-not-a-date. Holland looks like royalty with the top down, huge sunglasses, and her hair tied in a pale yellow silk scarf. Why did I choose a challenging drive, when I knew all I'd want to do is look at my bride?

"Are you cold?" I ask her over the wind.

"I'm great!" she is smiling so big I have to smile back at her. I'm such a sucker for her smile. "Naomi stashed this thick blanket for me, and I put on my boots. I'm good. Are you cold?"

"Nope," I say, returning my attention to the highway. Not for long, my heart. You will not be wearing boots or anything else in just a few short hours. I sound like an old-timey movie villain in my head.

After a scenic drive up the 101 and the 1, we arrive at our hotel to check into our private cliffside bungalow just as the sun is thinking about setting. The desk clerk acts like he's never greeted newlyweds before—a statistical improbability in this picturesque location—and fawns over Holland's dress, her rings, her tiny fur jacket-thing until I hear myself growling. Holland just turns to me and laughs. The desk clerk is still talking and assures us we'll be able to see the ocean from our bungalow's living room, bedroom, shower, and "huge indoor tub" (which seems a little weird to me until the clerk adds), and the outdoor hot tub on the sun deck.

Finally, at the door to the bungalow, I sweep Holland up into my arms and carry her over the threshold.

"How chivalrous of you," she says into my neck, kissing and nipping. I growl at her and it turns into a groan. Kicking the door closed behind us, I drop her legs, and then turn her so her back is pressed against it. I kiss her until we're both breathless—then I step back to look at my beautiful wife.

"Let's get you out of this dress," I say.

She unties the ribbon of her wrap and lets it fall off her shoulders. I slide my hands around her ribcage, filled with wonder at the feel of her skin, and pull the delicate lace top over her head. "You and your nearly invisible clothes," I say. Then my breath catches as my eyes devour her naked chest. "Holland, my love," I rumble. "You're perfect."

61

I slide down the hidden zipper of my skirt, then hook my thumbs under the satin waistband, and lower it to reveal the intricate ivory silk satin garter belt attached with twenty-four carat gold rings to ivory satin garters—but no stockings. This is why I've felt sexy as sin all day.

"Holy fuck." Kai falls to his knees. "What is this? You're magical." I just purr back at him. He runs his hands slowly over the six suspender straps. I step out of the skirt and stand before my man on his knees. I'm in my tall white vegan cowboy boots, lingerie, and nothing else. "Leave the boots on," he commands as he slides his hands between my legs to feel my already soaked silk satin thong. My butterflies begin country line dancing.

"Oh, Kai," I purr. He presses his big body against mine, kissing my stomach, running his hands over my lingerie-clad hips, my waist, my ribs, and then my breasts. He pulls one of my nipples into his mouth, and I immediately feel the same tug right down my center.

It's been a long time—but before I can get carried away, I tuck that anxiety away and remind myself to be present in this moment with this man. "Kai," I moan.

He hums as his lips and then his teeth lavish my nipple. He pulls aside my thong to slip a finger into my wetness.

"More," I say, dropping my head back against the door.

"More," he agrees. He slides his huge warm hands to my thighs, parting them. I shiver with anticipation. He puts his face against my center and breathes in deeply. "You smell so fucking good," he says. "I'm going to taste you, Holland. I've waited—" he doesn't finish the sentence because he presses the full flat of his tongue against my slit. I cry out.

"Waited so long," I finish his sentence as I wrap my fingers around his cleanly shaved head. His tongue caresses me slowly at first, and then hungrily. He grips my butt firmly with one hand and teases my nipple with the other. I am so close already and he is still fully clothed.

"So fucking good," he says, and then dives back in.

I moan as my orgasm builds in my belly. When he one more time sucks my bud into his warm wet mouth, I spill over the edge of my climax, crying out his name. He laps me up. Licks his lips.

"More," he says again.

"Please, Kai." I pant. In one smooth motion, he grabs the backs of my thighs, stands with me, and positions his rock-hard length against my center. I didn't even realize he'd unzipped his fly. This man. "Please." I beg. He holds me against the door, slowly pushes the head of his glorious length into my entrance.

"You okay?" he asks.

I open my eyes. "Yes." I breathe.

"Good." He slides his entire length into me smoothly as I stretch around him, feeling every inch of him.

"Oh fuck," I say (I know, I know, but what else is there to say?), "I needed you, Kai. I need this." He rocks his hips, and the feel of him inside me, the hard wood of the door against my back, his hands gripping my thighs, his lips on my neck, even the feel of the sweater he is (still!) wearing—it is all almost too much. "Kai," I say, wanting to tell him that I am deliciously close to my second orgasm but not able to say anything other than his name. "Kai," I say again.

"Cum on my cock, sugar," he whispers against my neck. Not a command, just a gentle push. And I fall harder this time. My climax washes over me, making me see the entire rainbow as I squeeze my eyes shut against the ecstasy, as I squeeze involuntarily around his hardness. "Fuuuuck, Holland," he says into my hair. "I don't want to cum yet."

After I take a minute to regain the use of my brain, I rock my own hips, encouraging him. "Please. Inside me, Kai," I beg him for his release. "Please, I need to feel you." I kiss and lick and bite every part of him I can reach, pinned as I am against the door. I dig my nails into his shoulder through his sweater. "Kai, please." I squeeze him with purpose this time.

And he growls his orgasm long and low and vicious into my neck. He falls against me—catching his weight with one arm so as not to crush me.

"Goddammit, Holland." He is panting now too. "I couldn't wait. Against the door? I needed you so bad. I should've at least gotten us to the bed."

"Are you kidding? I could not have waited that long. Don't apologize to me, husband." My legs under me again, I run my hands over the vast expanse of his chest. Lifting one eyebrow in my best Kai impression, I say, "But don't stop either."

He kisses me, butterfly-soft. "You're perfect. Let's go see all these views of the ocean we were promised." He zips up his jeans (sad face) and pulls off his sweater and shirt (happy face). I follow him.

Anywhere, I realize. I'll follow you anywhere, anytime, to do anything.

Especially if it is to christen our bungalow's bedroom, shower, bathtub, hot tub, and every space in between. My butterflies start singing Marvin Gaye.

EPILOGUE
forty weeks later

As Naomi holds my hand, I admire my husband holding our son. Elias Lemuelu Ipu looks remarkably small in his father's enormous hands. However, I know from experience that baby is not even a little bit small—and I can already tell the nine-pounds-nine-ounce tiny giant is going to take after Kai.

"He's so beautiful," I say.

"He takes after his mother." Naomi beams.

I'm so lucky to have this loving and lovely woman next to me. At every turn, from the moment we met to our engagement to our wedding to my nineteen hours of labor, Naomi has found ways to take the greatest care of our little family.

"Nomi," I say. "Thank you for—" but I am cut off by the arrival of Ximena and our foster babies.

"Here's Holly and KaiKai," Ximena says to the almost-three-year-old twins who have obviously been crying. "Tia didn't hide them, see?"

Naomi scoops up Cyrus, kissing his thick black curls. "Want to see the baby?" she coos to the sweet little boy.

Ximena picks up Shirin to bring her to me for a kiss. "Hello, my precious girl. Did you wonder what was going on?" I kiss her soft curls and smell her sweet baby head. "Look who KaiKai has, Shirin. It's a brand-new baby." I feel tears prick the back of my eyes, I'm so full of love for everyone in this room. Naomi returns to my side, holding her foster grandson. I try again. "Nomi, thank you for—"

"Holland, stop..." Naomi's eyes glisten with unshed tears. "I should be thanking you. Having you in my life is such a gift. Look at this family you have made for us. You have brightened all our lives. You have been my daughter from the first moment we met." Naomi runs a soft cool hand over my forehead and hair. "It brings me such joy to see you and my grandson—my grandbabies!—happy and healthy. Plus, you've named your firstborn after my husband." Naomi wipes a single tear from her cheek. "And look at your husband holding Elias…" She smiles widely at Kai and the baby. "Holland, I'm so glad you married this colossal, annoying, loving, wonderful friend of mine."

Kai rolls his eyes, but I can tell he's secretly swooning.

"Me, too," I say. "Mom."

ACKNOWLEDGMENTS

I could not have done this without the support of my writer
friends, my reader friends, and my coaches. I am deeply grateful to
Phoenix for making scrumptious dinners and walking the dogs
while I stared at my laptop. Without your support, y'all, I wouldn't
have gotten past the first draft.

I am thankful beyond words for the amazing mother gifted
to my sister and me—there's more of my mom in Naomi
than in anyone else.

A.J. Hackwith's *The Library of the Unwritten* inspired me to complete
this novel. I recommend her series to you from the bottom
of my slightly less-damned soul.

COMING SOON FROM
JENNIFER J. COLDWATER

The Badass Babes of The Bible Collection

unbreak my heart

An emotional, problems-in-paradise, witty, sexy romance with a
love triangle twist

my dissent

A sexy enemies-to-lovers courtroom rom-com with a
clairvoyant heroine

my temptation

A forbidden love, forced proximity, sexy, witty two-person-love-
triangle romance

my father's daughters

A sister's best friend (with a best friend's sister subplot)
sexy, witty romance

ABOUT THE AUTHOR

Loosely based on the Bible book of Ruth, **Holland, My Heart** is Jennifer J. Coldwater's first novel and the first in a collection of biblical women's stories retold as contemporary romances. She is currently writing **Unbreak My Heart** (based on 1 Samuel 1-2) and has her eye on Deborah (both a prophet and a judge), Eve (yes, *that* Eve!), and the five daughters of Zelophehad (who raised the case in Numbers 27:1–7 of a woman's right to inherit property).

When Jennifer moved to Los Angeles in the early aughts, her commute drove her batty until she developed an obsession for audiobooks. Now she's such an avid listener that she consumes audiobooks while doing housework, walking her four rescue dogs, eating her nephew's homecooked Italian meals, sitting for the interview for this bio. Look for **Holland, My Heart** on audio soon.

To learn more about Jen, visit jenniferjcoldwater.com.